unrivaled

USA TODAY BESTSELLING AUTHOR

KARA KENDRICK

Copyright © 2023 by Kara Kendrick

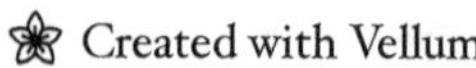 Created with Vellum

Read UNEXPECTED - the Prequel for FREE!
https://karakendrick.com/unexpected/

Dear Readers,

This book contains a dream scene that may be sensitive to some.

BLURB

It all started with a bang.

Literally.

Hooking up in the alley behind the local dive bar wasn't my usual style, but after one martini too many, I gave into my impulses. I banged Roman Montgomery, **former Marine and current hot AF bodyguard** to the mayor of Seaglass Beach.

But when I walked into court the next day and caught the eye of the defendant in my new land title case, well, let's just say shocked is an understatement. Now I'm suing my one-night stand and his family on a dubious land claim. Even an embarrassing disclosure to the judge about my sexy conflict of interest doesn't get me dismissed from the case.

I've lived my entire life following the rules and coloring in the lines. And I give my all to every case, every time. My dedication to my job and my passion for justice is unrivaled.

But this time, my heart's on the line—and I'm not sure I want to win.

Even to save my own father.

1

———————

SKYE

EVER HAVE ONE OF THOSE DAYS YOU DON'T WANT TO relive again? Like, ever?

Well, today's one of those days.

#worstdayever

I should've guessed that an eight-thirty a.m. phone call from my derelict dad wouldn't be good; it never is. I mean, I hardly see the guy, even though I moved to this tiny town to be near my only living relative.

But it's not like we frequent the same sorts of places. I work in a law office near the beach and he stays holed up in his half-rusted mobile home on the outskirts of town, set among a patch of grass that's technically overgrown weeds. At night, the ocean lulls me to sleep; he listens to the low hum of cicadas and the occasional errant shotgun.

Like I said, we live in different worlds.

"Hello?" I pick up my cell, distracted by my incoming emails and the seventeen Post-its littering my desk.

"Skye, baby?" He's slurring and it's not even nine a.m. yet.

Shit. Never a good sign.

"Yes, Dad, it's me. What do you need?" My voice hardens, a mix of irritation and low-lying anxiety pumping through my veins.

"Skye..." His voice breaks and now he's sobbing.
Good grief.

"Calm down, Dad. Pull yourself together." At this point, I've had years of therapy and can instantly recognize my tried-and-true pattern of parenting the parent. Taking a deep breath, I push away the panic, but I can't keep my right eyelid from twitching.

He inhales and exhales loudly, sighing directly into the mouthpiece. I hold the phone away from my ear to preserve my hearing while my father attempts to get his shit together.

"I need help, Chicky."

Original line, that. I can't even keep track of how many times I've helped him over the years. Groceries, rent money, cleaning up after one of his drinking binges. Then there was the time I bailed him out of jail while I was in law school. That was fun.

You need to cut the man out of your life. The stern voice of my therapist echoes through my head, but I silence it. Now's probably not the time—he sounds pretty desperate.

"What do you need, Dad? And come out with it already. I'm due in court in an hour."

"Fifteen grand."

"What the--? Are you kidding me? I don't have fifteen hundred laying around, let alone fifteen grand. What do you need with that kind of cash?" I swipe my hand down my black pencil skirt, trying to dry the clamminess.

"I have to pay off a debt. To the Capellis."

A chill slithers down my spine. I've been in town long enough to know the Capellis are the bad boys of Seaglass Beach—and it's best to avoid them at all costs.

"Dad. What kind of debt is this? Wait—I'm not sure I want to know. Is this illegal? If it is, don't tell me."

"Gambling, Chicky. I placed some losing bets on football this year."

"You know there's this cool thing called fantasy football. You should get some friends together, each throw like two bucks into the pot. Keep yourself out of harm's way." The eye twitch isn't getting better, even with my thumb pressed hard against my temple.

"I know. It was stupid. But now they're threatening to burn down my trailer—or worse—if they don't get the money."

"By when?"

"This weekend."

I glance down at my watch. Two days. My asshole father's calling me with two days left on the ticking time bomb.

A deafening rumble vibrates my cell, followed by the slam of a door.

"Oh no. They're here." My dad's voice tips up in panic, then there's a loud pounding on his door.

"Open up, we know you're in there, old man!" A deep male voice reverberates down the line.

"Hang tight, Dad. I'm on my way." I disconnect, grabbing my car keys and jogging out of the office.

Luckily, it's early enough that no one's in the office yet. I'm the junior associate, so I tend to log the most office hours. Face time and all that. Usually, I enjoy the quiet time in the mornings, sipping my coffee and strategizing.

Today I'm grateful I don't have to explain myself as I peel out of the parking lot and race out of town.

I weave through the morning traffic, fingers thrumming the leather steering wheel as I push as close to the upper limits of speed as I dare. Last thing I need right now is a speeding ticket. Drops of sweat bead on my lower back, even though the temperature's in the low sixties. Cold for Florida, moderate for the rest of the country.

The road turns to dirt and I'm forced to slow down, dust swirling around my Honda as I bump along the path. A green, grassy field blurs by on my left, a few cows standing together off in the distance, then my father's trailer comes into view. Sure enough, a lifted truck with ridiculous Monster Truck tires sits in the driveway, menacing and ominous.

Damn it.

I have no plan and no cash.

Slamming my car into park, I race over the gravel and up the steps, my heels clicking loudly against the metal. I pause at the screen door, peering in. My dad's cowering on the couch in his white undershirt and a pair of frayed shorts, while two of the Capellis hover near him, their biceps flexed and ready to deliver a punch or two to get their point across. A third Capelli, the stockier one, sits in my dad's ratty recliner, his feet kicked up like he's at the damn movies.

With a deep breath, I charge in. "Don't say another word, Dad."

The Capelli in the chair eyes me up and down. "Well, well, well. You didn't tell us you had a daughter, Larry boy."

He lowers his feet to the ground, then stands, circling me like a shark sniffing blood in the water. Icy fear trickles through me under his gaze, but I try to stay calm. He reaches out, running the rough pad of his finger down my upper arm and I yank it away.

"Don't touch me."

"Oh, she's feisty. I like that. Tell you what, Larry. Your daughter can pay off your debt. Might take a few nights, maybe a week, but I'm confident we can get it done."

"What? Fuck off." I spit the words out, not liking his tone, nor his implication.

He steps closer to me, his dark eyes hard. "That's kind of the idea." He winks and I shiver, skeezed.

"Your dad's not exactly in a great negotiating position right now, sweetheart. The old man owes us."

"Exactly. *He* owes you. Not me."

"And here I thought you'd be the dutiful daughter type."

"Jagger—" my dad rasps.

The thug in front of me swivels around, the fabric of his tight T-shirt straining with the effort. "What?"

"I can pay. Promise. I just need a few more days. Maybe a week or two. The holidays got me jammed up."

Under normal circumstances, I'd laugh at this line. My dad never works and I can't remember the last time he bought me a gift. Third grade, maybe? But the sight of him hunched over on the couch, deep worry lines marching across his forehead, has me all twisted up inside.

I almost feel sorry for him.

Almost.

The thug on the left lunges for my father, pulling him up by the shirtsleeve, and he's shaking like a leaf in a windstorm. Red-faced, his eyes puffy from crying and drinking.

Sad sack.

"Your time's almost up. No more extensions," thug number two says.

"Now, Cash, let's be reasonable here." The stocky thug taps his brother on the arm and he loosens his grip.

"Why, Jags? He's had a ton of time." Thug number one scratches his head.

The creepiest thug—Jagger, I guess—answers. "Boys. I'm sure there's something these two have that we want." He waves his hand first at me, then my dad.

"She's a lawyer, you know. You boys seem like you maybe could use those types of skills, right?" My father points at me, selling me down the river.

Nice.

"A lawyer, eh?" Jagger's slick head perks up, his eyes roaming my body, his gaze fixating on my boobs. Classy.

"I'm not in criminal law, sorry." I fold my arms across my abdomen, wishing I was anywhere but in this tiny, rusty hellhole smelling of stale beer and day-old takeout.

"Who said anything about us being criminals?" thug two grunts and I can't control my eye roll.

"Listen, lady—you want to help your dear old dad or should we just take what we want and burn this shithole down right now?" Jagger's so close to me his hot breath fans over my cheeks and I work to resist the urge to vomit.

"I can't—and won't—do anything illegal for you. Fair warning." I thrust my chin out and stand tall.

"We'd never ask you to do that." Jagger's thin lips curl into a pervy smile, and he knows he's got me. "Let's make a deal."

2

ROMAN

Wednesday's the night I meet up with my younger brother, Parker, at Manta Ray's for a quick drink and a game of pool. But seeing as how he just got married, he's away on his Caribbean honeymoon. Lucky bastard.

Which leaves me flying solo because our older brother King won't venture into town on a school night and most of my buddies are still active duty in the Marines.

Shoving into the dim bar, I rub absentmindedly at the twinge of pain in my lower back, reminding me why I'm currently working private security for the mayor of Seaglass Beach versus running special ops somewhere out in the great, wide world.

Getting grazed by a stray bullet will do that to you.

A year ago, the doc told me I'm lucky to be walking. A sixteenth of an inch to the left and I'd be paralyzed, so I guess I should be counting my blessings.

"Hey, Roman, what's it gonna be tonight?" Xander, the bartender, asks.

"I'll take whiskey, on the rocks." I lean up against the

bar, but don't take a seat. Sitting isn't great for the back, plus it's practically standing room-only since it's ladies' night. Hence why me and Parker come in on Wednesday night, although I suspect he'll be changing his ways now that he got hitched. Doesn't much matter to me, I rarely pick anyone up anyway. This town is way too small for that kind of thing. How Parker got away with it all this time, I'll never know. He's more charming than me, I guess.

"Here ya go." Xander slides the drink across the bar, not bothering with the nicety of a paper cocktail napkin.

"Thanks. Put it on my tab."

He nods, then moves down the bar to take the order of a vocal group of college girls, making me glad I opted for whiskey. Doubt I'm going to be here long, seeing as how I'm alone and the crowd's mostly college kids home on winter break.

"Is this seat taken?" A sort-of familiar, velvety voice hits my ears and I swivel, interest piqued.

An attractive brunette I recognize motions to the empty barstool. Skye, a lawyer I've seen around Town Hall.

"All yours." I pull the stool out for her and she shoots me a shy smile, sliding gracefully onto the pleather seat.

"It's Roman, right?" She pins her gaze on me, and my cock twitches in my jeans.

Good god. How long has it been, that all it takes to rev me up is an innocent stare? Sure, she has great eyes, sugar brown with long, thick lashes, but still.

"Yes, ma'am." I take a quick sip of my drink, swallow down the burn. "You're Skye, right?"

She nods and I can't stop staring at her deep red lips, the pendant lights reflecting off her gleaming white teeth.

The bartender sidles over to us and Skye doesn't hesitate with her order.

"I'll have an extra dirty martini, please."

"Coming right up."

She smooths her hair down over her shoulder, then clasps her hands on the bar.

"Long day?" I ask as she rubs her thumbs together, a tell-tale sign of anxiety.

"Yes, definitely."

"Work?"

"Sort of. More family problems than anything, though."

"Sorry. That sucks."

"Thanks." She purses her lips together in a wry smile and I figure I should probably drop the subject. A Bon Jovi song comes on and the college girls all scream like they're at a damn concert, then run out to the dance floor.

"To be young and carefree again…" Skye watches as the girls sway to the beat, a longing expression on her face.

She must have had a really bad day if that seems fun to her.

"Not all it's cracked up to be." I shrug, swirling the amber liquid in my glass.

"I honestly wouldn't know. I don't think I was ever carefree. Young, yes."

"You're still young."

A soft pink blush colors her cheeks and she smiles. "Not that young."

"They're babies. No life experience."

"Life experience is overrated."

The bartender deposits her drink and she takes a long sip, sighing.

"I'm probably going to regret this tomorrow, but right now, it's freaking amazing."

Sliding two fingers down the black swizzle stick, she pops an olive into her mouth and chews and I can't peel my eyes from her mouth, the delicate skin of her throat bobbing as she swallows.

"I've seen you around the courthouse. You're not a lawyer, are you?" She tips her head to the side, her white blouse shifting lower on her chest. It's a fucking monumental effort to keep my eyes on her face.

I chortle. "No. Definitely not a lawyer. I'm working security detail for the mayor."

"Ah. Got it. That makes sense. I see you with him a lot. How's that gig?"

"It's good." I take a sip of whiskey, try to focus on the conversation and not the way her breasts press against the sheer fabric of her blouse.

"You're a man of few words, I see." Her eyes sparkle beneath the glow of the pendant lights and I chuckle.

"Sorry. Small talk's not really my style."

"Agreed. Talk is cheap." She slides another olive into her mouth, dragging her lips down the stick this time, and I'm rock hard now.

Skye's sexy as fuck and I can't help thinking about her lips on other things.

Focus, Roman. Preferably on something other than her tits.

"So you're a lawyer, then?"

"I am."

"How's that?"

She picks up her drink and takes a big gulp.

"That good, huh?"

"Most days, it's fine. Today wasn't one of those days."

I scrub a hand over the back of my neck. "Relatable, actually."

"Have you worked for the mayor for a long time?"

"Not really. I was in the Marines, but sustained an injury and had to take a medical discharge. I could have worked a desk job, but I'm not really cut out for that sort of work." I roll my shoulders, attempt to relieve some of the tension between the shoulder blades.

"I get it. Long hours behind a screen must be pretty boring after you've been out in the field, running missions and shooting bad guys."

"Exactly."

We lock eyes for a long second, the thud of the music vibrating the bar.

"You need another drink?" Skye gestures at my empty glass.

"Sure."

I throw my hand up, signal for another round. A few minutes later, we both have fresh drinks in front of us.

"How long you been in Seaglass Beach?" I take a sip, the ice clinking against the glass.

"Only a few months. I was working down in Miami, but rent's really pricey down there. I saw a job posting here and decided to apply."

"Nice. You have family in town, I assume?" Most people don't just randomly move to Seaglass Beach. Typically, newcomers have familial ties or they stumble upon the beach during a vacation and decide to stay.

Skye nods, her dark hair brushing across her shoulders. "My dad's here. Although why I wanted to be near him again is beyond me." She bites on her bottom lip and my entire lower body tenses. *Fuck, she's gorgeous.*

I run a hand through my hair, lean forward close enough to catch a whiff of her deep floral perfume. "Sounds complicated."

"Not really. He's an asshole and I'm a sucker. Tale as old as time."

"Maybe you're just a good daughter."

She smiles wryly at me, our eyes locking, and I swear the air between us crackles with electricity.

"You're too kind. My therapist would disagree with you, you know."

"Not to disparage therapy, but sometimes it's psychobabble bullshit."

"True." She runs her finger around the rim of the martini glass, not breaking eye contact with me. "So Roman—how is it that a guy like you is alone in a place like this?"

I chuckle, shaking my head. "What do you mean by *a guy like me*, exactly?"

A hot pink flush climbs up her neck to her cheeks as she peers at me through lowered lashes. "You know—handsome, fit, friendly."

"I wouldn't say I'm friendly."

"You're not unfriendly."

"Well, thanks. I guess it depends on who you ask."

"I mean, this bar's crawling with women. I would have thought you'd be chatting one or two of them up."

"I'm talking to you." I level my gaze on hers and the pink spots on her cheeks darken to a crimson. She licks her lips and the tension between us is so thick I can barely breathe. Lynyrd Skynyrd blares over the loudspeakers and the college girls start screaming the lyrics to "Sweet Home Alabama" at the top of their lungs.

"You wanna get outta here?" I rise, setting my mostly empty glass down on the bar. She nods and chugs the remainder of her drink while I settle the tab. I shoot Xander a wave, then take Skye's hand and help her down from the stool. Her hand's soft and warm, small against my much larger palm.

"Thanks for the drinks."

"Any time." Sliding my hand across her lower back, I guide us around the edges of the dance floor, careful to avoid the flying elbows of the singing college kids. The air thumps with the bass, the floor vibrating, and my entire body's taut, coiling with tension.

We spill out into the chilly night air and Skye shivers, the thin fabric of her blouse definitely not enough to keep her warm, even in Florida.

"Here, have my jacket." I drape the leather over her slim shoulders and she snuggles into it.

"Thanks. I left mine in my car. I was kind of singularly focused on getting a drink and forgetting about this entire day."

"I hope your evening went better."

She steps toward me, moonlight bathing her face in a soft, white glow. "I don't want to forget tonight."

Reaching out, I cup the back of her neck, drawing her into me, then lower my mouth to hers. She tastes spicy from the drinks and her lips feel every bit as tender and delicious as I thought they would. With zero hesitation, I tease her mouth open and slide in. She meets me in the middle, our tongues tangling, and every nerve ending in my body's firing now. Her hands find the back of my neck, run through my close-cropped hair, as I press her to me.

It's been a very long time since I had this kind of connection with a woman.

I need her. Need to know what she feels like against me, on me, under me.

I need her more than I need oxygen right now.

I don't think I can wait another second without knowing.

My truck's parked right in front of the bar, directly beneath a streetlight. Less than ideal. And I don't want to make the ten-minute drive home.

"Come here." I take her by the hand and duck into the dark alley beside the bar. At least here we're shielded from the wind—and the prying eyes of the town busybodies.

Pressing her back against the building, I cup her face in my palm, crushing my lips to hers. She's sweet sin, right here in the alley, and I've never wanted to be repentant more in my life.

Skye moans softly into my open mouth, arching her back and thrusting her breasts against my chest. The sharp points of her nipples poke through the fabric of her blouse, and I snake one hand down, grazing my flattened hand across her chest. She pushes against my palm, so I squeeze until she moans louder.

"Roman..."

Tugging her blouse from the waistband of her skirt, I slide my hand under the gauzy fabric and up her torso, her skin silky smooth beneath my hand. She shimmies against me, wrapping her hands around my waist and squeezing my ass. I'm rock hard now as I knead her breasts, pinching at her nipple through the satin of her bra.

I drop my mouth to her neck, kissing a trail down the heated, tender skin. She untucks my shirt, her fingers exploring the ridges of my back, tracing my lats, my traps. Pressure builds low in my gut and I might explode from the tension.

But because I'm a gentleman and my mama raised me right, I pause, searching her face for any hint of hesitation.

"You okay with this?" My voice comes out deep and husky.

She bites down on her bottom lip and nods. "Yes."

That's all I need to hear. I hike her skirt, slide my hand up her toned thigh. Her breathing's shallow, her chest rising and falling fast, our eyes locked. I skate across her skin until I find her warm center.

Bright pink stains her cheeks as I press my thumb against her panties, find her clit. "So wet," I murmur, not breaking eye contact. She blushes harder, but doesn't move away. Instead, she wriggles under my touch, seeking more friction.

I give her what she wants, tracing tight circles until her eyes cloud with lust. Her fingers fumble with the button of my jeans, so I reach down and undo it, lowering my zipper over my painfully hard cock. I push her panties to the side, drag my fingers through her wetness. A moan falls from her lips as I dip inside her, her muscles clenching around me.

"Fuck..." she groans, spreading her legs wider, granting me better access. "Just so you know—I don't usually do this..."

"I didn't figure this was a typical night for you. For what it's worth, I don't either."

"Okay, wanted to set the record straight."

"Got it. Now do you want to keep talking or..." My

voice trails off as I gauge her response. Eyes dilated, chest flushed, breathing rapid and shallow.

"Or, please."

"Good." I seize her mouth in a hot, searing kiss, erasing any space between us. All that's left is physical sensation and liquid, molten need.

"Sorry, one last question..."

I pause, breaking away. "Yeah?"

"Do you have a condom?"

3

SKYE

I don't know what the hell I'm doing.

What I do know is I'm patently uninterested in stopping this hot-as-hell Marine vet as he finger fucks me in the alley.

It's the best I've felt in a long-ass time and exactly what I need right now.

All feeling, zero thinking.

Not my typical modus operandi. But whatever. Change is good, right?

"Oh…" A moan falls from my lips and I barely recognize the strangled sound, like it's coming from someone else. Someone a lot cooler and edgier. Someone who has sex with a near-stranger in a bar alley.

Roman picks up speed, moving in and out faster, black spots dancing at the edges of my vision. I'm embarrassingly close to coming and we haven't even fucked yet.

I reach down and stroke his steel shaft, vaguely considering if he'll even fit inside me. Not usually a problem, but nothing about today's been typical.

I'm glad I'm wearing heels because the height thing could be a challenge.

The random thought pops into my head and I can't help but giggle.

Roman slows down, but doesn't stop his movements, hitting all the right spots.

"What's funny?"

"Nothing. I'm happy I'm wearing heels is all. Because I'm a lot shorter than you and this would be more difficult."

Two seconds later, I'm lifted off the ground, my legs gripping his waist as he squeezes my ass.

This man is freaking strong.

His cobalt eyes glitter in the moonlight. "Wouldn't be a problem either way."

Hot, lusty desire glides through me like honey and I've never wanted to fuck a man more.

I twine my hands around his neck, smash my lips to his like he's the last damn meal I'm ever eating. And he tastes so fucking good, sweet notes of cinnamon and vanilla dancing on my tongue as I sweep into his mouth. He kneads my ass, sending hot bolts of pleasure straight to my core, all my muscles tight and needy.

With one abrupt movement, he tears off my panties, so fast and hard that it only leaves a slight stinging sensation on my left leg.

"Hope you didn't need those."

I shake my head no, too breathless to even form coherent speech.

He levers my hips up, then slowly, so slowly lowers me down onto his sheathed cock. Stretching me in all the right ways, filling me up and hitting the most sensitive spots, and it feels fucking amazing. My muscles spasm and clench around him and I vaguely wonder if this is some kind of out-of-body experience or dream state or something.

I sure hope the fuck not because I feel awesome. Sex with Roman—even in an alley—is better than the runner's high after a marathon. All my nerves fire and pressure builds low in my belly, my orgasm shimmering on the periphery. Just out of reach, but there.

Right fucking there.

"Yes, yes…" I'm making noise—too much noise—we're probably going to get busted. Roman solves the issue by seizing my lips in his, swallowing my screams as he thrusts harder and harder, racing toward climax. I'm undulating my hips, trying to match his rhythm, my breasts bouncing against his strong, muscled chest.

And then the dam breaks, hot pleasure sparking all over my body as I quake and shiver around him. As soon as I let go, he does too, and we both chase our release.

Quick.

Elusive.

Also, fulfilling, life-affirming, and one-thousand percent worth the effort.

After a few minutes, he lowers me gently to the ground, steadying me with his hands as I teeter on wobbly heels. Being fucked senseless in an alley will do that to a girl, I guess.

He pulls the hem of my skirt back down and I rearrange my shirt, fastening a button that came loose in the fury.

"Um, thanks." My voice is quiet and shy, a hot blush flaming my cheeks.

With one hand, he cups my face, his high cheekbones chiseled in the shadows. "Thank you."

Rolling off the condom, he buttons his jeans, then tosses the rubber in the trash can down the alley. I shrug out of his jacket, hold it out to him.

"Keep it. I'll walk you to your car." He winds his arm around my waist and I lean on him slightly for support as we make our way back down the alley out to the sidewalk.

"This is me." I tip my head at my Honda. The streetlight casts long shadows across the pavement, the ocean waves pounding off in the distance.

"You don't have to make any commitment or anything…" I gnaw at my puffy bottom lip, my heart hammering hard. "No need to exchange numbers, make promises we won't deliver on."

Roman pulls out his cell and hands it to me. "Send me a text. That way I'll have your number."

Anxiety unlocks in my chest, and I take a deep breath, punching in my digits and a text message.

> Skye: Thanks for tonight. Best alley sex ever

I hit send, then hand him back his cell. A low vibration cuts through the silence and Roman drops his eyes to the phone, then chuckles.

"Guess I'll have to work on getting you to drop the modifier."

"Just wanted to remind you of who I am. You know—in case you know another Skye."

"Nope. Only one." He steps toward me, grabbing me by the waist and pulling me up against his chest. The spicy scent of cinnamon and sex drifts off his skin and tiny bolts of pleasure zing through me, cascading up and down my body. He drops his lips to mine, delivering the slowest, hottest, most sensual kiss of my entire life, and thank goodness he's holding me tight because I'm pretty sure my knees buckle at some point.

Finally, we need air, so he breaks the connection.

"Good night, Skye."

"Good night, Roman."

I slide into my car and hand him his jacket. He waits until the engine roars to life and I pull safely away before he shoots me a wave.

And I only feel slightly bad about lying to him. Because obviously that wasn't the best alley sex ever.

It was *the* best sex ever.

Period, end of story.

I have a sneaking suspicion I'll never get over Roman— and I don't even know his last name.

4

ROMAN

No offense to Parker, but last night was the best time I've ever had at Manta Ray's.

And I've been going there a lot of years.

Skye's a hot piece of ass.

But more than that, she's smart, witty, fun. She obviously cares about her father, although he sounds like a real asshole. She's probably too nice for her own good.

Something about her pulls deep at my gut. A need to protect her, but I'm not sure from what. She seems perfectly capable of taking care of herself, but my instinct is to wrap her in my arms and shield her from something.

Or someone.

I shove this dark thought away, ignore the prickling at the back of my skull. Now that I'm a civilian, I need to stop looking for trouble lurking behind every corner when it's not there. We live in Seaglass Beach. Not exactly the murder capital of the U.S. Mentally, I understand this, but my brain's having a tough time accepting my new reality.

Hazard of the job, I suppose, past and present. A good bodyguard's always scouring for danger.

I'll chalk it up to that.

"Afternoon, Roman." Monty, the Town Hall security guard, waves me through the metal detector. "Big day today, huh?"

I nod and try to ignore the hard pit lodged in my stomach, the same pit that's been there since Thanksgiving. Even though I told my sister Poppy not to worry, I'm plenty concerned. I've tried to remain calm for her sake, but I've spent enough time around the courthouse to know that even frivolous lawsuits sometimes make it onto the docket. Depends on how good the lawyer is.

"Rome!" Poppy's high-pitched voice echoes off the shiny courthouse tile as she jogs up to the metal detector, tossing her cell phone and keys into a plastic tray.

"Come on through, Miss Poppy." Monty ushers her through and hands back her belongings, which she shoves into the back pocket of her jeans.

"Oh my gosh, I'm so nervous I might throw up my lunch." Poppy rubs up and down her arms, anxiety rolling off her body.

"It'll be fine, Poppy. It's a stupid lawsuit. The judge should dismiss the case right away." I try to reassure her, sounding much more confident than I feel.

"You think? I really hope so because I can't lose the inn." Worry lines etch her otherwise smooth forehead and I reach out, squeeze her arm.

"We'll be fine. Promise."

"Roman, Poppy. Come on back." Cleet, our lawyer and long-time friend of the family, motions us over to the double doors of one of the courtrooms. "Hey, y'all. How ya feeling?"

"Cleet!" Poppy throws her arms around him, catching him off-guard. He pats her back, shakes his head at me.

"Don't worry a bit, Poppy. We'll get this case kicked, sure as the sun rises in the east, darling. Take a deep breath, that's it."

Poppy exhales long and loud, her shoulders sagging. Cleet untangles himself from her arms, guiding her by the elbow into the nearly-empty courtroom. I'm not surprised; this isn't exactly the case of the century or anything. A ridiculous waste of taxpayer dollars is what it is. A low blow, even for the Capellis.

"Roman, you're going to sit next to me at the table." Cleet points to a long, black table at the front of the room. "Poppy, you'll be right here, directly behind us." He waves his hand at the row of wooden seats behind the half-wall separating the room.

"Don't you think I should be at the table? Since I run the inn?" Poppy scrunches her lips together and I shake my head vehemently behind her at Cleet.

"It's probably best if Rome sits up with me. The less emotion we show, the better."

"Hmmph." Poppy crosses her arms over her chest, but folds one of the wooden seats down and collapses into it.

I follow behind Cleet, taking my place at the table. He unpacks his briefcase, setting stacks of manila folders out, along with his yellow legal pad and a pen. A few bystanders shuffle in to watch the proceedings, including a guy I recognize as a reporter for *The Seaglass Beach Record*.

Super. I don't love the idea of our family business being splashed all over the front page of the local paper, but the free press amendment and all that. Not worth my time or energy worrying about it right now.

At ten minutes to one, Cash and Damon Capelli saunter into the courtroom. Dressed in ill-fitting suits—their attempt at looking presentable and upstanding—the two of them shift uncomfortably in the scratchy polyester material. Doesn't stop them from snickering and acting like the couple of thugs they are, though. They leer at Poppy and I fix my eyes on them, shooting them a death stare. They grunt and flip me the bird, but do manage to tear their eyes away from my sister. Message received.

The ticking of the clock on the wall is deafening, and sweat beads on my back. I doubt the Capellis can afford a decent lawyer, so this lawsuit shouldn't even get off the ground.

With one minute to spare, in comes Jagger. Unlike his brothers, Jagger's not wearing a suit. Instead, he's wearing a button-down shirt with a leather motorcycle jacket and dress pants. He swaggers to the table at the same moment the judge enters.

"All rise."

Cleet and I stand, Poppy jumping up so fast her chair groans with the effort of the forceful swing.

"You may be seated." The judge is an older woman with wavy steel-gray hair, one I recognize but don't personally know. "I'm Judge Ratler and I'll be hearing your case today. Is the plaintiff ready?"

I glance over at Jagger, sitting alone at the other table. *The Capellis didn't hire a lawyer at all?*

This is gonna be an open and shut case, a freaking slam dunk, because there's no way in hell the Capellis know how to make a land dispute case.

"Um—just one second, Your Honor. Our lawyer had to pick up a file from the office. Must be running late. Traffic." Jagger throws the final excuse out in a lame, last-ditch effort. "Oh, here she is now."

I peer over my shoulder as the Capelli's lawyer breezes through the swinging door, file in hand, and hurries to the table apologizing profusely.

"So sorry, Your Honor, I regret my tardiness." She smooths her dark hair over her shoulders before glancing over at me and Cleet. Her face blanches at the same time a deep pink flush blooms over her chest, a pretty contrast to the silk white of her blouse.

A shirt very similar to the one she wore last night, except this time she's wearing a sharp navy blazer to match the skirt, looking every bit the professional lawyer.

A lawyer helping the Capellis try to steal my family's land.

Skye's mouth opens and closes, her hand fluttering up to her throat.

The same throat I sucked and licked yesterday, her skin smelling like exotic flowers from some far-off rainforest. From my seat, I can make out a faint trace of a bruise, a reminder of the passion we have between us.

Had. Past fucking tense.

Because anyone representing the Capellis is dead to me, no matter how gorgeous and fuckable they are.

5

———

SKYE

No.

No, no, no.

This can't be happening.

Of all the cases, in all the courtrooms in the world, I'm being forced to try this one.

Against the hottest guy I've ever hooked up with in my life.

Burning shame washes over me as scenes from last night scroll through my mind like an X-rated movie: Roman leaning up against the bar, ass perfectly outlined in his jeans. Roman's hand on my back, guiding me to the dark alley. His lips on mine, tasting like fiery cinnamon and sex. My back up against the wall as he drove into me.

Oh my god.

Embarrassment pricks at my scalp, the tips of my ears scorching. His expression's flat and impassive, eyes icy cold, steely.

I'm sure he hates my guts right now.

I hate my guts right now.

If it weren't for my father's gambling debt, I'd never in a million years take this case. It's far-fetched at best, a total fabrication at worst. But it's my job to help my client and that's the oath I swore to the courts—an oath I always uphold—no matter what.

Except now I have a clear conflict of interest, what with my personal relationship with the defendant.

"Your Honor, permission to approach the bench?" I force out the words, willing my voice to stay strong, though my insides are shaking.

"Granted. But make it quick—I'm already running behind schedule and the delays aren't impressing me."

Jagger's dark brow rises and he scowls in my direction, but I ignore him. There's no way he'll understand the ethics—I'll cross that bridge in a minute. I scurry forward, the clicking of my heels echoing off the barren walls.

"Your Honor, I need to be dismissed from this case."

Judge Ratler's brows scrunch together, a deep valley forming across the bridge of her nose.

"Explain, Counselor."

"I have a, um...personal connection to the defendant."

The judge narrows her eyes, her lips pursed. "What sort of *connection?*" She air quotes the last word and I grimace, my face heating.

"Um...a relationship. Sort of."

She stares at me, unblinking, then folds her hands together. "Explain, Counselor. I'm going to need more detail than a *sort of relationship.*"

A hot tingle sweeps over me, from my head down my neck. "We have—had—an intimate relationship."

"Why did you take the case then, Counselor? You should have passed it to a colleague from the start."

My insides twist like a pretzel and I don't think I've ever felt this humiliated in my life. How can I stand here and admit to the judge that I had an alley tryst with Roman just last night—and didn't even know his last name? Worse, how do I sidestep the circumstances of how I came to have the Capellis as my clients in the first place without throwing my father's illegal gambling into the court record?

I take a deep breath. "I was only assigned to the case this morning, Your Honor, and didn't realize the identity of the defendant until now."

"So what I'm hearing is you came late to court, unprepared, and now have an ethics concern? Am I correct in these assumptions, Counselor?"

"Yes, Your Honor." I drop my gaze to the floor, swallowing hard over the lump in my throat. This case is definitely not off to a good start.

"In my chambers now. With your client."

Standing, she swivels and heads back to chambers. Jagger glares at me as I wave him and his brothers over, and we all tag along behind the judge into her office.

The room is dim and cool, the back wall lined with tidy rows of hefty legal tomes. She sinks into a chair behind the desk, then takes off her glasses and squeezes the bridge of her nose. I sit in one of the leather club chairs and motion for Jagger to do the same. Cash and Damon lurk behind us, their thick shadows threatening.

"Gentlemen, it has come to my attention that Ms. Adams has a conflict of interest in her representation of your case."

"What the hell?" Jagger's beady eyes bore into me, the scar above his brow a fiery scarlet.

"I'm sorry, but I didn't know the defendant is Roman."

I rub my silver thumb ring, the cool, smooth metal somewhat comforting.

"One of the defendants, Ms. Adams," the judge corrects and I nod.

"Right. Yes, the entire Montgomery family, I get it."

"So you have a hard-on for Roman or something?" Jagger asks with a snicker.

"Language, Mr. Capelli. Need I remind you that you're currently sitting right outside a court of law?"

"My apologies, Judge. Skye, what's the deal with you and Romeo?"

"We, um..." I bite the corner of my lip, my face burning. "Have kind of a relationship thing."

Probably not anymore, by the glower on his face back there, but no need for the Capellis to know that. Either way, I shouldn't be the lawyer on this case.

"What kinda relationship thing? Are y'all banging or something?"

Judge Ratler tsks at Jagger, but he leans forward, hands resting on his knees, and I swear he's practically drooling at this new intel.

I shift in my seat, wishing I were anywhere but here right now. I'm sure guilt's written all over my face. Clasping my hands together in my lap, I sit up straight, trying to appear as prim as possible.

"Not that it's any of your personal business, but we may have shared an intimate moment."

Cash and Damon snicker behind us, guffawing like middle schoolers taking sex ed for the first time. Jagger's lips twist as he digests this juicy nugget of gossip.

"So, Mr. Capelli, you have the option of taking a continuance and gaining new representation."

My stomach sinks with leaden dismay. I'm not sure how this change of plan will affect my dad's debt. Maybe we can come up with a new deal?

"What if we really like Ms. Adams here and want her to stick it out on the case? Because we don't want to drag this out even longer. We've already been screwed out of our land for decades. We're ready to get it back." Jagger lays his palms flat on the judge's desk, leaning forward to emphasize his point.

Judge Ratler picks up her glasses, twirls them around as she contemplates his request.

"I suppose that would be up to you. Should you wish to retain Ms. Adams as counsel, we can continue with today as planned."

"Wait, what?" My gut twists harder and the salad I ate for lunch threatens to make an encore appearance. "But I'm in clear violation of the code of ethics here. I *know* the defendant."

"I understand that, Ms. Adams. And so do your clients. It will go into the court record that the Capellis are aware of the conflict of interest, but have chosen to proceed. The court cannot and will not hold you responsible for any prior relationship with the defendant. Going forth, however, you're advised to cease relations with the defendant—to the best of your ability, I do realize Seaglass Beach is a small town —for the remainder of the case. But I can appreciate the Capelli's desire to move ahead with their claim. Frankly, the court wishes to settle the matter as expeditiously as possible as well." She slides her glasses back into place, sitting back in her oversized chair.

"Your request to be removed from the case, Ms. Adams, is denied. Your clients have made an informed decision to retain you as counsel. We will proceed as scheduled."

The air's sucked from my lungs, evaporating, and I'm lightheaded. Clutching the edges of the chair, I struggle to remain upright as the room swims before me.

I cannot believe this.

This judge expects me to go back out there, into that courtroom, and stand in front of Roman—the same man I had sex with less than twenty-four hours ago—stare him dead in the eye and question him about deeds and boundary lines?

It's going to be my job, my duty, to try to fuck the man out of his land. Land his family's owned, farmed, and developed over generations. Land I'm sure the family plans to pass on to their children, and their children's children.

And God forbid I don't win. Because then the Capellis will probably burn my father's house down, and then what? He moves in with me? Goes on a bender and drinks himself to death? They kill him?

I've never wanted to try a case less in my life, let alone win the damn thing. But it appears I have no other choice.

"Ms. Adams, can you do that? Set aside your personal feelings and fulfill your legal duty? Or should the Capellis reconsider their decision?" Judge Ratler peers over the rim of her glasses at me, and cold dread replaces the hot panic from earlier.

Jagger taps the face of his watch, sending me a silent reminder of the ticking clock and my father's debt repayment plan. Bile rises in my throat and I struggle to swallow it down.

"Yes, Your Honor. I understand. I can represent the Capellis."

"Very well, then. Let's resume."

With shaky legs and a pounding heart, I stand and follow Judge Ratler out to the courtroom, keeping my gaze directly ahead of me to avoid the hard stare of Roman. I catch Jagger smirking in that direction, but I'm too flustered to worry about him and his bad behavior at the moment.

Taking my seat, I rifle through the thin file on the Capelli case. It appears not much work has been done yet. A tiny flutter of hope wings around in my chest. Maybe the case won't go to trial at all. Maybe Judge Ratler reviewed the documents and decided it's all bullshit.

"Now that we're all back together again—" The judge clasps her hands together and my heart rate kicks into overdrive. "I've taken the documents filed by the Capellis into consideration."

I bite my lip, holding my breath.

"And I do believe this case may have merit. Therefore, I move that we go to trial."

An audible gasp sounds from behind me, but I don't dare turn around and risk making eye contact with anyone in the courtroom.

"Of course, either party may request a settlement. Now would be a good time, before we go to all the trouble of assembling a jury."

The judge pauses, waiting for someone to take the bait. I lean over, getting closer to Jagger than I'd like.

"Any chance you'd want to settle?"

Because honestly, the sooner I can be done with the Capellis and pay off my dad's debt, the better.

"Only if they're handing over the keys to the Seaglass

Inn." He shoots me a wolfish grin over his steepled, meaty fingers and my skin crawls.

"That seems highly unlikely. Not to mention unfair, given the small section of land in question."

"Whose side are you on? Theirs—" Jagger hikes a thumb at Roman—"or ours?"

He doesn't want to know the truth here.

I drop my voice to a whisper. "Listen, Jagger. I'll try your case to the best of my ability, but I'm not going to knowingly screw the Montgomerys out of their rightful land. Are we clear?"

Jagger inches closer to me, the strong smell of his musky cologne stinging my nostrils. "I think you're forgetting who has leverage here, darling. And it ain't you." Under the table, he squeezes my kneecap hard, pain racing down my shin.

I hate my client.

"I told you I'll do my best. That's all I can do." I force the words out, but my stomach's clenching so hard I feel sick.

"So no settlement then?" I scooch away as far as I can, trying to put as much distance between me and this asshole without rousing suspicion.

"No. No settlement."

I clear my throat, wishing I wasn't in this courtroom, in this predicament, right now. "My client wishes to proceed with the trial, Your Honor."

"As does mine." Roman's lawyer booms his response and I press my lips together, trepidation settling over me like a weighted blanket.

"Trial date is set one month from today. Please endeavor to prepare as quickly as possible. And I don't want any unnecessary motions for continuance. Let's resolve this matter efficiently and not waste anyone's time or money. Court is adjourned."

The bang of the gavel echoes in the quiet room and then chatter erupts behind me. All I hear, though, is the swooshing of the blood pulsing in my eardrums. I just want to get out of the courtroom before I suffocate, the sharp claws of anxiety already pulling at me and the trial hasn't even yet begun.

"Daddy's safe so far. But we're watching you," Jagger leans in and hisses against my ear.

I shove my files into my satchel and stand. "Don't try to intimidate me. I'm doing my job. That's the deal."

Straightening my blazer, I head out of the courtroom and away from the prying eyes of the judge.

I need to explain myself to Roman. He may not forgive me, but at least he'll understand the truth—I didn't know he was involved and never meant to hurt him.

6

———

SKYE

"Roman, wait!" I run after him as fast as I can manage in my stilettos, leaving my clients to lumber out of the courthouse on their own.

I may have been coerced into taking their case, but that doesn't mean I have to hang out with them in my free time. Or explain my relationship—or anything else, for that matter— to them, either.

Roman doesn't stop. He doesn't even slow down, taking long, angry strides across the slick floor of Town Hall. I feel slightly pathetic racing after him, but I need to explain myself, let him know I had no idea he and his family would be sitting on the other side of this case.

Convince him I'm not the bad guy here, without giving away my family's secrets.

This should be fun.

Roman shoves through the glass doors, jogs down the stone steps. I'm panting and out of breath, a thin sheen of sweat collecting in my armpits. Sexy.

"Roman, please wait!" I call after him again, and he

finally slows a little. Probably only because he's at his truck, but it's something.

"Pretty sure you're not supposed to be speaking to me." He spins to face me, growling the words, his jaw flexing with tension.

"I'm definitely not. But it's a risk I'm willing to take. Because I felt something last night—something real—and I want you to know that."

"I'm pretty sure you felt something last night." A mixture of pain and pride flashes across his face, a vein pulsing in his neck.

"You know what I mean. Besides the physical part, which was amazing. I felt a connection with you. And that's something that doesn't happen to me. Ever."

His lips press together, full and perfect, and I fervently wish we were back in the alley, his hands all over me.

"Did you plan it, Skye? Our little rendezvous last night? Feels suspicious right now, from where I'm standing. What was your angle? Try to mine me for intel before court this afternoon?"

"We never even talked about the case!" I throw my hands out in exasperation, frustration bubbling inside me. "What kind of ambush is that if I didn't even mention the trial?"

He shoves a hand into his pocket, but stays silent.

"I didn't know this case was against you and your family. Swear."

"Well, now you do. And you're still representing those scumbags."

"I know and I'm sorry. I asked the judge for a dismissal from the case due to conflict of interest, but no dice."

"Great. So now she and the Capellis know about last night?"

A hot blush floods my cheeks and I fiddle with a loose thread on my blouse. "Sort of, yes. I mean, obviously not all the details. But, um, they kind of know the broad strokes of the relationship."

"Shit, Skye. You may as well have blasted that we had sex on social media. The whole damn town's gonna hear about it by suppertime."

"I had to try to get off the case, Roman." I cross my arms over my chest. "I needed some legitimate reason, so I went with the truth."

He heaves out a long sigh. "Whatever. If you're doing business with the Capellis, you're not the person I thought you were."

Ouch. Shots fired.

"You don't understand." My voice is quiet, my fists balled at my side.

"I think I do. You're on the wrong side of this case, so we're done."

He unlocks his truck and climbs in, slamming the door shut. The window slides down and my heart jumps, a glimmer of hope flickering inside me.

"Lose my number."

He fires up the engine and roars out of the parking spot without so much as a backward glance in my direction. Hot tears prick at the corner of my eyes and I will myself not to cry.

"Naughty girl, already breaking the judge's orders."

A low rasp taunts me from behind.

Fucking Jagger.

I spin to face him, masking my emotions with a scowl.

"What I do off the clock is none of your business, Jagger. Got it?"

He steps forward, grabbing my forearm so tight I'm sure I'll have a thumbprint-shaped bruise tomorrow. "Listen, Chicky. That's the little nickname from dear old dad, right?"

All the blood drains from my face, an icy trickle of fear slithering down my spine as I stare into his beady eyes.

"I don't give a shit if you talk to soldier boy. Kiss him. Fuck him. Whatever you want to do with him. Bring us back information and we're all good. Understand, Chicky?" He draws out my nickname, making my skin crawl.

"I can't do that. You heard the judge, Jagger."

He steps in closer, his face inches from mine. My stomach turns, knowing I'm sharing the same air as this vile man.

"You'll do as I say. Or there will be consequences."

Even though my insides quake, I straighten my shoulders and put on a brave face. "I can't—and won't—break any laws for you, Jagger."

"Last time I checked, it's not illegal to fuck a Montgomery. In poor taste, sure. But still legal."

Cash and Damon laugh behind us at the lame-ass joke and for what feels like the hundredth time today, I fight back nausea.

"I can't, Jagger."

"I can't, Jagger," he taunts me, his voice a ridiculously high imitation. "Bring us insider info and Daddy keeps his miserable little shithole of a trailer. No info and the trailer goes boom." Jagger spreads his fingers wide in a mock explosion.

"You can't do that." Despite my best efforts, my voice wobbles, giving me away.

"Don't push me, Chicky. I've done worse things."

"He has," Cash chimes in and Damon nods and grunts in agreement.

"Roman's not even speaking to me."

"I don't give a shit how you get the info. Take your clothes off again. Show him your tits. I'm sure soldier boy will give some stuff up when he's distracted by those knockers." Jagger's gaze drops to my breasts and I pull my jacket tight against my chest, covering as much of my body as possible.

"I can't..."

Jagger shrugs. "Suit yourself. You have five days to come back with something good—or Daddy's house goes bye-bye."

He drops his grip on my arm abruptly and I stumble backward, nearly falling without the tension holding me up. The three of them don't spare me a second glance. Jagger unlocks his truck, and he and Cash climb in. Damon launches himself into the back of the truck, either unaware that it's illegal, or—more likely—just not giving a shit. I'm betting few cops in Seaglass Beach bother with the more minor legal violations when it comes to the Capellis. Not worth the paperwork.

Jagger revs his engine, once, twice, vibrating the sidewalk, then roars down the street. Damon grins and flicks me off from the back, just for funsies.

And here I thought yesterday was bad...

7

ROMAN

Ninety-seven. Ninety-eight. Ninety-nine. One hundred.

I drop the weighted ball onto the rubber mat in my home gym, sweat dripping down my back after the fifth set of Russian twists. Core burning, I stand up and grab the forty-pound weights, cranking out twenty biceps curls, then twenty more, and another twenty after that.

Ring, ring. My cell screams from the weight bench and I debate picking it up. There aren't many people I want to speak to at the moment.

Ring, ring. Dropping the weights, I check caller ID.

King.

"Hey." My voice is tight and breathless—from the workout as well as the strain of the lawsuit. I've been dealing with this shit for a while now and it's starting to wear on me.

"How'd it go today, really? Poppy called me crying, but figured I'd call you and get a reality check of the situation."

To an outsider, my brother sounds neutral. But I know

King better than anyone, and the worry carries straight through the phone line.

Truthfully, I feel the same.

Blowing out a sharp breath, I collapse onto the bench. "Shitty. The judge decided to hear the case. I hoped it would get dismissed as total horseshit, but the judge—and I quote—sees merit to the claim. So we go to trial in a month."

Silence fills my ears.

"Well, that sucks."

I nod, even though he can't see me. "It does. And I wasn't worried before today because, c'mon, it's the Capellis. But they somehow managed to hire a decent lawyer."

"Who? And how do you know he's decent?"

Heat floods my system, remembering the way Skye held my gaze last night in the shadows of the alley as she bounced on my cock.

"He's a she, actually. Her name's Skye Adams. I did some digging—"

And a little fucking, but no need to bring that up right now.

"—and she's good."

At several things, including hot-as-hell alley sex. But King doesn't need to know all the dirty details.

"Graduated top of her class from law school and has a winning record."

Also, fantastic tits, but I shove the visual out of my mind. That's not part of this current conversation.

"But the claim's bullshit, right? I mean, it has to be. The Seaglass Inn's been in our family for four generations. We have all the paperwork to prove it. Surely Cleet can get this thing thrown out?"

I sigh, the adrenaline from my workout leaking out of me as quickly as it built up.

"Honestly, I don't know. I have a meeting with him tomorrow. I think you should be there."

Another long silence, then King mutters in agreement. "I'll come. But I'm not putting on a tie or anything. And I'm wearing my boots."

"Understood."

King disconnects and guilt weighs heavy on my chest. That was the perfect opportunity to tell him what happened with Skye, but something inside me wouldn't come clean.

Even to my big brother and best friend.

Fuck.

Scrubbing a hand through my hair, I flash back to the scene in the Town Hall parking lot. The haunted look in her wide eyes, the pleading note in her voice as she begged me to listen to her side of the story.

No. Just no.

I can't go getting soft now, not with my family's land and livelihood hanging in the balance.

And definitely not with someone working actively against me. Against us.

As much as I hate it, I need to steer clear of Skye Adams. Even if my body—and a gentler part of me that I suspect is my heart—screams otherwise.

True to his word, King meets me at the law office the next morning. He's in his typical uniform of T-shirt, jeans, boots, and his cowboy hat, but at least he showed up. I didn't tell Poppy about the meeting. No need to get her riled up any more than she already is. The last thing we need is full-blown hysterics. Or worse, her doing something stupid, like confronting the Capellis. I have enough on my plate, what with my security job for the mayor and handling the lawsuit; I don't want to provide twenty-four-seven protection for my baby sister, too.

"Rome." King tips his head at me, his tanned face stoic. You don't want to play poker with my brother.

"Hey. Thanks for coming."

Together, we head into the office. A secretary greets us, offering coffee, but we both decline. I don't need any caffeine at the moment, I'm jumpy enough as it is.

"He'll be with you gentlemen in a minute. Please have a seat." She motions to the bank of chairs in an empty conference room, all mahogany wood and red leather. We do as instructed and she sashays out, leaving us alone.

King shifts in his seat, clearly uncomfortable, the leather squeaking beneath his weight. He looks out of place here, sitting amongst the thick law books and framed college degrees, wooden plaques of recognition lining the wall behind us. King rarely ventures off the ranch, much more at ease with the trees, horses, and hay bales than people. Right now, I'd rather be out there too, truth be told.

"Gentlemen..." Cleet strides in and King and I both rise to greet him. He shakes King's hand, patting him on the back, then does the same with me before sitting at the head of the long table.

"It's good to see you, King, although I wish it were under better circumstances. Frankly, I'm shocked Judge Ratler agreed to hear the case, but that's where we are right now."

"Pardon my French, Cleet—" King leans forward in his chair, palms flat on the shiny table. "but the lawsuit's bull-shit. There's no way the Capellis own that land. We gave you the deed, the survey, the purchase agreement. Every-thing we have says that land is ours, free and clear. Bought and paid for by our great-great-grandfather." He taps the file folder on the table in front of Cleet hard with his thick index finger.

"I understand. But the Capellis must have something, some type of document, that calls the land into question. Otherwise, Judge Ratler wouldn't be hearing the case." Cleet fiddles with a pen, twirling it round and round between his fingers.

"When will we know what they have?" I ask, already wondering about the calendar and how much longer this thing's gonna drag on.

"And how will we know it's legit?" King adds.

"Well, the judge fast tracked this case, but we still have a month before the trial. They may or may not submit documents to the court during that time." Cleet flips through the trial paperwork in the file. "The Capellis would be pretty bold to falsify documents in court. That's perjury, a punishable offense."

"Probably not a deterrent for them. And leave it to the Capellis to wait until the last second to deliver any sort of evidence. They're not exactly known for fighting fair." I shake my head, remembering all the times the Capellis started shit with us. The list is long, stretching all the way back to grade school. And I'm pretty sure the bad blood runs deep, pumping through multiple generations.

"My team will do their best to determine legitimacy of any documents they bring forth. That's the best we can do." Cleet's lips press into a thin, tight line, his years of experience etched in deep furrows across his forehead.

"So our entire strategy is a defensive one? Isn't there something we can do right now? Someone we can talk to?" My legs bounce up and down beneath the table with nervous energy.

Cleet's gray brows scrunch together in a frown as he stares up at the ceiling, thinking. After a long pause, he cracks his neck, first to the left, then to the right, before speaking.

"The one thing you could do right now is comb through any family files you can find that may hold information. Maybe something will turn up that we can use."

King huffs out a deep sigh. "I went through all the files in the office out at the ranch. But maybe there's something up in the attic." He glances over at me. "Guess we'll have to make a trip up there."

My stomach clenches, every muscle tense. The last thing I want to do is head to the attic, the landmine of family memories. Each box a potential minefield, threatening to detonate if I lift the lid, blowing the fragile normalcy I've constructed since our parents died to bits.

I crack my knuckles and stand. "It must be done. I'll be over tonight, King. And we'll get back to you with anything we find, Cleet."

8

———

ROMAN

MUCH AS I'M NOT LOOKING FORWARD TO THE ATTIC TRIP down memory lane, I head straight over to the ranch when the mayor leaves Town Hall for the day. Figure the sooner King and I start the search, the quicker we'll finish. And then hopefully I won't have to go back up to the attic again anytime in the near future.

I let myself in, not bothering to knock on the front door of my childhood home. That would be too weird, even if this is King's house now.

"Hi, honey, I'm home," I call out in a joking voice, attempting to lighten the mood. I know King's dreading the task as well, maybe even more so than me. Although I'm the Marine, King's less emotive—and that's saying a lot. I'm not exactly a therapist's dream client or anything.

"In here." King's voice echoes off the high wooden rafters as I make my way to the kitchen. He's standing at the island sipping a beer.

"Want one?" He tips the green glass bottle at me and I shrug.

"Sure."

Grabbing a beer from the fridge, he pops the top and hands it to me.

"Thanks." I take a long pull of beer and relish the cold liquid as it slides down my tight throat. I really don't want to be doing this right now.

"Tree looks good." I gesture at the tall, twinkly fir Christmas tree standing in the corner of the room. "Poppy did a good job."

Ever since the death of our parents, our sister's made a point of having a tree delivered to each of us and decorating them all herself. She's good about things like that, family traditions and stuff.

"She did. If it wasn't for her, you know I wouldn't have a tree."

"I'll bet she's glad Parker got married. One less tree for her to have to decorate."

"Knowing Poppy, she probably snuck into his house while he was on his honeymoon and did it anyway."

I shake my head, chuckling. "Probably."

The sun sets and darkness falls over the ranch, a comfortable silence settling between me and my older brother. King and I have an easy relationship. Neither of us is a big talker and we don't push the other into idle conversation. Poppy and Parker are a different story altogether; the two of them got all the sociability genes King and I lack. And that suits both of us just fine.

After we finish our beers, King chucks the bottles and rolls his shoulders, a frown settling in between his brows.

"Ready?" He glances over at me, his face set with determination.

"Let's do this."

We head to the second floor and King pulls the rope for the attic ladder, the rickety wooden stairs unfolding.

"After you." He waves a hand and I climb into the hot space, clambering through the small entrance. It takes a second for my eyes to adjust to the dark, then I find the string for a bare lightbulb and click on the light. A golden glow washes over the dusty space as I survey the piles of boxes covering most every surface.

"Shit. This could take a while." I heave out a sigh, already wishing I was back home watching television or filing reports—basically, anything other than hunting through Montgomery family heirlooms on a wild goose chase.

"You take the right side, I'll take the left." King points at a tall pile of plastic bins, all neatly labeled.

"Fine."

A solid hour later, I've rummaged through my baseball card collection, a weird array of Parker's trophies, a box of dress patterns our mom used way back in the day, an assortment of Poppy's baby dolls, and a bunch of King's 4-H stuff. But nothing that could help us in the land dispute.

"Damn, this was a dead end." I shove the lid back on our parents' record collection. We should probably sell it—some of those albums are worth a bunch of coin—but none of us has the heart to.

I stack bins back up in the corner, then peer over at King. "Listen—and maybe this is a long shot—but have you spoken to Juliet?"

King keeps his head down, avoiding eye contact at the mention of the youngest Capelli, the only daughter in the family.

"No."

A gruff, one-word response. *Super.*

I clear my throat, swallowing down over the dusty tickle. "Maybe it'd be worth reaching out? See if she knows anything?"

A few beats of silence pass between us, then he shakes his head. "I'm sure she doesn't know anything."

"How do you know that? Even if her brothers didn't loop her into the details, she may have overheard something, seen something that could help us."

"I said *no*, Rome. Drop it." The line of his broad shoulders and the deep furrow of his brow tell me to do as he says, but I can't help myself.

"I'm just saying it could be worth a conversation."

"Damn it, Rome!" King's voice booms through the small space, his fists clenched at his side. "I don't want to talk to her. Understood?"

I only half-understand, but figure now's not the time to dig deeper. We're both too pained from the task at hand and the pressure of the lawsuit, and neither of us is thinking all that clearly.

"Sure." I drop the subject for now.

Buzz, buzz. My cell vibrates in my pocket and I pull it out, read the text.

Skye: I know you told me to lose your number. And I will. But I want you to know I never wanted this case and had no idea it was against you and your family

Skye: Swear

I scowl at the screen, hot anger swirling in my gut. I

can't believe she's texting me, after I told her to never contact me again.

"You okay?" King narrows his navy eyes at me from across the attic.

"Yeah." I shove my cell back into my pocket and ignore the buzzing of yet another text, vowing to block her number as soon as I leave the ranch.

"Hey—I think I might have something." King holds up an old leather diary, carefully flipping through it. "This is Great-Grandma Alice's diary. And look here—" He points at a pencil sketch—"She talks about Great-Grandpa Theo's family buying the land. When Great-Grandpa Theo died, the land passed on to Grandpa Thomas and Grandma Cornelia. And here's the family tree."

"Nice find, King. More written documentation that the land belongs to the Montgomery family. Free and clear. No mention of the Capellis anywhere in there, right?"

King skims over the page again, then flips forward and back, searching for any mention of the Capellis.

"Nope. Nothing that I see. Maybe this is enough to shut the case down for good. Maybe we won't even go to trial." His voice tips up in a hopeful lilt.

I shrug. "Maybe. Probably not, but that's definitely a plus for our side. Mark the pages and I'll photocopy them tomorrow and run them over to Cleet."

"Good plan. That's enough digging for tonight. You want another beer?" King clicks the box lid back into place before hefting it up and shoving it on the top of the stack.

"Nah. I should get going. I need to be at work early tomorrow. Thanks, though."

"Sure. Hit the light, will you?" King heads down the ladder, leaving me up in the dusty attic alone.

As soon as he disappears, I slide my cell out of my pocket and read the text.

> Skye: Please forgive me

I heave out a sigh, my chest aching at the raw words. *Please forgive me.*

Deep-down, I want to. Would love nothing more. But as a soldier, I instinctively know this is war. And she's on the wrong side of the battlefield. Forgiving her is tantamount to treason, and I can't do it.

I shove my phone back into my pocket without responding and click off the light, climbing down the ladder.

One lesson my mom taught me that stuck: sometimes the best thing is to say nothing at all.

And this feels like one of those times.

9

———

SKYE

I STARE DOWN AT THE TEXT, WILLING ROMAN TO WRITE back. But the little blue text bubbles never appear.

Damn it.

Not that I thought he'd write back. But a girl can hope, right?

I fling the phone down onto the couch cushion beside me and close my eyes, trying to visualize my next move. Jagger threatened to destroy my dad's trailer if I don't come up with some kind of insider info on the Montgomery family. Which is going to be damn near impossible, considering Roman won't even speak to me.

Not to mention unethical and going directly against what Judge Ratler warned me about back in her office: *Try to minimize contact with the defendant.*

Unfortunately for me, Roman was making that super easy. And I'm sure Jagger and crew aren't going to care one iota about the fact that he isn't talking to me. They're probably out buying dynamite—or whatever they plan on using to blow up my dad's trailer—right now.

What are you going to do about it?

Sitting on the couch, while comforting and cozy, isn't exactly solving the problem. Maybe I can concoct some fake tidbit to satisfy Jagger? A pretend hot tip, juicy enough to quench his thirst, but nothing real that could hurt Roman or his family.

Probably not my best plan, but it's all I can come up with right now and it's certainly better than nothing. Besides, how will Jagger know it's not the real deal? He's not the brightest bulb in the circuit, that's for sure.

Maybe you should go to the judge and tell her the truth about the Capellis—they're low-level thugs, intimidating you with threats against your father and his property instead.

I kick my feet up on the coffee table, cross my arms over my chest, and fidget with the thin silver of my ring.

No, I can't do that. Because then the judge will ask questions, ultimately revealing the real reason I'm on the case—to pay off my dad's illegal gambling debt. Then my dad will be in trouble with the law, the Capellis will be pissed and seeking vengeance, and I will have lost my firm a client. Not a very valuable one, but still.

No, confessing the truth is out as a strategy. One hundred percent.

Even though it's kind of late already, I need a change of scenery to think better. It's too dark to go walking alone, even in this idyllic little beach town. Instead, I grab my car keys, settling on a drive.

Five minutes later, I'm cruising down A1A. Traffic's light, most people home from work and after-school activities. Probably done eating dinner and now the kids are doing last-minute homework or they're asleep, giving parents time to catch up on the latest episode of whatever bingeable show's popular on Netflix at the moment. I'm partial to true crime drama myself, hence my growing unease with the Capelli case. Last thing I need is to end up on one of those shows—especially as the victim.

A cold shudder rips through me and I turn the heat on full blast, even though the outside temperature is a moderate sixty degrees. Not all that chilly, but thinking about Jagger and his bros gives me the creeps.

The stoplight turns yellow and I slow down, easing to a stop. The radio pumps out a tinny yacht rock tune I recognize, but can't name. Humming, I casually glance out at the traffic and something registers deep in the recesses of my brain.

The truck diagonal to me looks like Roman's.

Could it be him?

I crane my neck, trying to see, but the light turns green and the truck takes off. *Shit.* What if it's him? Should I confront him? Try to get him to talk to me? Explain myself again?

Or should I follow him and spy, try to get some innocent piece of info I can pass on to Jagger to spare my dad's trailer?

Figuring the best option is to follow him either way, I step on it, careful to leave one car between me and the truck. Not that Roman's looking for me or anything. But still, better to be on the safe side.

Another traffic light stops us and I duck down behind the wheel, trying to stay low. He has a major height advantage, being in a truck, so I need to be even stealthier. The light's short and the truck again sprints off the line. I rush to keep up, hot adrenaline racing through me now.

Suddenly, the truck makes a quick right onto a side

street. I follow, but slow way down because in the quiet neighborhood I'm a lot easier to make. The truck abruptly slides over to the curb and cuts the engine. I quickly debate what to do—should I pull behind him and take the risk of being seen? Or keep driving past, make a fast loop, and circle back, praying he'll still be here?

I speed up and keep driving down the road. But not without taking a little peek at the driver of the truck.

Yep, it's him. Definitely Roman, his square, chiseled jaw highlighted beneath the streetlight.

And—because I'm a very good attorney—I've already done some digging and know for a fact this is *not* the street where he lives.

Why did he stop? Is he meeting someone? Maybe he has another girlfriend I don't know about. Or a nighttime security gig.

Circling around the block, I turn back down the street and the truck's still there. I squint out into the darkness, trying to figure out if Roman's still in the vehicle. But I'm too far away and I can't tell from this distance. I think I see him, but it could also be a shadow playing tricks on me.

I ease my car up against the curb and kill the engine, cutting the lights. My breathing's shallow, pulse racing. I have no plan and no agenda, but it feels like I'm in some kind of high-stakes game of cat-and-mouse—and I'm not sure which one I am.

Sliding down low in my seat, I duck my head and peer over the dash through the gap in the steering wheel. Minutes tick by, slowly, so slowly, and nothing happens. No movement. Now I'm sweating, regretting turning the heat up so high, and I have to pee. And still nothing. I tap my foot on the floorboard, antsy, as time crawls by. Gawd, it must be almost midnight by now, I've been sitting here for hours.

I check my watch. 9:30. I've probably been staking out the truck for less than ten minutes. This is so freaking boring. It's a good thing I'm an attorney and not a private investigator because this is *so* not my jam.

Tap, tap, tap. A loud rap on my window scares the daylights out of me and I scream at the top of my lungs.

Standing right outside my car is Roman, his cobalt eyes blazing—and not in a good, lusty way, either.

Cover blown.

He motions for me to roll down my window, so I do, my chest heaving, what with my hyperventilation at the jump scare.

"Why'd you scare me like that?" I hiss.

The best defense is a good offense.

"Why are you following me?" He folds his arms over his broad, muscled chest, his eyes narrowed.

"Me? I'm not following you." I hold my hand against my heart, acting affronted.

"Really. Then what are you doing on this street at 9:30 at night?"

"Maybe I live here." I jut my chin out, daring him to call my bluff.

"No. Because if you lived here, you wouldn't be sitting in your car. Ditto for any explanation other than you're following me. So what's the story, Skye? Is this all part of making the case against us? You're going to follow me around town until you find something out?"

"No. Absolutely not." My chest squeezes, knowing that's only a half-truth.

"Cut the crap, Skye, okay? There's no other reason for

you to be out at this time of night, on this street, where I happen to be."

"For your information, Roman—" and I put heavy emphasis on his name here, just to piss him off— "that's not what's going on at all. I was out for a drive and then my, um, check engine light came on, so I pulled over. You know, to be on the safe side. Don't want my engine to explode or something." I somehow manage to hold eye contact, even though I'm making this whole story up as I go.

"Really? Huh. Well, why don't you let me take a look then? I'd hate for you to blow up."

He feigns sincerity and my heart flip-flops in my chest, half-wishing there's some truth behind his words.

"Um, okay. Sure." I climb out of the car, handing him the keys, my oh-shit meter clanging loudly inside my head. But what can I do? I've spun a web of sticky lies. Now I need to try and untangle myself as carefully as possible.

Roman edges past me, our bodies brushing, and I catch a whiff of his cologne, the scent of cedar. He smells really nice and I wish I was wrapped in his strong arms again.

Like last night.

But clearly *that's* not gonna happen.

Lowering himself into the driver's seat, he pushes the ignition button and my car sputters to life. I lean over, making a big show of scanning the dash. Roman's face is close to mine, peppered with a dark five-o-clock shadow, and I vaguely wonder how the scruff would feel against the inside of my thighs.

His deep voice interrupts my fantasy. "No check engine light."

"Huh. Weird. Looks like the problem's fixed, at least

for now. Don't you hate it when that happens? The dealer won't be able to repair it because they can't see the issue." I bob my head, as if this happens to me all the freaking time.

"Uh-huh." Roman's lips press together in a tight line of disbelief.

"Well, thanks for checking it for me. I appreciate it."

His hand darts out and grabs my wrist. Startled, a harsh gasp falls from my lips.

"Stop with the games. What are you really doing out here?" Roman's voice is low and husky. Much to my dismay, a hot flash of desire rips through me and settles low in my belly. Apparently, my survival instincts aren't exactly on point.

"I told you—I was out for a drive. Honest." I level my gaze on his, figuring this is my best play since that's the actual truth.

He stares at me for a long second, his jaw tense as he debates the veracity of my statement. The air between us is charged, but unlike last night, it's not just lust. Now there's distrust, hurt, and probably a hint of betrayal.

And I hate it. I want nothing more than to come clean with Roman—right here, right now—but I can't.

God knows what Jagger would do to my father.

And that's not a risk I can afford to take, even for Roman.

"I don't believe you." Roman breaks the fragile silence between us, a frown marring his handsome face.

"Fine." I shrug, as if his words don't sting, cutting me right to the core. "You don't have to believe me. That's your prerogative."

His thumb feathers out over my wrist, tracing a whisper-soft line across my vein. My pulse rate shoots up under his tender touch. The lines around his eyes soften as he locks eyes with me.

"Why'd you take the case, really? And don't feed me some bullshit line about how you couldn't get dismissed, blah, blah, blah. I already heard that story once."

I swallow hard over the ginormous lump in my throat, blood pounding in my ears.

Chance number two to tell Roman the truth. But at what cost? My dad's trailer blows up? Or worse?

I can't do it.

"I had to." I whisper the words, so quiet they almost blow away on the wind.

"You always have a choice, Skye. In every situation. I've been in more than one tough spot, times when I had to make a life-or-death decision. And you know what? I always chose to do the right thing. You could have too."

The anguish in his voice, the hurt in his eyes, cuts me all the way to the bone. I hate that he feels this way. Hate that he believes the worst of me.

But still, the words don't come.

Because I can't admit my dad's predicament. Because I'm ashamed. Because I don't want to put anyone else in danger, including Roman.

No. I can handle this on my own. I have to.

"You're wrong, you know." I pull my arm out of his grasp, instantly missing the warmth of his fingers against my skin. "Sometimes you don't have a choice."

"I guess we'll have to disagree on that. You have a choice here—" Roman gets out of my car, squares his body with mine, and now we're inches apart. We're sharing the same air, but it feels like we're worlds away from each other right now.

"—you're just making the wrong one." Roman walks away, disappointment radiating off his body.

My stomach swirls, bitter acid rising in my throat. I resist the urge to scream after him, hot indignation pulsing through me.

Instead, I climb into my car and slam the door shut, locking the doors.

"Fuck you, Roman," I mutter into the dark interior of my car, swiping away the tears shimmering in my eyes.

In my heart, I know I'm doing the right thing—but it sure doesn't feel like it at the moment.

10

ROMAN

She was lying.

Skye stared straight at me, held my gaze with those wide, brown sugar eyes, and lied to my face.

Her pupils dilated, her pulse picked up beneath my thumb, her breath quickened.

All the signs were there.

And yet—I don't want to believe it.

There has to be a good explanation, some reason for the lies.

A reason she took the Capelli's case in the first place.

I may not know her that well, but one thing I am is a solid judge of character. And I believe Skye's a good person, even if she's lying to me right now.

But why would she lie?

Am I deluding myself here because I made a mistake, a bad decision, in the alley?

What could be so terrible, so horrific, that she can't tell me the truth?

And what's all this horseshit about not having a choice?

People always have choices, even if sometimes both choices suck.

I have to find out what's going on. Maybe if I can do that, I'll figure out a way to win this lawsuit and life can go back to normal.

And you can have another shot with Skye.

I shove that thought out of my mind, unlocking the front door of my house. It's been a long day and all I want to do is shower and go to sleep.

Setting the diary on the kitchen counter, I open the fridge and survey the contents. Not many options. A loaf of bread, some expired yogurt, leftover Chinese take-out.

I grab the white take-out box and a fork, eating cold fried rice in the dark, directly from the carton. Far from the dinner of champions, but it's past ten p.m. now and I can't be bothered with any type of cooking.

A few minutes later, I toss the empty carton into the trash, drop the fork into the dishwasher. A dull pain throbs in my lower back and I know I pushed it too far in the gym yesterday. Hopefully a hot shower will take the edge off.

I head to the bathroom, twisting the shower faucet all the way to the left, the hiss of the spray echoing off the white porcelain subway tiles. Pulling my shirt over my head, lingering notes of floral perfume tickle my nose. Skye. I inhale the soft cotton, my dick instantly hard.

Shedding my jeans and boxer briefs, I fist myself, running my hand up and down the hard shaft. Muscles tight, tingly pressure builds at the base as I step into the shower and adjust the water temperature down from scalding to chili-pepper hot. The spray hits my back and the throbbing pain eases. Or maybe I'm distracted by my dick as I stroke up and down, harder and faster, using slippery body wash as lube. Water sluices over my shoulders, down my chest, and I close my eyes, surrendering to feeling.

The heat, the pressure, the tension coil low in my gut.

I'm back in the alley, Skye's long legs wrapping around my waist as I thrust into her hot, wet pussy. Soft moans against my ear sending an excited shiver down my spine. Her muscles clenching, milking my cock as she grips my shoulders. The salty, briny taste of her perfect, pillowy lips, her tongue pressing against mine.

"Fuck..." I hiss as hot, white cum hits the tile wall of the shower, my dick pulsating in my hand.

I sigh, the excitement of release seeping out of me, leaving me bone-tired. I take a few more lazy swipes up and down the shaft, then grab the showerhead and rinse the wall. Erasing the evidence of my solo session.

Of all the women in Seaglass Beach, why'd the Capellis have to hire Skye Adams?

She told me she just got the case—and I tend to believe her. When we met at the bar, she'd had a bad day.

Dealing with the Capellis always puts me in a bad mood. Most other people, too. And I'm betting Skye's no different.

What did she say exactly? I rack my sleepy brain, trying to remember. Something about family problems and her dad being an asshole. But what did any of that have to do with the Capellis?

Rinsing myself off, I cut the water and grab a towel. The steamy shower drained me, the last bit of energy sucked out of me. My body's heavy and sleep's imminent, my brain fuzzy with exhaustion.

I wander into my dark bedroom, pull back the

comforter, and climb into the cool sheets buck-ass naked. One of the benefits of living alone.

Closing my eyes, I surrender to the sweet siren call of sleep, visions of Skye dancing straight into my dreams.

I WAKE UP TO A FULL VOICEMAIL BOX, EVERY MESSAGE from Poppy.

Good grief. How long are these messages? I hit the button to listen to the first voicemail.

"Rome, it's me. Call me as soon as you can. Justin Johnson texted me and said he saw King in town yesterday. Any idea why? Did you two meet or something? Is King alright? What's going on? Call me."

Trashing the message, I listen to the next one.

"Rome, where are you? Why haven't you called me back yet? It's already six-thirty. I need to know why King was in town. What was that about? Please call me back."

Delete.

Next message: "Roman. It's your sister. I heard from Mary Katherine Jetty that you and King had a meeting with Cleet. How come you didn't tell me? I would have loved to come, you know. Anyway, call me."

Next message.

"I can't believe the two of you had a meeting with the lawyer and didn't invite me. Rude. You *know* the Seaglass Inn is my baby. The least you could have done is ask me to the meeting. I want to be involved with this case, Roman. Because if anything happens to the inn..."

Poppy's voice cracks and now I feel shitty. Although this is the very reason King and I didn't invite her to the meeting in the first place. She's too close to the case, too emotional. Poppy wears her heart on her sleeve—for good or bad—and there's no room for that with the law.

She must have exceeded the voicemail time limit because there's a click and the message ends.

I listen and delete several more voicemails, finally clearing the mailbox. Before I can set my cell down and climb out of bed, the metal vibrates in my hand.

It's Poppy.

Might as well answer this and get it over with. She's obviously not giving up any time soon.

"Good morning, sunshine."

"Don't sunshine me, Roman. Why haven't you returned my calls?" Her voice is shrill and filled with fire. I scrub a hand over my face, wiping the rest of the sleep away. I'm gonna need all my energy to deal with my baby sister.

"I just woke up, Pops."

"How can you sleep at a time like this?" she shrieks. "We're about to lose the inn, our parents', our grandparents', and our great-grandparents' life work. Our legacy. And you're sleeping?!"

"Calm down, Poppy. The trial hasn't started yet." I swing out of bed, pulling on a pair of boxers.

"Calm down? Calm down? You want me to be calm?" Tapping the speaker button, I toss the cell onto my bed and hurry to get dressed. She does have a point—it's already past seven a.m. and I promised King I'd stop by Cleet's office with the diary first thing.

"Yes. I need you to be calm. King and I have this under control."

"So it's true, what Mary Katherine said. The two of you did have a meeting with Cleet. And didn't feel it necessary to invite me." Sadness and anger lace her words and my gut clenches.

I'm uncomfortable with high levels of emotion, especially first thing in the morning.

"Try to ignore the town gossip, will you?"

"Nice punt, Rome. Way to avoid answering the question."

I shrug into my dress shirt, buttoning as fast as I can. "Listen, Poppy. I can meet you at Coastal Coffee in thirty minutes and I'll fill you in. But right now, I gotta run."

She exhales loudly and the cell speaker rattles with the force. "Fine. I'll see you there."

Another click and Poppy's gone, never saying good-bye. She must be pretty mad. I hope buying her a coffee will salvage the situation because I don't particularly want to be fighting with the Capellis, Skye, *and* my sister.

I hurry out of the house, grabbing the diary on my way out. Thirty minutes later, the critical pages are photo-copied and handed over to Cleet and I stroll into Coastal Coffee. The scent of fresh roasted coffee beans hits me as soon as I step into the small café. There's no sign of Poppy yet, so I order her favorite, an iced mocha, along with an extra-dry cappuccino for myself and then snag a table in the back. I sit facing the window, a hold-out from my military days.

Never have your back to the door. Always be ready.

Minutes tick by, and still no Poppy. I should have known. Punctuality's never been her thing.

The door chimes tinkle and I glance up from my coffee,

fully expecting my sister to charge over and start jawing. But the customer isn't Poppy.

"I'm not following you, swear." Skye holds her palms up, waves of dark hair falling around her shoulders.

Fuck, she's sexy, in her tight black skirt and a light blue blouse, a deep V highlighting her ample chest. Sunlight streams through the window behind her, the lacy outline of her bra faintly visible through the sheer fabric.

Of course my dick takes notice and I shift, leaning back in the wooden chair.

"I said nothing." I level my eyes at her and keep my face neutral.

"No, but you were thinking it. I could tell."

Despite my best efforts, the corner of my lip tugs into a smile. I cover it up by taking a sip of my drink.

"I'm grabbing a coffee, that's all. I had no idea you'd be here." She smooths her hands down her skirt, her silver ring glinting in the sunlight.

"Uh-huh." I stare over the rim of the demitasse cup, watch as her cheeks flush a soft shade of pink. "How's that check engine light? Did it come back on this morning?"

"Thankfully, no. That's a problem I do not need." She flips her hair back over her shoulder, lying effortlessly.

"Good. Glad to hear it."

The door chime rings out again and this time Poppy does fly through the door, muttering her apology for being late.

"So sorry, Rome, a guest stopped me in the lobby as I was leaving and asked me a million and one questions about the restaurant menu and if they could order anything gluten-free. The chef wasn't in yet, so I had to get his room number and promise I'd investigate.

Anyway, tell me everything about your meeting with Cleet."

Poppy stops short at the table, pulling up right next to Skye. Only then does she realize she's in the presence of opposing counsel. She glances first at Skye, then at me, then back at Skye again, her aqua eyes narrowed.

"Oh, sorry. Am I interrupting?" Poppy asks.

"No. Skye was just leaving."

"Er, yeah. I was. Am. Leaving." Skye stumbles over the words, clearly flustered, her chest flushing. "See you."

Spinning on her heels, she heads to the counter and places her drink order. Poppy peers over her shoulder at Skye, then sinks down into the chair across from me.

"I hope I didn't say anything incriminating." She cups her hand to her mouth and whispers loudly enough that I'm sure Skye hears.

And that's reason number two why King and I didn't loop Poppy into the meeting. She has a big freaking mouth.

I shrug, distracted by Skye's perfect round peach of an ass and her mile-long legs. "It's fine."

"Rome."

I tear my eyes away from Skye's ass and attempt to focus on my sister, although my pants are now uncomfortably tight. Much as I want to hate Skye, my dick has other ideas.

"Earth to Roman." Poppy waves her hand in front of my face, then her eyes go wide in recognition. She checks over her shoulder before leaning in close to me. "Oh. My. Gawd. You're hooking up with her!"

To her credit, Poppy lowers her voice so Skye most likely doesn't hear this, but I still kick her foot beneath the table.

"Shh. And no, I'm not."

"C'mon, Rome. There's no way that's the truth," Poppy presses, one brow arched high. "You're never this distracted."

"Fine." I huff out a breath. "Not currently, at least. We slept together once. *Before* I knew she was the Capelli's lawyer."

"Roman Montgomery! I cannot believe this." Poppy shakes her head, her blonde ponytail swish-swishing behind her.

"Anyway, my sex life is none of your business." I fold my arms over my chest, hot embarrassment prickling my skin. "I have no desire to talk about this with my little sister."

Poppy keeps glancing over at Skye, presumably assessing the situation.

"Stop. You're so obvious, Poppy."

"I mean, normally I'd be thrilled about this. She seems cool and you two would make a really cute couple."

Warmth floods my face and I drum my fingers on the table, avoiding eye contact.

"But she's playing for the other team, Roman. I'm shocked, honestly. You of all people, Mr. Loyalty..." Poppy twists her hair around her finger absentmindedly, takes a sip of the iced mocha.

"I told you. It was a one-time thing. Drop it, will you?"

Up at the bar, Skye gets her coffee and shoots us a quick wave before ducking outside. I keep my eyes on her narrow hips as she sashays across the street over to Town Hall.

"She's gone. Now I can tell you about the meeting. And don't go spreading it around town that Skye and I had a thing. Emphasis on *had* there, Poppy."

Poppy scrunches her lips together and nods. "Fine. I'll keep your little secret. But on one condition."

I tip my head back, already seeing where this is headed. "What's the condition?"

"You and King involve me every step of the way. No more secret meetings, with Cleet or anyone else. Deal?"

Much as I'd like to decline her terms and conditions, I don't figure I have a choice if I want my relationship with Skye kept quiet.

"Fine. But keep your mouth shut. About me and Skye, the case—everything. Got it?"

"Got it."

She thrusts her hand out to shake on it and a nagging worry tugs deep in my gut. I love my sister, but discretion isn't her strong suit.

Poppy leans forward, all business. "Now tell me about the meeting."

11

———

SKYE

Bumping into Roman at Coastal Coffee first thing this morning isn't exactly how I wanted to start my day. Not after our run-in last night.

Although my panties tell a whole different story.

He may be on the other side of the trial, but it doesn't hurt to look. Stare. Drool. In the end, it's all semantics.

The man is gorgeous, no doubt about that. I haven't even seen what's under his dress shirt, but I am certain Roman's all muscle. That jawline, his strong, broad shoulders. And those eyes. I could drown in that deep cobalt blue.

"Morning, Skye." Sahara, the office admin, waves at me from the reception desk. "You have a message on your desk."

"Okay, thanks. Did anything come over on the Capelli case?"

"Not yet. But as soon as it does, I'll get it over to you."

"Great."

I head past the conference room to my office, a tiny, windowless room that I'm pretty sure used to be a supply closet. Flipping on the light, I spy the pink Post-it on my desk.

Message

For: Skye Adams

From: Jagger Capelli

Tick-tock.

And that's it. The entire message. The asshole actually called into my office—my place of freaking employment—to deliver a verbal threat. I'm glad I didn't give him my cell number.

Crumpling the sticky note into a tight pink ball, I toss it into the metal trash can next to my desk and pull out the Capelli file. The manila folder's thin—not much to go on yet. There's a copy of the current land survey, several zoning ordinances from the town, the operating license of the Seaglass Inn, a deed to the land. Nothing screaming that the Capellis have a case, but for some reason the judge moved for a trial.

What am I missing here?

I flip through again, then pull everything out of the folder and arrange it on my desk. Move all the papers again, rearranging them in a different order. Sometimes if I switch positions, the pieces of the puzzle click into place.

But not this time.

Shit. I might need to meet with the Capellis to discuss the case. The very thought sends an icy shiver down my spine. I don't love all my clients, but I've never had clients I disliked quite this much. The entire case stinks and something feels very off to me.

Starting with the reason you're on the case to begin with.

I should have given up on my dad a long time ago, I know that. But after my mom drank herself to death, he's all I have left.

And maybe not for long if you don't figure out how to save his ass. Again.

Dropping my head into my hands, I squeeze my eyes shut. What am I missing? There has to be a critical piece of information the judge has that warrants a trial.

I can't see Roman or his family intentionally stealing land though. What I *can* see is the Capellis doing something nefarious to steal the Montgomery's land after they worked hard to build a thriving, successful business.

This line of thinking is getting me nowhere. I need to pay the Capellis a visit and try to figure out what they have on the Montgomerys—and if it's legit. Because I meant what I said to Jagger. I won't be complicit in anything illegal, my father's predicament be damned. I've worked way too hard to get where I am to risk it all on some bad debt.

But I do owe it to my client to try the case to the best of my ability. And that means at least attempting to discover the truth.

Grabbing my bag, I head out of the office on a research mission.

"I'll be back later, Sahara. If the Capellis call, let them know I need to meet with them as soon as possible."

"Got it." She scribbles a note to herself, then promptly goes back to scrolling through TikToks on her phone.

The air's chilly, a salty breeze biting at my face and whipping my hair around. Dark gray clouds build to the east over the ocean, and rain's heading our way. I pass Town Hall and turn right, walking the two blocks over to the Seaglass Beach public library.

Shoving through the glass door, the earthy, vanilla scent of old books hits me and I take a deep, calming breath. As a kid, I always loved to read. Anything, really, but especially mysteries. Nancy Drew was my favorite. Ironic, given the private investigation skills I displayed last night. Nancy was better at fifteen years old than I am at thirty-three.

I head over to the Reference desk in the corner, a white-haired woman hunched over the keyboard of the computer. I stand there for a long minute, then clear my throat, the sound echoing through the almost-silent room. Only then does she glance up.

"Oh, hello there, dear. What can I help you with today?" She peers at me over the dark green rims of her bifocals, her name tag glinting in the overhead fluorescent lights.

"Hi, Beatrice. I'm interested in learning about the town's history. Specifically, the settlement of the land." I hike the strap of my bag higher on my shoulder, shifting my weight to the other foot.

"Certainly. We have lots of information about the history of Seaglass Beach. This is a marvelous town, with an interesting past." She taps on the keyboard, jotting reference numbers down on an index card in a loopy scrawl.

"Here's where you'll find books on the early town

settlers. And in this section here—" she points at the second set of numbers—"are the written logs the town's historical society donated to the library. A real treasure trove."

"Wonderful." I beam at her, hoping she'll know the answer to my next question. "And do you have the town's early maps here too? Like land surveys? Or would I need to go to the courthouse for that?"

"As a matter of fact, we do have some of the early land surveys for the town here. But they're in the vault and require special permission to be handled." She purses her lips together, her face serious.

"Oh shoot. I was really hoping to get this done today. How do I apply for special permission?"

"You need to fill out this paperwork—" She slides a pastel green form over the counter to me— "and send along a copy of your photo identification and then wait for a date."

"And how long does this process typically take?"

"Three to four weeks, but since we're bumping up on the holidays, it will probably be closer to six, what with Christmas and New Year's."

I bite at my lip, thinking. "Well, that won't work."

"Can you be more specific about what you're looking for? Maybe then I can steer you in the right direction."

"I'm interested in the Seaglass Inn."

Beatrice stands stock still. "Is that right?"

"Mm-hmm. I'm interested in the history of the land and when it was built."

She crosses her arms over her blue gingham shirt. "And why's that?"

I shift from foot to foot, not used to this type of questioning when I'm researching a case. Welcome to small-town living, I guess.

"I'm trying to get the facts straight."

"Well, I've lived in this town my whole life and I can tell you the facts, you don't even need to bother accessing the vault. The Montgomerys have owned that land, free and clear, for almost a century. Theo Montgomery inherited that land, then built the inn and passed it on to his kids, and then the kids after that. Now sweet Poppy holds the land, and rightfully so. Those Capelli boys are bullies and they have no right to the inn." She juts her chin out, bright pink spots coloring her cheeks.

"Thank you for the oral history, Beatrice. But I'm afraid that won't hold up in court. So if you wouldn't mind terribly—could you please help me find the information?"

Beatrice pauses for a moment, the deep lines between her brow furrowing. "Fine. I think you may be able to find newspaper articles about the inn online. We used to have microfilm here, but a few years ago everything went digital and we sent the microfilm over to the library at Florida State University. The state got a big grant and put a bunch of the newspapers online. Follow me."

She circles from behind the desk and waves at me to follow. I trail on her orthopedic heels in the wake of her heavy floral perfume, scrunching my nose up to hold in a sneeze. Way too quiet in here to do something so gauche as sneeze.

We march through the tall stacks of books, all the way to the rear of the library, then duck into a room off the main reference section. A row of computers line the back wall and Beatrice slides a plastic chair out for me.

Huffing out an aggravated breath, she leans over my

shoulder and taps on the keyboard, pulling up the Florida Digital Newspaper Library. A few keystrokes later and I'm staring at grainy black-and-white images from the *Milton Gazette*.

"I'll leave you to it then, dear."

"Thank you, Beatrice. I appreciate it."

She doesn't respond, striding out of the room and leaving behind a cloying perfume cloud.

I grab my notebook from my satchel, flipping through the pages of notes I've already scribbled. The Seaglass Inn was built in 1928. I enter the search date of 1928 and then do an advanced search, typing in the keyword *Montgomery*.

Bingo.

Several articles pop up and I click on the first one, zooming in. The quality's deteriorated over time, some of the ink smudged. The font's so small I have to blow the image up 400% to read.

The construction of the Seaglass Inn being announced. A Theo Montgomery and the mayor shaking hands.

I hit print, then scroll to the next article.

A groundbreaking ceremony. Theo Montgomery holding a shovel, with Alice Montgomery in the background, smiling and dressed to the nines.

Goosebumps rise on my skin as I take in the smiling faces on the screen. These must be Roman's great-grandparents. I print this article as well, then move to the next.

1928. Opening day at the Seaglass Inn, a row of black Studebakers lining the circular drive, the inn looking very similar to how it looks today.

All great info worth having, but none of this proves the land belongs to the Montgomerys, only that they developed the land for commercial use all those years ago. I still need to get my hands on the land surveys or find the original deed of sale.

I click out of the newspaper database and snag the papers off the printer at the back, shoving them into the manila file folder. Guess I'll fill out the paperwork with Beatrice and hope the Seaglass Beach powers-that-be will grant me access to the vault before we go to trial.

"Thanks again for your help, Beatrice."

She gives me a barely perceptible nod, her lips a thin line, as if she's disappointed in my life choices.

Same, Beatrice, same.

"Listen, I'd like to complete the paperwork requesting permission to access the vault."

"Fine." She slides the green sheet across the counter. "Fill everything out completely. I'll also need to make a copy of your photo ID."

I dig through my wallet, producing my driver's license. Taking it from me, she eyes the photo as if it could potentially be a fake or something.

"Not my best angle," I joke and the tips of her ears turn crimson. She frowns and scurries away to make a copy of my ID.

A few seconds later, she's back and we swap the completed form and my license.

"Thanks again. Have a good one." I wave and smile in an attempt to be friendly, but she only bobs her head in my direction before averting her eyes. Like she can't stand the sight of me for taking the Capelli's case.

Great.

Not only do I have a difficult case—and even worse clients—but now everyone in town's going to despise me for going up against the beloved Montgomery family. Challenging a Seaglass Beach institution and potentially destroying a landmark piece of the town's history.

I really hate my life right now. I only hope I can get my dad out of his debt. Then the Capellis can forget they ever met me or my father.

12

ROMAN

No matter how hard I try, I can't get Skye or the damn trial off my mind. Usually, I'm good at this sort of thing. Compartmentalizing is a skillset practically woven into my DNA. But something about this whole situation stinks.

Figures. The Capellis *are* involved.

After I escort the mayor out of Town Hall and load him safely into the waiting vehicle, I'm officially off-duty until after the first of the new year. He's taking an extended holiday break, which means I am too. Leaves me plenty of thinking time, I guess.

I check my watch. Only four p.m., which means the records department should still be open. Cleet's on top of things, I'm sure, but after finding the diary, I'm curious to see what else I can dig up. Maybe the original land survey might be a clue.

Jogging down the wide marble steps, I descend to the lobby level, then take the smaller, less-grand staircase down to the basement level where the town keeps the records. It's much darker down here, the only outside light spilling in from narrow horizontal transom windows. Overhead, fluorescent box lights throw off a weird greenish cast, along with a low-level buzz that would drive me nuts if I worked down here.

I stride up to the lone desk. "Hey, I'm looking for the land survey of the Seaglass Inn."

"I'll need a copy of your ID." The female clerk holds out her palm and I dig my city ID badge from my back pocket and hand it to her. She shoves a thick black leather-bound log across the desk. "Sign in. I'll be back in a jiffy."

The clerk disappears as I open the log, tracing my finger down to the next blank rectangle.

The name above the empty space catches my eye.

Skye Adams.

Dated today.

My gut swirls, my heart hammering harder. Of course she's been here. Doing due diligence, at least, I'll give her that.

"Here's your ID back." The clerk plops the plastic badge into my hand. "Come with me."

She ushers me into a small room to the left of the desk and waves at the wooden table and chairs. "Have a seat. I'll bring the documents out to you."

Then she vanishes again, leaving me sitting alone in the cold room.

I'll bet it's the same room Skye was in a few hours ago. Maybe her perfect ass even sat in this very chair.

But what did she find?

"Here you go." The clerk returns carrying a thick, oversized brown leather book. She drops it onto the table, a loud thud echoing off the bare walls and the concrete floor.

"Geesh, that thing's heavy." She rubs up and down her biceps before shoving a hand in the pocket of her corduroy pants. "If you need anything, give me a holler. Bring the book back to the desk when you're done so I can lock it up. And no food or drink while you're in here. For obvious reasons."

I nod. "Sure thing."

"And be careful with the pages. Some of those surveys are really old and it's my butt on the line if anything happens to them." She frowns, squishing her lips together.

"Got it. I'll be careful. Listen—can I get a copy of any of the land surveys I find in here?"

"Sorry, no. Unless you have an official order or something, I can't let you do that."

"Okay, no problem." I could always send someone from Cleet's team over if I see anything critical to the case. "Thanks."

"We close in thirty minutes."

Then she pivots and leaves me alone. I carefully open the book to the first page, dated March 1905. There's a line drawing of a plot of land and it looks similar to the main square of Seaglass Beach today. I flip through the dusty pages, recognizing the layout of the Town Hall, the corner grocery, the public library. Finally, I find what I'm after.

A land survey taken in 1926, commissioned by Mr. Theo Montgomery. My great-grandfather. Chill bumps rise on my skin as I run my finger along the graphite pencil sketch, tracing the line of the property.

Our land. Bought and paid for back in 1900 by Hugh Montgomery, my great-great grandfather.

I tap the camera icon on my cell and snap several photos: one of the entire two-page spread of the survey, then close-ups of each corner of the drawing. The outline is exactly as the Seaglass Inn stands today, down to the last detail. We've not expanded since opening day in 1928, mainly because we're oceanfront and have nowhere to build. Plus, Poppy's running the inn now and the rest of us have other things going on. The land's plenty big and more than enough to manage.

I lean back, crossing my ankles and staring up at the square tiled ceiling. The land survey further proves the Capellis have no claim to the inn, so what's got the judge so bound and determined to hear the case? What do the Capellis have that we don't know about?

Closing the cover, I stand and stretch before returning the heavy book to the front desk.

The clerk pulls a yellow number-two pencil from between her lips. "Find what you were looking for?"

"Yes, thanks. I appreciate it."

"Anytime." She flips her mousy brown hair over her shoulder and stares at me, unblinking.

"Well, thanks again."

I head back upstairs, pausing in the lobby to forward the photos to both King and Poppy.

> Roman: Here's the land survey on record at Town Hall. Notice anything?

Less than one second later, Poppy texts back. Not a surprise. She's probably sitting at the front desk of the inn, scrolling through Instagram.

Little Sis: Looks accurate. Just like the
current property lines of the inn. Why?

Roman: That's what I thought too. Not
sure why judge is hearing the case

Little sis: Me neither

I head outside and cross the street, making my way to
my truck. The sun's almost set, even though it's barely five
p.m. The white lights of the town Christmas tree in the
square twinkle in the dusky twilight, the streetlamps flickering on as I unlock the truck and climb in.

Buzz, buzz.

A text from King.

King: I don't see anything notable, but I'm
not a land surveyor. I'll forward to Cleet
and his team to look over

Roman: Ok, thanks.

Firing up my truck, I glance over my shoulder and start
backing out of the parking spot. That's when I spot a
certain curvaceous attorney, satchel slung over her arm,
walking my way. I freeze, wait for her to cross the street
and slide into her Honda. She glances around nervously,
but somehow doesn't spot me. Taking a call on her cell, she
peels out of the spot and speeds away.

Instincts kick into gear and I reverse out of the lot,
following her. I'm careful to stay several car lengths away
so she doesn't notice I'm tailing her. Skye drives fast. Like,

race car-driver fast. She blows through not one but two yellow lights, and I have to gun it to keep up with her.

I wonder where she's headed in such a damn hurry.

We drive straight through town before she makes a sharp right onto A1A and heads west. There are fewer cars on the road now that we're out of the town center, so I drop even further back. The sky's fully dark and I train my eyes on the bright red of her taillights. Houses on either side of the road spread further and further apart as the grass gets taller and less manicured. We're on the outskirts of town and there's not much out here.

Where the hell is Skye going?

The road narrows from two lanes down to one and I drop back, keeping as much distance between us as I dare. There's no way she lives all the way out here. Hardly anyone I know lives out here.

She slows and takes another sharp right onto a dusty dirt road. I pause, waiting until she's a good ways down the road before turning and following behind. Bumping along, I squint into the darkness, noting the absence of string lights or any holiday decorations at all on the few houses we pass. Then the houses turn into mobile homes, tiny metal boxes liable to blow away in the next hurricane.

Eventually, she slows even further, pulling up to a nondescript trailer. From this distance, I can make out a lawn chair, a rusty old car sitting up on blocks, and a familiar lifted truck with huge wheels.

Jagger fucking Capelli's truck.

I park my pick-up in the drive of a darkened trailer and pray nobody's home. I'd rather not get shot at this evening by someone protecting his property. Cutting my lights, I peer over at the Honda. Skye gets out and sprints up the steps of the trailer, flinging the door open, not bothering to knock.

Minutes pass and nothing happens. Then the trailer door swings open again and Jagger and Cash walk out, laughing. Jagger's holding something in his hand, but I'm too far away to see what it is. Jagger shouts something at Cash and his brother jogs over to the truck, grabbing something from the rear. A big bag of trash, from the looks of it.

Jagger keeps walking toward the truck, yelling at Cash over his shoulder. Cash snickers, then pulls out a long lighter and ignites the bag. He flings it toward the trailer and laughs maniacally as red flames engulf the trash bag. Both he and Jagger hop into the truck and then they squeal out of the driveway, racing past me doing sixty miles per hour on the dirt road, easy.

Skye runs out of the trailer, screaming. An older man in a sleeveless white T-shirt and jeans stumbles outside, then heads back inside with Skye as the flames start to spread, the dry grass kindling. I reverse out of the driveway and speed toward the trailer, ready to help extinguish the fire. But before I pull in, Skye and the man run back out, pouring buckets of water onto the bag and the grass. The man stomps at the ground as Skye continues the water assault and soon the fire's out.

What the hell? Who is the man and why is Skye out here? And why is Jagger lighting shit on fire?

I mean, besides the obvious reason of being an all-around menace to society. Why would he be committing petty crimes against his attorney?

None of this makes any sense.

After a few further seconds of assessment, making sure

Skye's safe, I reverse direction and head back to town more confused than ever. Nothing adds up. Not the random man in the trailer, not the Capellis, and definitely not Skye's involvement with any of them.

A nagging feeling tugs at my gut, a feeling I recognize from my time running special ops in the Marines.

Something's not quite right about all this—and I need to figure out what it is before we lose the inn.

13

SKYE

Jagger's a real asshole. I can't believe he almost torched my dad's trailer, even after I paid him half the money.

Dickhead.

After dousing the fire, I leave my father on the sofa watching a rerun of *Law & Order* and make the drive back into town. Humming loudly to Mariah Carey's "All I Want for Christmas Is You," I try to take my mind off the case and get in the holiday spirit, but my heart's not in it. I'm not feeling the least bit festive, despite the sparkly lights and the huge Christmas tree glowing in the middle of Town Square. All I want for Christmas is the Capellis to leave me the hell alone and I don't see that happening anytime soon.

The only way to make my wish come true is winning the case for them—and destroying Roman's family in the process.

A lose-lose, the type of case I try to avoid at all costs.

The big—and only—winner in that scenario is Jagger

and he's the last person I want to win anything. Ever. And I barely even know the asshole.

I can only imagine how the Montgomerys feel.

The pained look on Roman's face when I walked into that courtroom still haunts me. I'm not sure I'll ever be able to erase it from my memory. And what's going to happen if I do manage to win this case?

A knot squeezes tight in my gut, a wave of nausea rolling over me.

Moving to Seaglass Beach was a mistake.

After the case is over, I'll probably leave town for good. I don't own property, have no friends (unless you count my sweet landlady or the barista at Coastal Coffee), and I'm lead counsel against the most popular family in Seaglass Beach. If I win the trial, everyone's going to hate me, and if I lose, the Capellis will come after me.

Lose-fucking-lose.

I pull to a stop at the red light and scan the area. Shit, I'm way past my street. I'd been so caught up in my life problems, I must have driven right on by and now I'm adjacent to the Seaglass Inn.

Might as well hop out and walk the property, lay eyes on the small square of land Jagger believes belongs to him. Since I'm here and all.

I bypass the circular drive in front of the main entrance, continuing straight instead. The beach is to my left, along with villas, the pool, and a tiki bar. I manage to find an empty spot near the bar and park my car. Leaving behind everything except my keys and my cell, I lock up and casually stroll down the sidewalk, acting like a typical guest. Beachy holiday music's drifting from the tiki bar, the thatched roof sparkling with white string lights. Soft laughter carries on the wind and a sharp pang radiates from my chest.

I wish I were at the tiki bar, drinking an extra-dirty martini. Laughing and flirting with Roman.

Just like the other night, which may as well have been a lifetime ago. So much has changed in the last few days. I doubt Roman would even sit next to me, let alone flirt with me. And he definitely wouldn't kiss me.

Shoving this depressing thought away, I focus on the task at hand. I pull the photo of the land survey up on my phone, compare it to the modern-day inn. The corner in question must be down the street a little further. I keep walking, passing by cute all-white beach villas, the happy sounds of the tiki bar fading behind me.

The line of villas ends at the far edge of the property, the main building behind and diagonal to me. There's a small side street and beyond that, dark green rectangular blocks of tennis courts shielded by tall mesh netting. I glance down at my cell to verify this is the corner in question.

"What are you doing here?" A deep voice rumbles behind me and I spin around, clutching at my chest, my heart hammering hard against my palm.

"Dammit, Roman, stop sneaking up on me!" I fan my face, trying to calm down and catch my breath.

"You didn't answer my question." He takes a step toward me, our bodies inches apart. Silvery streaks of moonlight highlight his high cheekbones, a contrast to the dark shadow of stubble over his flexed jaw, and my breath catches in my throat.

Somehow, I manage to force out words. "Just out taking an evening stroll. Not that it's any of your business."

"Bullshit." His hand darts out and grips my forearm, sending a shock of desire racing through me.

Not fear.

Desire.

Fuck. Not the time, Skye.

"Some might view this as trespassing." He narrows his cobalt eyes and I swallow hard, staring at his full lips and straight white teeth, wishing our circumstances were radically different. I'd much rather be doing a horizontal song-and-dance instead of this cat-and-mouse crap.

"The sidewalk's public property."

"You're standing on the grass." Roman nods at my foot, the heel of my shoe touching the manicured emerald blades.

"Barely." I inch my stiletto out of the Bermuda, bringing me even closer to his broad chest. "Better?" I gaze up at him, tipping my chin in challenge.

"Not really."

I totally blank, all snappy retorts vanishing beneath his hot gaze. Waves crash against the shore, the sound whooshing loudly in my eardrums, and I can't think with his palm searing my skin. His scent winding around me, mixing with the salty sea breeze and intoxicating me.

It's like I'm drunk on Roman Montgomery and all he's doing is touching my freaking arm.

"You shouldn't be here." His voice is low and growly, and heat unfurls low in my belly. I take a deep inhale and force myself to focus.

"You shouldn't be talking to me." I challenge him, but he doesn't back down, not even a little bit. Instead, his thumb runs back and forth across my skin gently, tiny sparks of pleasure zinging up my arm.

Double fuck.

He's making this whole covert-operation thing really difficult. And thinking on my feet even tougher.

"The judge never gave me any specific orders about who I can and can't talk to, Counselor."

Wetness pools in my panties as he continues his tender assault, making slightly wider circles on the sensitive skin. Every nerve ending in my body's on high alert and I might actually combust.

"It kind of goes without saying that the plaintiff's lawyer and the defendant aren't supposed to have contact during a trial." The words pain me, cutting me to the core, because there's nothing I'd rather do right now than kiss Roman, let him take me any damn way he pleases.

Twice, for good measure.

"Too bad. I really liked you, up until the point when you took the Capelli's case." His nostrils flare, the only tell that he's angry.

"I wish things were different," I whisper, my heart squeezing so hard my chest hurts.

"For what it's worth—me too."

We stand there beneath the stars for a long moment, taking each other in, a weird frisson of tension flowing between our bodies.

"You should go."

I nod, a lump stuck in my throat, preventing me from saying all the things I want to but can't.

He finally drops my arms and I shiver, hugging my body tight to replace the warmth of his touch. Then I walk away before I say anything stupid.

I TOSS AND TURN, VIVID NIGHTMARES OF JAGGER SETTING fires tormenting me all night long.

Finally, at five a.m., I give up on the concept of sleep altogether and head to the kitchen. Fixing myself a strong cup of coffee, I doctor the steaming beverage with cream and a heaping teaspoon of sugar, then lean against the kitchen counter to think.

The land survey I found at Town Hall matched up with the property lines at the Seaglass Inn. I may have been distracted by Roman last night, but I got what I needed from my little investigation.

Still, something's gnawing at me. A nagging feeling in the back of my mind that something's not quite right. I set my coffee cup down and grab the Capelli file from my satchel, pulling everything out and arranging it on my kitchen table. Then I grab my phone and zoom in on the land survey from Town Hall, comparing the two documents inch for inch. Everything lines up.

Everything but the far-right corner, the section of the property in question. The survey in the file folder is different than the official survey on file at Town Hall. The land map the Capellis have show the property line ending a few feet before the side street, effectively giving them ownership of a small portion of the land on which the inn is built.

Did the Capellis submit a fake document to the court? Why are the two surveys different?

If they forged documents, they have no legitimate

claim to the land, and therefore no case. Plus, it shouldn't be that difficult for the Montgomery's lawyer to prove the land survey is fraudulent. This entire case may not even go to trial once I submit the documents to the court.

But then what will happen to my dad? Not gonna lie, yesterday was fairly terrifying, what with Jagger trying to burn the yard down. And I have complete faith he's capable of doing much, much worse things than a little foliage arson.

FML.

Here I am again, spinning round and round in a no-win situation.

I bite down on my lip and stare out the window at the sky streaked with the pink of sunrise. I have a few options, none of them palatable:

1. Move forward with the case, pretending not to notice the forged document. The defendant's lawyers will most likely catch on, but if I say nothing maybe I won't be culpable. The cons: ignorance as a defense strategy is weak and I will most likely lose the case, thereby ruining my record. My dad is fucked.

2. Talk the Capellis into dropping the case. Honestly, my best option, but it assumes the clients are logical, reasonable, law-abiding citizens and I'm pretty certain we're oh-for-three on that. My dad's still fucked.

3. Go to the judge and beg for a withdrawal from the case. The obvious con being she already rejected this plea once. And my dad's still fucked.

Super. Three bad options. I may as well spin the wheel of misfortune and go from there.

Downing the rest of my now-lukewarm coffee, I shoot a text off to Sahara asking her to set up a conference with the Capellis at the office as soon as possible. Because after last night, there's no way I'm meeting with those thugs anywhere other than the safe confines of the office with multiple witnesses around.

Then I hit the shower to get ready for what promises to be another not-so-great day at the office.

14

ROMAN

ALTHOUGH I'M OFF-DUTY FOR THE NEXT TWO WEEKS, I'M not exactly in a festive mood.

Maybe it's the stress of the impending trial, maybe it's general holiday blues—Christmas hasn't been the same since our parents died.

Maybe it's a certain off-limits, hot-as-hell attorney you can't seem to get out of your head.

No. Definitely not that last one.

I'm fine alone. Have been my entire life. No sense changing things up now. Even if I could go there, we probably wouldn't work out anyway. She's awfully stubborn for my taste. And headstrong.

And vivacious and witty and sexy as fuck.

My cell vibrates, rattling against the coffee table and knocking me out of my going-nowhere-productive thoughts.

> Little Sis: You meeting us at Milk & Cookies Movie Night in the square?

> Roman: I'm skipping it

Little Sis: Aww, c'mon! Parker & Liv are back from the honeymoon & Griffin's in town for the weekend. It'll be fun!

This I doubt. Whenever Poppy's overly enthusiastic about something, it doesn't turn out well.

> Roman: Rain check.

Little Sis: Rome. I even talked King into coming. Come on. Please

Little Sis: He'll back out if he knows you're not coming

> Roman: So don't tell him

Little Sis: He'll figure it out pretty quick when you don't show up. Don't be a holiday hater—the movie's not even the Grinch this year

> Roman: Fine. But I'm not staying long

Little Sis: Deal. See you soon. Oh, and bring a chair for me, will ya? I can't find mine. I'm pretty sure it blew away during Hurricane Clementine

I roll my eyes and scrub a hand over the back of my neck. My sister's a real piece of work. Wonder what her back-up plan was on the chair situation. She was probably gonna make Griffin hold her in his lap all night.

Despite my lack of holiday cheer, I shower and head over to the Town Square, mainly to avoid the wrath of Poppy.

The Christmas countdown is on in Seaglass Beach and the town's fully decked out. Every streetlight has a huge teal bow and string lights twinkle on the storefronts lining the square, illuminating the grassy space. The highlight of the whole scene is the glittering tree in the center, towering high above the buildings. The movie screen's set up off to the side, with the beach behind. Tons of people are already here, mingling and munching on cookies. Every year, the town bakery, *Sandy's*, donates hundreds of treats to the event, and it appears that this year is no exception. I hope there's a few chocolate chip cookies left—they're legendary around here.

"Rome!" Poppy runs across the grass and jumps into my arms like she hasn't seen me in a year or something.

I pat her back and covertly unwind her legs from around my waist. "Here's the chair."

Thrusting the beach chair at her, I nod at her boyfriend, Griffin. He's a professional baseball player in Atlanta, but his Aunt Jess is a local. "Hey, man." We clasp hands, then bro hug. "Glad you could make it down."

"Happy to be back for the holidays." He wraps his arm around my sister's waist, pulling her closer to his body, and a tiny part of me is a little jealous.

Poppy's my baby sister. I can't believe she's locking it down before me.

But it's fine. Good for them.

"How's Atlanta?"

"Cold. It's nice to be warm again—for a little while at least."

Poppy snuggles into his chest, and honest to goodness, I've never seen her this calm in my life.

Too bad dude can't stick around permanently.

"Hey, Rome." Parker, Poppy's twin, slugs me on the arm. Liv—Poppy's best friend and Parker's wife as of a few weeks ago—smiles at me.

"Hey. How was the honeymoon you two?"

"So awesome, man. The snorkeling in Trunk Bay is amazing. So many fish, it's crazy! Loved it."

"Just the snorkeling, Parks?" Poppy teases and Liv's cheeks blush a deep crimson.

"Well, I mean, obviously Liv being there was pretty cool." Parker wraps his hands around Liv's waist and kisses her on the cheek and I can't right now. The twins—my two younger siblings—are coupled off, while King and me are both as single as the day is long.

How in the hell did this happen?

"They have anything stronger than milk here?" King's deep voice rumbles from across the lawn as he sidles up to us wearing his uniform of jeans and cowboy boots.

"Spiked eggnog? Rum horchata?" Parker waves at the makeshift bar next to the cookies and milk display.

"Whiskey on the rocks?" King tips his head, surveying the scene over the crowd of children huddling around the cookies.

"Probably. Come on, I'll go with you." I start walking toward the bar with King, while Parker, Liv, Poppy, and Griffin set up camp toward the back of the lawn.

"How're things?" King keeps his eyes on the bar, only glancing at me for a second.

I shrug. "Fine."

"No new developments?"

"No. And I promised Poppy I'd tell you both at the same time. If I don't, you know she'll somehow ferret it out and hold a grudge for roughly a century or so."

King chuckles and I'm happy I have my older brother to commiserate with.

"That she would. You didn't find anything out at Town Hall?"

"Not really. Everything seems to be in order. I can't figure why the judge is hearing the case at all."

We join the line at the bar, two couples in front of us. I drop my voice to minimize eavesdropping. "I saw Skye at the inn last night."

"Really." King folds his arms across his abdomen, the jolly holiday music the wrong soundtrack for his mood.

"Yeah. She pretended to be out for a walk, but she was definitely up to something."

"Wonder what..."

"Not sure. And the Capellis have dirt on her, I think. Something's off about the whole deal, but I'm not sure what."

The first couple at the bar shuffle off and King and I move up in the line. I drop my voice even lower, to a near whisper. "Maybe reconsider reaching out to Juliet?"

King's jaw flexes, a vein pulsating in his neck. He stares straight ahead, not bothering to look at me. "I said 'no,' Rome. Drop it."

His tone's sharp, so I heed his words. King says what he means and means what he says, and he's my biggest ally. It would be unwise to piss him off.

"Fine. But it may come down to you reaching out. Just sayin'."

His head spins and he locks his gaze on mine. "I'm not reaching out. Period."

"Even if it means saving the inn?" I shove a hand in my pocket, wait for his response. I know the two of them have bad blood, but this is a real situation. One that could be a big, big problem for us. Seems like he could take one for the team here.

His brows furrow, his lips a tight line. "I can't, Rome."

I don't understand his position on the topic, but I respect my brother. "Okay. Heard. I'll figure out another way."

We move up in the line and order drinks—two whiskeys, two beers, and two spiked eggnogs—then juggle all the beverages and make our way back to the family.

"Bro, I would've helped." Parker jumps up, snagging the eggnogs for the girls, and Griffin takes the beers, and soon we're all sprawled on the now-crowded lawn. *It's a Wonderful Life* plays on the pop-up movie projector screen and we snack on popcorn and cookies. The weather's decent—the wind's not too bad—but the temperature definitely dropped after the sun went down and I kind of wish I had some extra body heat like Poppy and Parker.

Lucky bastards.

The movie rolls on and my mind replays the events of last night—the fire at the outskirts, Skye's panicked face as she doused the bag of trash. Then running into her at the inn less than an hour later, and she acted like nothing out of the ordinary happened.

Maybe extinguishing fires and fighting with clients isn't

out of the norm for her, I don't know. But seems to me that a sharp attorney like her would have a better pool of clients. I can't fathom why she'd take on the Capelli case.

Unless she had to for some reason.

Now that scenario makes more sense. Skye was probably pressured into taking the case.

But I still stand by our earlier conversation—she had a choice. Because you always do. And she chose the Capellis.

Why the fuck would she do that?

That part still doesn't add up.

I lean over to my siblings. "I'm going to get a water. Anybody want anything?"

The only response is King standing and heading to the periphery of the lawn, weaving his way through the sea of blankets and lawn chairs. I follow behind his long strides and soon we're all the way across the field. There's no line at the bar this time, the bored bartender leaning across the table and squinting at the movie screen.

"King?" a quiet voice calls out from the shadows.

King and I both swivel, trying to locate the source of the sound.

Juliet Capelli appears out of nowhere. Almost as if she'd been lurking around all night, waiting.

King's face blanches as Juliet approaches. He swallows hard, stuffs a hand in his pocket. "What do you want?"

Her eyes dart around the open space and she wrings her hands, but she still steps toward us. King's shoulders stiffen, tension practically rolling off him in waves.

"I need to talk to you. Alone." She smooths her hair down, searching his face with her wide hazel eyes. It's hard to believe she's a Capelli because unlike her thug brothers,

Juliet's attractive, even wearing her *Tipsy Taco* T-shirt and jeans. If I were her, I'd pretend I wasn't related.

"Anything you need to say to me, you can say in front of Roman."

She bites down on her lip, shifting from foot to foot, weighing her options. Taking a deep breath, she leans in close to King. He bends back a touch and disappointment flashes over her face, but she recovers quickly.

"I don't know the specifics, but Jagger's lying about the inn."

"No kidding." King's voice is flat, his face impassive.

"Listen, I'm taking a big risk even talking to you. If Jagger finds out..." She shudders, wrapping her arms around her flat stomach.

"I'm gonna need more than that, Juliet. I can't go to the judge with an accusation of lying. I need evidence, proof. Can you get that?" King locks his eyes on Juliet and I feel like I'm intruding on something, but I'm not sure what.

Juliet tips her head, hair feathering over her forehead. "Maybe?"

"Maybe's not good enough."

I swear her eyes mist up, but then the movie ends and the streetlights come up. Chatter rises around us, happy shrieks of kids hopped up on holiday cookies filling the night air. Juliet gives King a tiny nod and then dashes away as quickly as she appeared.

"That was unexpected. You okay?" I touch King's forearm and he shakes his head, breaking his stare at the Juliet-sized space.

"Yeah. Do me a favor."

"Oh-kay." I stretch the word out, not liking where this is headed...

"Don't tell the others about this. I doubt she'll come through with anything concrete and I'd hate to get Poppy's hopes up over nothing."

I swallow, my stomach churning. This is exactly what I told Poppy I wouldn't do, keep things from her. My gut instinct is to tell King no—and it's rarely off. Hell, it kept me alive through three tours of duty.

"You know you're putting me in a bad position, right? I promised Poppy I'd keep her in the loop."

"And we will. If Juliet comes up with anything useful, we'll tell her."

Heaving out a sigh, I scrub a hand over my neck and kick at the grass. "I don't like it, but I'll do it."

"It's for the best." King seems so certain, but the situation is sticky.

"As long as Poppy doesn't find out, yeah. But if she does, there'll be hell to pay."

"Don't let her find out then." He shrugs, like that's the obvious—and best—solution here. "It's not like you don't know how to run covert missions. And Poppy can't be worse than an enemy of the state."

I raise my eyebrows at my older brother. "You have no idea, bro. She definitely could give a few of them a run for the money."

A rumble of laughter shakes King's broad shoulders, and his mood lightens a touch. "We better get going before we have to face an interrogation. Remember—we never saw Juliet."

"Yeah, I got the order. I just don't like it."

I shake my head, but slam my hands in my pockets and follow his lead back to our crew.

Typically, King has good instincts, especially about

family stuff. But when it comes to Juliet Capelli, all bets are off.

I only hope he doesn't drag me into something we both regret.

15

SKYE

Christmas is almost here, but sugarplum fairies, Rudolph, and Santa are nowhere on my radar at the moment. All I can think about is the forged documents and getting the hell off the Capelli case. Sahara's called Jagger for me a half-dozen times, but so far he's been non-responsive.

What the fuck?

I've had bad clients before, but these boys take the cake. What client doesn't bother calling their attorney back, especially after the sixth freaking message?

I stare at the blank computer screen, the cursor blinking at me.

Blink. Blink. Blink.

I have several other trials to prepare for, but I'm struggling to form a coherent thought at the moment. I need to ditch the Capellis before Christmas. I'd figure out some other way to help my dad repay his debt. Within strict legal limits and as far away from the Capelli brothers as I can possibly get.

The phone on my desk trills and I jump, my rear lifting clear off the ergonomic mesh cushion.

"Yes?" I hit the speaker button, trying to sound calm and professional.

"The Capellis are here." Sahara's voice echoes around my office and my stomach turns, acid rising up my throat.

You can do this.

"Send them in please."

I throw my blazer back on, fastening every button, mainly to cover as much of my chest as possible. The last thing I need is one of those creeps staring at my boobs.

The door slams open and Jagger swaggers in, with Cash and Damon lurching along behind him. The trio sidles up to my desk and I automatically rise, happy I wore my highest stilettos today, giving me the best height advantage I can get.

"You wanted to see us?" Jagger cocks a dark brow at me, a smirk on his face. His hair's slicked back and he reeks of motor oil and stale cigarettes.

I swallow down a dry heave and make eye contact with him, his blue eyes icy. "I found an inconsistency in the land survey you gave me."

He blinks, screwing his mouth up. Cash and Damon slump down into the desk chairs, but Jagger remains standing.

"So?" He folds his thick arms over his chest, an angry vein popping on his forearm.

"What do you mean, *so*? So—that's a big deal. A case-ending deal." I rub my ring, my heart pounding wildly in my chest. I don't care for the way Jagger's glaring at me, as if he may jump across the desk and shank me any minute now.

"You can't end the case. That's not your call." He juts out his chin and I can't stop staring at the deep cleft cut down the center. A butt chin, we used to call it back in grade school. I almost snicker, but manage to hold it together.

"It's not my call, and that's not what I'm getting at. What I'm saying is if I found the discrepancy, I'm certain the defendant's attorney will too."

"You better not have snitched on us." His gravelly voice cuts through the thudding of my pulse pounding in my eardrums.

"I haven't said anything because I'm your attorney. However, I strongly encourage you to drop the case. The court could charge you with perjury when the defendants discover you submitted forged documents."

"Not if no one finds out."

I huff out an exasperated sigh and speak slowly, trying to get him to understand the situation. "What I'm telling you is they *will* find out. The defendants have access to the same materials I do and they're smart enough to piece it together."

Jagger rolls his eyes, unconvinced.

"Trust me, they are. Guaranteed. It's my professional legal counsel that you drop the case."

I pause and try to appear calm even though my mouth's so dry I can barely swallow and my palms sweat against the polyester blend of my blazer. Jagger cracks the knuckles on his right hand one by one, each pop deafening in the quiet office.

"Fuck. The. Fuck. Off." He enunciates each word, pairing it with a knuckle crack on the left hand. If he were smarter, he would have added the word *bitch* to round it up to five, one per knuckle.

What a missed opportunity.

"Gee, wish I could. Unfortunately, I'm sworn to do my duty by my client. So again—I strongly recommend dropping the case."

Jagger slams his palms down on the desk so hard my coffee cup rattles and the office phone falls off the hook. I calmly reach down and replace it, straightening all my papers and trying to get a hold of my breathing.

"Listen, bitch..."

There it is...

"We're paying you to be our lawyer. So do it."

"Actually—" I drop my voice—"because of my father, I had to take the case pro bono. So you're not really paying me. I've already repaid half of his debt. I can get you the other half by the end of January."

Jagger's face cracks into a grin and he reaches back and punches Cash in the arm. "You hear that? This stupid bitch wants extra time to pay back Daddy's debt. Isn't that funny?"

Then he turns around and inches closer to the desk, his face hardening as he stares at me.

"No more delays. You pay the debt by handling our case. And by handling, I mean winning. Capeesh?"

Guess Jagger fancies himself the Godfather of Seaglass Beach all of sudden.

I huff out an exasperated sigh. "I just told you there's no way you're going to win with the evidence we have."

His fist finds my desk again, pounding down. "Then go find some more fucking evidence!"

"I can't go out and *find* evidence, Jagger! That's illegal."

Damon guffaws behind Jagger. "Like that matters."

"It definitely matters to me. I'm a lawyer. I could lose my law license for way less than that."

"Not our problem, sweets." Jagger shrugs and my stomach roils, a hot flush of anger burning my chest. His above-the-law attitude's really starting to piss me off.

"I told you, I'm not doing it."

"Your funeral, Chicky." Jagger twirls his finger in the air and Cash and Damon both jump up, ready to do his bidding. "You have until the day after Christmas to make a choice. Keep the case and dear old Dad's safe and sound. Or fuck this up for us and kaboom." He fans out his fingers and his brothers chuckle like the immature goons they are.

"This is a huge mistake, Jagger. You're risking possible jail time."

"So don't fuck it up." He locks his gaze on mine, squaring his shoulders. A minute passes, then the three of them stroll toward the door. Cash and Damon file out, but Jagger pauses at the threshold, glancing over his shoulder at me.

"Have a great fucking holiday, Chicky." He winks, then saunters out of the office. An arctic chill slides down my spine as I sink into my chair, my heart hammering.

Now what? I have a mentally unstable, pyromaniac of a client intent on revenge against the one man I've really and truly clicked with. A man who's an actual decent human being, with a good, hardworking family. A man who risked his own life to protect and serve his country.

I have literally no case—and my dad's life depends on me winning.

Jagger's right about one thing—I am fucked.

Laying my head down on the cool mahogany desk, I

stare at the black-and-white grid of the monthly desk calendar until everything blurs, the lines dancing in a chevron pattern.

I know what I need to do. But I don't like it and it's not going to be pretty. Feels like my only option at this point, though.

With a deep breath, I stand up, the blood rushing straight to my head. The room spins for a second and my stomach flip-flops. After a few seconds, I'm okay. Grabbing my satchel and the Capelli file, I head over to the courthouse to pay Judge Ratler a visit.

16

SKYE

After talking (more like pleading) with Judge Ratler, I'm finally given the green light to withdraw as counsel from the Capelli case. I manage to bite my tongue and hold back everything I know about the Capelli's dirty documents, but I meant what I said to Jagger: the defense *will* figure it out. The Montgomery family lawyer is good, with a winning reputation. I'm positive he'll drill down to the truth.

And that's not going to go well for Jagger and his bros. But at least I'm off the case and don't have to worry about preparing for the trial anymore.

I can only imagine standing up there, Roman on the stand, all chiseled cheekbones and broody stares. Me questioning him about the land and trying to cobble together a convincing case when I know the Capelli's claim is total bullshit.

No, thank you. I became a lawyer to do good and protect people, not destroy lives and reputations with falsehoods and blatant manipulation.

I slink back to the office, shoving through the heavy door into the balmy reception area. Maybe I could get a raise if the thermostat wasn't cranked to ninety degrees.

"Hey, Sahara. Is Joe still here?"

Sahara taps the screen on her cell, pausing whatever she's watching. "I think so. Haven't seen him leave. You okay?" She scans my face and I purse my lips, shaking my head *no*.

"Not really. I withdrew from the Capelli case."

"Shit. That bad, huh?"

"You've met the Capellis."

She grimaces. "Unfortunately. Now Joe's going to have to reassign the case. And weren't you supposed to go to trial right after the holidays?"

"Yep. I have all my notes." I tap the manila folder in my hand. "But doubt anyone's going to be too thrilled with the state of the case."

The phone rings and Sahara answers, shooting me a sympathetic smile as I head down the hall toward Joe's office. A cape of heavy dread hangs over me and my stomach's a tight knot of anxiety.

I know I'll feel better having unloaded the case, but this convo isn't going to be fun.

"Knock, knock." I rap lightly on Joe's door and pop my head in.

"Hey there, Skye. You ready for the holidays?" Joe's cheeks are rosy, like he may have already hit the eggnog. I hope that bodes well for this discussion.

"Sure. Listen, Joe—" I move to his desk, tightening my abs and focusing on breathing in and out from my diaphragm. "I withdrew from the Capelli case."

There, I said it. Just ripped the bandage right off, quick and dirty.

"Come again?" He freezes, the tip of his pen pointing straight at me. Like a ballpoint dagger to the heart.

"I withdrew from the Capelli case. I'm sorry, but there are things you should know." I toss the file folder on his desk, lean over and start pulling out the land survey.

He holds his palm up, a fleshy stop sign. "Stop. Maybe I don't want to know."

"But you'll figure it out." I frown at him, popping a hand on my hip. "And don't you want the next attorney going into trial prepared? I spent quite a lot of billable hours doing research for this case."

"I'll reassign the case and you can give the details to the next lawyer." He reclines in his chair, rocking back slightly. *Inching away from me.*

"Okay, that's fine. But I'm warning you—this won't be a good look for the firm. I think we'll lose the case. If we go to trial at all."

"Maybe, maybe not. You never really know in matters like this." He twirls the pen like a baton in a damn parade, a blue swish cutting through the air.

Huh? The law's pretty damn clear here—I'm one-thousand percent sure forged documents are a big no-no.

I tuck my hair behind my ear, my mind swirling. "I don't want to know what *matters* you're talking about." I hold my fingers up in air quotes.

What in the actual hell is going on here?

"Probably for the best. I'm assuming you dropping the case has to do with a certain former Marine and your relationship outside of the courtroom?"

My cheeks burn and I can barely breathe. *How the fuck does Joe know about Roman and me?*

"Um, not exactly. At all, really. I disclosed my prior relationship with the defendant to the judge and the client—asked to be dismissed right then and there for a potential conflict of interest—but the judge left the decision up to the client and they retained my services."

"This is a sticky situation for the firm, Skye. I assume you're telling me about the withdrawal and now you're here to resign your position with the firm?"

That's a sucker punch to the gut. I hadn't planned on quitting my job two days before Christmas, but his tone coupled with the accusations have me rethinking this decision.

"Resign or—" I force my voice to remain steady, but inside I'm shaking with anger and panic.

The unspoken threat hangs heavy in the air, my scalp prickling because I already know the answer.

"Let's part ways on a good note, shall we? I'll write you a reference. Have your desk cleared out by the end of the day."

Ouch. So much for that Christmas bonus.

Hot tears sting at the corners of my eyes, but I hold them back. I won't let Joe see me cry.

"Thanks." I spit the word out, bitterness strong on my tongue.

Joe ducks his head, pretending to concentrate on the papers scattered all over his desk. I pluck the Capelli file up and retreat to my office. Joe's too tipsy with the afternoon's holiday cheer to notice.

I have photos and scans of all the documents on my phone, but my gut tells me not to trust Joe with that file.

Somehow, the Capellis got to him too. And maybe the judge or someone else at the courthouse.

Ethically, I can't tell Roman what I found. But I can make sure the next lawyer at this firm at least gets all the facts. I slide the file into the desk drawer and lock it, tucking the key into the inner pocket of my blazer. I want to personally hand that file to the next attorney and I'm not taking any chances.

Grabbing an empty box from the mailroom, I load my meager personal belongings into the cardboard square and clear my desk out in under an hour. I power down my laptop and cut the lights in my cubby of an office for the last time.

I would have liked to say good-bye to Sahara, but she's long gone, off for the holiday break.

Shoving out of the office, I trudge down the sidewalk toward my car, the salty air cool on my heated face. This day definitely sucked. I never thought I'd be unemployed going into the new year—my job's been my life since I moved to town—but here I am. Maybe I should start a side hustle and it'll be so great, I can quit law altogether. Although the thought of hocking makeup or leggings or body transformation plans on social media makes me physically nauseous, so that's probably out. I don't even have a Facebaby account anymore.

Balancing the box in one hand, I pop the trunk, ready to load my work life into the Honda. But bright red ink (gawd, I hope it's ink) catches my eye and I freeze.

BITCH is scrawled across the rear window in huge capital letters.

Gee, wonder who did that?

A potent combo of fear and fury mix in my veins and

my heart rate triples. How dare the Capellis deface my vehicle? I shove the box into the backseat, snapping several photos of my vandalized Accord.

I probably won't press charges. Too much effort required, but at least I'll have evidence of the Capelli's malice toward me if I ever need it.

With shaking hands, I slide into the car, locking the doors as fast as I can.

Jagger's probably watching me from nearby, hoping I lose my cool. But I won't give him the satisfaction.

Instead, I drive straight out of town with no destination in mind. I want to put as many miles between me and the Capellis as possible while I figure out my next move.

17

———

SKYE

I SPEND THE NEXT TWO NIGHTS AT A CHEAP MOTEL somewhere in the Panhandle, drinking boxed wine and watching cheesy holiday movies on cable. Thank goodness for Uber Eats because the last thing I want to do is go sit in some shitty chain restaurant and face the holidays alone.

Again.

My only personal nod to Christmas is attending the midnight service at a tiny church I spotted driving into town. Wearing my slightly rumpled black skirt and blazer, I'm dressed all wrong for the candlelight chapel service. But it's sparsely attended and I stick to the back pew closest to the door, so it's fine.

The scent of pine and melted candle wax swirls around me as I stare up at the ornate stained-glass window. The deep crimson, bright blues, and shiny golds meld together to tell a story and I let myself get lost in the images of pain, suffering, hope, and redemption. The organ music vibrates the wooden pew in the small space and the five-person choir lifts their voices up to God, singing of the holy night and a baby being born in a manger.

A calm settles over me as the soft glow of candles glimmers in the dark church, lighting up the night.

"Merry Christmas!" the pastor shouts from the pulpit, and I absorb his words, his energy.

Everything's going to be alright.

I don't have the answers or much clarity still, but I do have peace.

And honestly, that's a Christmas miracle in and of itself.

CHRISTMAS MORNING SHINES BRIGHT AND CLEAR, AND I'm ready to head back. I check out of the motel and hit the diner next door for coffee and pancakes before my return trip to Seaglass Beach.

I haven't heard a word from my father, which I take as a good sign. Honestly, no news is good news in his department. That's always been the case—even before the Capellis.

Back home, I shower and change into jeans, a navy sweater, and boots. Then I do a quick Google search of an address and decide to throw a Hail Mary.

There's someone I need to see, and it needs to be today.

With shaky hands, I slide behind the wheel again and drive through town. I'm practically the only car on A1A since most everyone's home with their families, opening gifts, drinking mimosas, and watching *A Christmas Story* on loop. All the boutiques, cafes, and restaurants are closed for the holiday and the grassy square's empty as I pass by. A lone seagull soars overhead, flying out toward the ocean, and I try to ignore the butterflies winging around my stomach.

Roman's been on my heart this entire time, but especially last night in the chapel. Praying and reflecting on my life choices, everything kept coming back to him. Wild, since we had one night together. But I can't get him out of my head.

Don't want him to get out of my head.

He may not want anything to do with me, but I need to clear the air between us. Let him know I'm not the person he thinks I am.

The road narrows from four lanes to two and now the landscape's changed from quaint beach town to countryside. Mostly flat browns and dull greens due to winter, but the grass still stands tall, waving in the wind.

Eventually, I come to a limestone road and make the right turn. Slowing down over the gravel, my insides quiver like they do every time I stand up in trial to make an opening statement.

I don't even know if he'll be here. I drove by Roman's house in town, but his truck wasn't in the driveway. So this was the next logical place to come. King's house. His family seems tight and it is Christmas Day. Stands to reason they'll all be together for dinner somewhere.

Stalk much.

I silence the harsh inner critic and idle in the driveway behind a row of trucks and SUVs, including Roman's. I'm breathing hard and fast, like I just ran sprints, and if I don't get it together I may hyperventilate right here in the

Accord. That would solve all my current problems, at least.

Cutting the ignition, I smooth my hair over my shoulders, check my reflection in the mirror. Dark circles ring my eyes, but at least they're not puffy from crying anymore. It's been almost twenty-four hours since I shed a tear and I really hope I can maintain that record.

I climb out of the car, stretching, then walk up the steps. The Montgomery house is lovely, a white two-story with rocking chairs and a front porch swing. Very modern-day farmhouse chic. The property's surrounded by a sprawling, well-maintained lawn and large oak trees. A wooden swing hangs from one of the larger trees and I can picture a young Poppy flying through the air, her feet kicking and her head thrown back with glee.

Heart racing, I ring the doorbell and wait. A few seconds later, the door opens and my breath hitches in my throat. Even though I practiced my speech over and over on the drive here, the words evaporate as soon as I meet Roman's steely glare.

"Uh...Merry Christmas. And I withdrew from the case." The words tumble from my mouth in a rush.

"What?" Roman's dark brows squish together, his jaw tensing.

"I withdrew. Then I resigned before I got fired."

He stares at me for what feels like an eternity, the wind whipping around us, cold on my cheeks.

Maybe he doesn't care. Maybe I can never take away the hurt I saw swimming in those cobalt eyes that day in the courtroom.

Maybe I did the right thing, but it's too late.

His chest rises and falls and I drop my gaze to the light

gray T-shirt peeking out beneath his flannel shirt. Every nerve in my body's twitchy, but I stand rooted to the wide-plank front porch.

Finally, he breaks the silence.

"Why?"

Taking a shuddery breath, I lick my bottom lip, choosing my words carefully.

"Because I couldn't in good conscience keep representing the Capellis. I wish I could say more, but I'd rather not get disbarred for breach of confidentiality. I doubt I'll be very good at side hustles, my social media game's not strong. But I wanted you to know that I won't be the reason anything happens to your family or their legacy."

Roman steps onto the porch, closing the door behind him. His body's inches from mine, the spicy scent of cinnamon and pine rolling off his shirt. He cups my face with his large hands and his touch is soft, yet strong. Running his thumb over my cheek, heady anticipation skitters through my veins. He drops his lips to mine and in that moment, everything negative between us melts away.

All is forgiven.

Distrust, betrayal, harsh words, all swallowed by this kiss in this perfect moment.

Well, besides the fact that I'm now unemployed in the world's smallest beach town and the Capelli brothers still want my father's debt paid by tomorrow.

My stomach clenches with anxiety, but I push away the negative thoughts and sour emotions and instead focus on Roman.

Even better, Roman and me together and how very, very right everything feels when I'm in his arms.

Safe, protected.

I've never felt like this before and I don't want it to end. If I could freeze time, I definitely would. I'd gladly stand on the front porch of the Montgomery ranch in the dead of winter if it meant I'd be here with Roman.

"Thank you." He murmurs the words so quietly they'd float away on the wind if our lips weren't touching.

He's so sweet, so earnest.

So vulnerable.

I've never seen this side of Roman before.

I pull away, gazing up at him. "You're welcome. I mean, who needs a job, right? Employment's totally overrated." I try to laugh, but the sound comes out strangled and raw.

"You can check comedienne off your list of future careers."

"Ouch. Going straight for the jugular."

"Oh, sorry. I didn't figure you were interested in a stand-up routine. My mistake." He brushes a stray lock of hair from my eyes and suddenly I feel very exposed. Way more so than I did the night in the alley, bare-assed with my skirt hiked up around my hips.

"Are you okay?"

I bite down hard on my lip, hot tears pricking at my eyes. *Damn it.* My no-crying streak's slipping away.

"Mm-hmm."

"You don't have to pretend with me, Skye."

"I know."

His hands move from my face to my shoulders, dropping all the way down to my waist, pulling me in closer to his body. My heart thuds hard in my chest and I'm so freaking torn. I want to tell him the truth, but I can't.

A bird chirps, long and loud somewhere off in the distance, and I flash back to a grade school field trip. For the first time ever, my dad agreed to chaperone. He was between jobs and I begged him to do it.

But he didn't come to the school. All the kids, parents, and teachers got on the bus and I thought maybe he mixed up the time. That somehow he would still make it and meet us at the aviary.

He never showed.

I spent the first half of the trip scanning the crowd for him and the second half piecing together a plausible explanation for his absence.

Turns out he was at the racetrack betting on horses instead of going on the third-grade field trip.

Looking back, the big surprise wasn't his absence—it was the fact he signed up in the first place.

I take a quick breath, swallow hard, my throat arid. "The truth is, I took the case because of my dad. He owes the Capellis money—gambling debt—and I was paying it off for him. Because he can't pay." My voice breaks and I'm right back in the third grade, hot shame and disappointment washing over me.

I hate my dad, but I can't stop caring about him. And that makes me hate myself even more.

"Hey." Roman brushes a hot tear away with the rough pad of his thumb. "Come here."

Wrapping his arms around me, he pulls me into his broad chest and I do what I swore I'd never, ever do.

I fall apart.

Not just a little bit, shedding one teensy-weensy, delicate tear.

No.

I unleash an entire ocean of tears into Roman's flannel shirt that smells like Christmas and masculinity and home-spun goodness. Hard, wracking sobs shake my body and Roman absorbs them like a human sponge.

He doesn't have to. He owes me nothing and I'm sure he's uncomfortable as hell. He already told me emotions aren't his thing. (P.S. They aren't mine either, but here we are.)

But instead of pulling away, he holds me tight until my throat's scratchy from crying and I have no tears left, his hand rubbing comforting circles on my back the entire time.

"I'm sorry." I mumble the words into his shirt, my face burning with embarrassment even though inside, I feel better than I have in years.

"For what?" The deep timbre of his voice vibrates against my cheek.

"Ruining your shirt, for one."

"I own a few more. And a washing machine."

"And having a mental breakdown on your porch. On Christmas Day, no less."

"I've seen worse. I do have a highly emotional sister. But don't tell her I said that." He smooths his hand over my hair and a tiny flutter of hope wings around in my chest.

Maybe this can work between us.

I hadn't dared to hope for a relationship. The most I could ask for was forgiveness.

But this, right now? This feels like more—and it's even better than I dreamed it would be.

"I hope I didn't ruin your holiday." I tip my head up, swiping at my wet face and regretting my mascara choice.

"Santa already came, it's all good."

I smile up at him, my heart pounding in my chest. Honest to goodness, I'm weak in the knees, just like the damn expression as I stare at his astoundingly perfect face.

"Do you want to come in?"

"Me? No. I couldn't possibly impose on your family's Christmas."

"You have somewhere you need to be?"

Only if you count sitting on the couch crying into a peanut butter-and-pickle-sandwich and drowning my sorrows in Cabernet.

"No."

"Come in then."

"Are you sure? I don't want to intrude."

"You're not. We have plenty of food. Poppy, Liv, and Jess Carter are all here, so you won't even be the only female. Come on."

His hand rests on the small of my back as he guides me into the house. A simple gesture that sends tingles straight to my belly.

"You can dry your face in the bathroom. I'll wait for you."

Emotionally depleted, I follow his suggestion and duck into the guest bathroom to regroup. I should feel awkward and uncomfortable, crashing Roman's Christmas dinner with his family.

But instead, all I feel is cool relief.

Relief that I don't have to lie, obfuscate, or omit.

Relief that I can be honest and do the right thing.

Relief that I can act on my desires.

I still need to figure out how to repay my dad's debt by tomorrow, but right now, all I want to do is be here in this moment.

And maybe, just maybe, things will work out this time. I can definitely see a future with Roman Montgomery.

I only hope he feels the same way.

18

ROMAN

The last thing I expected this Christmas is Skye Adams showing up at the ranch, but here she is. Sitting at the Montgomery dinner table, smiling and sharing stories with my family.

Unbelievable. If I didn't have my hand on her upper thigh beneath the table, the floral scent of her perfume wafting off her skin, the high, tinkly notes of her laugh trilling in my ears, I'd never believe it.

I didn't anticipate this turn of events, but I'm not mad about it.

Her fingers lace with mine under the table and a surge of protectiveness rushes over me. There's something fragile about her, beneath the tough, kick-ass exterior, and I want to shield her, keep her safe.

Maybe it's the Marine in me, always assessing. Maybe it's the bodyguard duties I'm accustomed to. Hell, maybe it's the Montgomery blood running through my veins. My dad taught us to look out for each other, and he always took care of my mom, treated her like a queen.

Poppy's telling a funny story about some guest at the inn, complete with voices and accents, but I'm not really listening. Instead, my focus is on Skye, the long, delicate column of her neck, the way the candlelight dances in her brown sugar eyes, the tiny mole sitting at the base of her collarbone.

I long to touch that sensitive spot, suck and kiss the flesh until she's writhing beneath me. Hear her scream my name as she shudders around my dick, clawing at my back.

"Rome?" King's deep voice rumbles through my fantasy, bringing me firmly back to reality. "I need help with the horses."

He nods in the direction of the barn and I give Skye's hand a quick squeeze under the table. "I'll be right back."

King and I head out of the house in silence, make our way across the yard toward the stables. I wait for him to say what he needs to say, the air crisp as the sun sinks lower in the sky.

"What's going on?" King keeps his eyes straight ahead, his voice tense.

"Skye withdrew from the case. And resigned from her firm. Sounds like that part wasn't really in the plan, but her boss forced the issue."

"Hmmph." A half-grunt from King. He's clearly suspicious and doesn't trust her.

"She was upset about the whole thing, if it makes you feel better."

He works his bottom lip, thinking, his face blank and impassive. King's a tough one to read and an even harder one to win over. Skye's going to have an uphill battle with my older brother.

Which means King and I may clash, and that's not something I'm looking forward to.

"What'd she say about the case?" He lifts the iron latch on the log fence, swinging it open wide for us to pass through. Then he closes and locks the gate behind us.

"Summary version: she withdrew because she didn't feel good about representing the Capellis. She can't say anything else because that's a breach of client confidentiality. But she didn't want to hurt our family."

"Kinda late for that."

I shrug. "If it wasn't her, it would have been some other lawyer and you know it. The Capellis get something stuck in their craw and don't let go until someone breaks their jaw."

"Still. Any decent human being doesn't work with the Capellis."

"I thought the same. But there are extenuating circumstances."

"What the hell does that mean?" Deep lines furrow between his brows, his jaw clenched.

"It means Jagger and his bros threatened her father if she didn't take the case."

King stops outside the barn, the horses neighing at his voice. "And you believe her?"

I nod. "I do."

He stares at me for one long second, an icy wind kicking up, sending tiny wheat-colored cyclones of dirt blowing across the ground.

"I don't like it."

Thrusting a hand deep in my pocket, I level my gaze on his. Brother to brother, man to man.

"You don't have to."

He licks his bottom lip. "Fair enough."

King lifts the nearest bag of feed, emptying brown pellets into a metal bucket hanging in the first stall. I follow his lead, grabbing another bag of feed, and together we move down the line, feeding the horses. Not another word passes between us for twenty minutes as we work.

King chucks the final empty feed bag to the ground. "What I'm trying to say is be careful. You don't know this girl or her intentions."

A sharp bolt of anger flares deep in my gut and I snap. "Not sure you're the best one to be giving advice on women."

Pain flashes across his face, replaced quickly with a tight expression. His lips press into a thin slash and I know I crossed the line, but I don't care.

"Shut the hell up, Rome."

"No. You've made mistakes before and now you hide out here with the horses, doling out advice and pretending you're perfect. Like you have all the fucking answers. And you don't."

King's knuckles flex, loosen, flex again. My stomach tosses around and I'm seriously regretting the second helping of mashed potatoes Poppy pushed on me at dinner. King and I rarely fight, but when we do it ain't pretty.

"You don't know what the fuck you're talking about, Rome. So why don't you stop saying stupid shit before you really piss me off."

"It's not stupid shit, King. Someone needs to knock some sense into you. And since Mom's not here to do it, I guess it's gonna be me."

At the mention of our mother, King's nostrils flare and I instantly know I've gone too far. But it's too late now, so I might as well say what I need to say because the damage is done—he's already furious.

"You need to man up and talk to Juliet, King. It's important. We could lose the inn. I don't know what the Capellis have, but it's not good. So stop being a damn crybaby and talk to her. Find out what she knows. And get the fuck over yourself."

King shoves me hard in the shoulders, pushing me backward. Instinctively, I shove back and now we're wrestling, grunting, the horses stomping their hooves at the excitement. King wraps his arm around my neck, pulling me down and into his body. I stumble and he follows right behind, both of us tumbling down onto the hay-covered ground. We land with a hard thud, shockwaves of pain rippling up my spine, but I block it out. My sole focus is gaining the upper position.

My brother's strong from years of manual labor, with a broad, barrel chest and a vice-like grip. His arms wrap around me and squeeze and I can hardly catch my breath.

"I'm not a crybaby, motherfucker. You don't know what you're talking about." King pants out the words, sweat beading on his forehead. "Take it back."

I scissor out of his grip and we roll along the ground like teenagers.

"No."

Another barrel roll and King's back on top. "I said— Take. It. Back."

Adrenaline races through me, pouring fuel on the fire. A surge of anger bubbles up inside me—I'm tired of taking King's shit, him playing the boss while I clean up every-one's messes.

"Not a fucking chance."

I kick his legs out from under him and roll, pinning him to the ground. I lock his arms down and he struggles against me, his face red and sweaty. We're both panting with exhaustion, but I'm younger and in better shape.

"I know what happened with Juliet sucked. I get it. And if there were any other option, I'd let it go. But there's not, King. We need her help." I loosen my grip and he shoves me off of him, sitting up and brushing hay from his shirt. Worry lines crinkle the skin around his eyes and I feel sorry for him.

King, the newly minted patriarch, out here in the country all alone. He didn't ask for this. This was never the plan. It was always supposed to be him and my dad running the ranch together.

He stares blankly at the barn door, his chest still heaving from our wrestling match.

"I'm sorry to put you in this position, I really am. But it's been almost fifteen years. You've gotta move on."

King swallows hard, his Adam's apple bobbing with the exertion. "I have."

"Really? With who?"

A horse stomps a hoof and another neighs while my brother contemplates his answer. He rises to his feet, brushing the dirt from his hands onto his jeans.

"I'll talk to her. But you have to come."

I follow his lead, standing and straightening my shirt, plucking hay from my hair. I'm surprised he'd want company.

"In case her idiot brothers come around. I may need back-up."

"Deal.".

Without another word, he walks out of the barn and

heads back to the house. I'm guessing he's still angry, but with King who the hell knows?

I shuffle out behind him, a sinking feeling in my gut.

This thing between us definitely isn't over. And if my relationship with Skye gets serious, King probably won't approve. Not that I need his permission, but he is my brother and closest friend. I'd rather have his blessing than not.

Shoving my worries down, I head into the house, pretending like nothing happened.

19

ROMAN

"Everything okay out there? You guys were gone a long time." Poppy studies King and me as we saunter into the kitchen, doing our best to act normal. Not like two grown-ass men who just had a full-blown wrestling match in the barn.

The table's been cleared and a variety of pies and cakes line the granite island, along with plates and forks.

"Ran out of feed," King says, dismissing Poppy's concern. "Had to haul in some more bags. But we're all good."

Poppy reaches her hand out, plucking a piece of hay from the back of King's collar.

"Mmm-hmmm." She cocks one brow high, her mouth twisting up, but drops the subject. Most likely because we have company. "Who wants pie? Chocolate cake?"

She and Griffin slice up thick slabs of pie and slices of cake for everyone and we all head to the family room. King has a fire going, the red and orange flames dancing in the stacked stone fireplace. Skye and I take a seat on the leather couch, Poppy and Griffin sliding in next to us. Skye scootches closer to me until our thighs touch, the glow from the glittering Christmas tree highlighting the apples of her cheeks. A dull pang hits me in the chest and squeezes.

My mom would have loved Skye.

I swallow hard over the lump in my throat, the tightness in my gut. Sometimes I miss my parents so much it physically hurts and holidays are the worst. Especially Christmas. They loved Christmas.

Skye's foot taps against mine, rubbing against me, and the ache lessens a little bit.

I could love this girl.

The thought floats into my mind and catches me off guard. Where the hell did that come from? We haven't even gone on a date or spent an entire night together. I need to get a fucking hold of myself.

"Skye, do you have any brothers or sisters?" Poppy asks before taking a big bite of chocolate cake.

Skye shakes her head. "No, I'm an only child."

"How was that? It must have been fun, getting all the attention. I've never been by myself, even for one second." Poppy glares across the room at Parker and he grins back.

"Some people get lucky, Pops," Parker teases, chuckling, and Poppy scowls at him.

Skye shrugs. "Kind of lonely. And my parents weren't exactly the PTA type, so it's probably for the best that they only had me."

"Oh. Sorry." Poppy's mouth forms a perfect pink 'O' and the room gets quiet. I swoop in to rescue Skye, changing the subject.

"Anybody have fun plans for New Year's?"

Poppy and Liv start chatting about some event at the inn and I tune them out, focusing my attention on Skye instead. She listens intently to the girls' conversation, but doesn't chime in. She gazes at them longingly, almost like a child on a playground waiting for someone to ask them to play.

I lean over, my lips close to her ear. "You ready to get out of here?"

She shoots me an appreciative look and nods. "Yes."

Standing, I stretch my arms above my head, ease the tension that settled in my lower back. The skirmish with King didn't do the injury any favors.

"Thanks for dinner, everyone. We're going to head out." I stack Skye's dessert plate on mine, the silverware clinking against the china. "Everything was great."

Skye follows my lead. "Thanks so much for having me. It was a lovely dinner, so nice to meet all of you."

Poppy jumps up from her spot on the couch, wrapping her arms around Skye in a hug.

"Thanks for coming. And for dropping the Capellis. You're on the right team now."

Skye flashes her a quick smile. "Thanks."

Liv, Parker, Griffin, and Jess all say their goodbyes. King tips his head at us, but doesn't get up.

Guess he's still pissed.

"Y'all need help with the clean up?" I ask, heading toward the kitchen.

"No, go. We've got it." Poppy waves, shooing us out.

Not one to turn down a free clean-up pass, I link hands with Skye and we walk outside.

The sun's gone now, the moon taking its place. Bright beams of light filter through the clouds, casting a soft glow over the grass. Gravel crunches beneath our feet as we move toward the cars.

My heart's pounding hard, my mind racing. It's been a long time since I dated anyone and I'm twitchy with nerves.

"Thanks for inviting me in, Roman. That was the nicest Christmas I've had in a long time." Skye's voice is soft, her hand warm in mine, and I don't want the night to end.

"You're welcome. Glad you came."

We're at her car and she hits her key fob, the Accord beeping loud in the quiet night. She doesn't open the door, though. We stand facing each other, still holding hands. I make the move, dropping my hand to her waist and pulling her up close to my body. I'm certain she can hear the thudding of my heart as I press my lips to hers. She tastes sweet, like cinnamon and apples, as I tease her mouth open with my tongue. I slide in, exploring, my cock hardening in my pants as she reaches up and wraps her hands around my neck. Her fingers trace along my neck and tension coils low in my gut.

"I should go," she murmurs. "Your family's probably watching from the window."

"Probably." I don't move away, instead lowering my hands a fraction of an inch, cupping her ass.

"Rome—" She giggles, sending a wave of pleasure rolling through me. I love her laugh. It's rare, and that somehow makes it even more special. Like she saved it just for me.

I inch away, my thumb tracing the soft skin of her cheeks, her jaw. She's so beautiful, with the moonlight kissing her skin.

She presses her mouth to mine, then opens the car door.

"What's on your window?" I squint in the darkness, then step closer to the glass. The word *BITCH* is only faintly visible.

"How'd that get there?" A hot gurgle of anger bubbles up inside me as I stare at the faint traces of red ink.

Skye shrugs. "It's no big deal. Probably Jagger."

"No big deal? That son of a bitch." I grit my teeth so hard shooting pain radiates up my jaw. "Did you go to the police?"

"What? No. They wouldn't do anything anyway." She waves her hand, dismissing the idea. "It's merely a threat."

"He can't go around threatening you. No more." Squaring my shoulders, I pluck the keys from Skye's hand, slide into the driver's seat.

"What are you doing?" She gnaws on her bottom lip, frowning down at me.

"Moving your car around to the back. You can leave it here for awhile. I don't want you staying by yourself. It's not safe. Come home with me."

The tip of Skye's tongue darts out, licking at her lip back and forth as she contemplates my proposition.

"I can take care of myself, Roman." She folds her arms across her chest, but her voice is unconvincing.

"I know. But let me take care of you for now."

Closing the door, I hit the ignition and reverse down the driveway, ending the discussion before she can brook any further argument. I drive around the line of cars, head back toward the barn. Best to stow the car out of sight, not that anyone comes all the way out here. But just in case.

Two seconds later, I'm ushering a feebly protesting

Skye into my truck. I sit and listen to her misgiving for a few minutes before pressing a finger to her lips.

"Sshhh. Enough. I get it—you can take care of yourself. Heard and understood. You're strong and resourceful and took self-defense. But I'll sleep better at night knowing where you are. Okay?"

She heaves out a sigh, sinking back against the seat. "Fine. But only because I know you'll sleep better at night."

She rolls her eyes at me, but her body visibly relaxes.

"Good. Now that that's settled—what do you want to listen to? Classic rock? Country? Pop?"

A slow smile spreads across her face, her lips turning up. "Christmas music."

I groan as she fiddles with the radio, finding the local station still playing holiday music until the new year.

"You're lucky I like you." I shake my head and drive us back to town, Mariah Carey yodeling all the way home.

20

SKYE

I can't believe I let Roman talk me into staying with him. But I've been making all kinds of rash decisions lately, starting with taking the Capelli case in the first place, so I guess I shouldn't be all that surprised at myself.

And I hate to admit it, but he's right. I am a teeny bit afraid of Jagger and his brothers. I'll feel much safer here, with him. No way will the Capellis try anything now. Even Jagger's not that stupid.

Plus it's nice having someone look after you for a change.

I push that thought out of my mind as the garage door thuds down behind us. I can't get too used to this. Staying with Roman will be temporary, I'm sure.

He takes my hand in his and leads me into the house. Hitting the hall light, he kicks off his shoes and leaves them by the door. I follow suit, bending down to unzip my boots. The air smells like him, a blend of crisp soap mixed with the spicy scent of his cologne and I'm not surprised by the tidy counters in the kitchen. No dirty dishes in the sink here, folks.

The family room's small and cozy, with a leather couch in the center of the room directly in front of a large television. A two-person table stands next to the galley kitchen and on the left is a hallway that leads to the bedrooms.

"I can lend you a shirt to sleep in tonight and I probably have an extra toothbrush in the bathroom. We can swing by your house tomorrow morning, grab some of your stuff."

"Sure, that sounds good. How long are you thinking this little arrangement should last?" I wave my hand through the air. "It's nice of you to be my bodyguard and all, but I don't think you want me moving in."

He gazes at me, his deep blue eyes serious. Tiny creases of worry crinkle around his eyes as he reaches out and cups the back of my neck. Heat flames my cheeks, then unfurls low in my belly.

"We'll see. Let's take it one day at a time, okay?" He lowers his lips to mine, brushing softly against me, and I melt into him. He's so strong, yet so gentle. Holding me delicately, as if I'm fragile and might break.

I'm so tired of thinking and analyzing. Worrying and stressing. For once, I'm going to give in and let go. Let someone else take the lead.

Because—for the first time in my life—there's someone capable besides me. Standing right here, offering to protect me. Help me. Comfort me.

"Sleep with me, Roman," I whisper into the darkness, my breath catching in my throat.

He says nothing.

Instead, he lifts me into his strong arms and carries me down the hallway to his darkened bedroom. Setting my bare feet on the wood floor, he wraps his arms around me and grabs me by the hips, pulling me into his strong body. My hands flutter to his shoulders, then his neck. I twine my fingers in his hair and get totally lost in the kiss.

His lips warm and gentle on mine. Soft at first, then more urgent. I open to him, tangling my tongue with his, tasting. He's delicious, sweet and spicy, and I don't think I'll ever get enough.

Without breaking our connection, I ease my sweater up, pull my arms from the sleeves. I'm desperate to feel his skin on mine, to run my hands over the ridges of his muscles, to writhe beneath him until I call out his name.

I strip out of my clothes as fast as I can, chucking them on his floor, leaving only my bra and panties. His pupils widen as they drink in the curves of my body. Without hesitation, he unbuttons his shirt, tossing it to the ground, then lifts off his T-shirt.

He's even more gorgeous than I imagined, all tan, rippling muscle.

My breath hitches as I feather my hand over his chest, trace along the lines of his defined pecs. Move down to trail my fingers over each individual ridge of his abdominals.

"Wow."

He chuckles, the vibration tickling the pads of my fingers. "Bodyguards have to stay in good shape."

"I'm feeling even safer now." I gaze up at him, my heart pounding.

The alley was good, but this? This is far better. I'm torn between taking my time and savoring him or devouring him in one delicious bite.

Reaching down, I unbutton his pants then lower his

zipper, the sound loud in the quiet room. He helps me out, kicking his jeans into a dark puddle on the floor.

Then he cups my ass, squeezing, and a hot shiver of pleasure ripples through me. My thighs clench and wetness seeps into my panties.

"I love your ass," he murmurs against my lips and I smile as he kneads the flesh.

"Thanks. Not sure anyone's ever said that to me before."

He pulls away, one brow raised high. "Really? It's perfect."

I giggle. "Really."

"Well, you have definitely been with the wrong men. Because if they don't appreciate this peach of an ass, they're not right." He rubs his hand over the silky fabric of my panties and a happy flush spreads through me.

I could love this man.

Slipping my tongue into his mouth, I kiss him with passion, determined to suck every drop of pleasure from this moment. He responds, skimming his hand over my breast. My nipples harden, chill bumps rising on my skin.

I need to feel him on me, in me. I want his body pressed up against me, driving into me so hard I can barely breathe.

He thumbs my nipple into a diamond-sharp point, pinching lightly and my thighs clench. Hot pressure's already building inside me, each nerve zinging with every stroke of his hand, every caress.

"Fuck me, Roman. Please."

He skims his thumb over my lower lip, locking a heated gaze on me. "So polite. Such a good girl."

His words wash over me like warm, sweet honey and

my insides quiver. The tip of my tongue darts out, licking the rough pad of his thumb and he groans, soft and low. I suck his thumb into my mouth, swirling my tongue around and around, until his cock bulges in his briefs, straining against the black cotton.

"Fuck, Skye," he hisses.

Scooping me up, he gently tosses me onto his slate comforter, the fabric smooth against my sensitive skin. Then he spreads my legs open, pushing my thighs wide apart, before drawing my clit into his mouth through the satin of my panties. The heat combined with the pressure is exquisite and I'm swollen and ready. I arch, trying to get more contact, but he presses my hips down.

"Relax and enjoy, baby. We've got time."

I take a deep, shuddery breath and close my eyes, giving in to the sensations. Waves of pleasure roll through me, from my toes all the way to my core, then up through my torso. I'm relaxed, but on edge, a strange and wonderful combination.

Roman hitches his thumbs into the sides of my panties, easing them down, and the cool air on my bare skin shocks me. Seconds later, he's sliding his tongue through my wetness, tasting me, licking and sucking until I'm a quivering mess.

"I'm so close—" I moan, fisting the comforter.

He slides two fingers inside me and my muscles clench around him as I arch off the bed.

"Oh my...Rome..." My voice comes out strangled, black spots dancing at the edges of my vision. He works another finger inside, hooking to hit my sensitive bundle of nerves.

I can't take it any longer. I explode around his hand, bucking wildly, as he thumbs my clit.

He keeps working me, stroking and pinching my breasts with his other hand as he gazes down at me and watches me come all over his fingers.

"So beautiful." He trails his free hand up and down my belly as I shiver with my release. "Such a good girl, coming for me."

Pressing his lips to mine in a searing kiss, I flush with his praise.

"Thank you," I whisper, my hand cupping his face.

"My pleasure," he murmurs, his hands running over my curves.

"No, I believe it was mine. And it was good—"

"But?" He cocks his head, staring down at me.

"I want to feel you inside me."

21

ROMAN

Fuck. Seeing Skye come, her guard down, her body unraveling for me, is sexy as hell. I like this side of her.

Unbridled. Uninhibited. Wild.

Dark hair splays all around her and she's so damn fuckable, a real-life pin-up model here in my bed.

She definitely doesn't need to ask me twice to fuck her. I can't wait to be inside her, feel her clenching around my dick as I drive into her tight pussy.

I pull my briefs down, my hard cock springing out, and her eyes widen.

"What?"

"Nothing. It's, um—you're bigger than I remember." She stares at my hand fisting my steel shaft.

"It was dark and you did have two martinis. That might have something to do with your memory."

She squeezes her eyes shut tight. "Yeah, two martinis and no dinner maybe wasn't my wisest decision ever."

"I kinda like how it's turning out though." I stroke her

cheek and she opens her eyes, gazing up at me through thick lashes.

"Me too."

I dip down and kiss her, and in this moment all that exists—all that matters—is me and Skye.

Teasing her mouth open with my tongue, I slide in and explore. She's sweeter than any dessert I've eaten and I don't think I'll ever get tired of tasting her.

A tiny mewl of pleasure falls from her lips and I want more.

More noise, more touch, more everything.

"Come here." I roll her over onto my chest, and she straddles me, her long hair tickling my bare skin.

I reach around and unhook her bra, the lacy undergarment falling away to reveal lush, round breasts.

"Magnificent." I palm one, then the other, and she responds to my touch, nipples puckering to rosy peaks. I roll one sharp point between my finger and thumb, her skin supple. Her hands spread on my chest and she drops her lips to mine, easing her tongue inside. I feel her wetness on my skin and my cock pulses, ready.

I play with her breasts for a while longer, until her hips writhe against me, a soft pink flush rising from her chest to her neck.

"Hang on one sec." I break away and Skye slides off me. Leaning over, I root through my nightstand for a condom. Ripping through the foil, I roll the rubber over the swollen head of my cock as she stares, lips parted.

I lay her back against the pillows, smooth a dark lock of hair from her face. "You still good?"

She nods, biting down on her puffy bottom lip.

"Good." I position myself above her, trail my dick

through her wetness. She inhales, a quick little gasp, her breasts rising, and my heart pounds even harder.

She's so damn beautiful. I can't wait to bury myself deep inside her.

With a gentle push, I ease in, her muscles tense. "Ssh, it's okay. Relax. I'll go slow."

I kiss her eyelids, her cheeks, her chest, and she calms down, her thighs falling open wider.

"That's good, just like that." I push inside her, inch by inch, and her body receives me as if I'm a gift she's been waiting for.

"You feel so good, baby," I murmur, kissing the dark chocolate freckle on her collarbone, the one I've been staring at for days.

She doesn't say anything, only arches up to meet me, our bodies now fully joined. I'm all the way inside her, my balls tingling as they smack against her ass. We find a rhythm, me giving, her receiving, her pussy milking my thick cock. I try to hold on as long as I can, stroking her clit until she's moaning and bucking beneath me.

"Rome..." Her voice is strained and needy, her hips bowing off the bed. A light sheen of sweat glistens on her skin as our bodies slide together. I piston in and out, harder, faster. Her nails claw at my back as I drill into her, going deeper than I thought I could.

I'm close, so close to exploding. Every muscle coiled and ready.

"Come for me, Skye."

The words send her spiraling over the edge, spasms of pleasure tearing through her body. She contracts on my dick as I chase after my release. Finally, I get there, detonating and spurting hot cum into the rubber.

Collapsing next to her, I pull her limp body onto my chest and she shivers, a happy sigh blowing over my skin. I run my hand over her bare back, down to her ass, squeezing the soft flesh.

"Thank you." I press my lips to her hair, breathing in the deep floral scent of her shampoo.

She wraps her legs around mine, snuggling in close to me. She fits perfectly in the crook of my arm, like she was made for that exact position.

"Thank you. This is the best Christmas I've had. Maybe in forever."

I hug her tight to my body, wanting to revel in the closeness of the moment. "It was a good day. I'm glad you came to find me at the ranch."

Her fingers trace over my abs, her touch whisper soft. "Me too. Thanks for letting me stay with you. I feel a lot safer."

Every part of me wants to protect her, keep her wrapped up in my arms, safe and sound.

"No problem. The Capellis won't be able to hurt you, I'll make sure of it."

With a contented sigh, she curls up against me and falls fast asleep. I lay awake, her inhales and exhales light on my skin, and wonder about what's next. With the lawsuit, the Capellis.

With us.

Watching Skye sleep, her face calm and relaxed, my heart pounds. Beating harder and faster—*because of her.*

For the first time in my life, I see an *us.*

And it's exciting, and strange, and oddly terrifying. I've never put myself out there before.

Unlike Poppy, I don't share things easily. I'm not Parker,

the life of every party. And I'm definitely not King, trapped in the past, brooding over a long-lost love.

This is a first for me and I don't want to fuck it up.

I wish my mom were still here. She'd be able to talk me off the ledge.

Somehow, I'm going to have to find the courage to take the leap—and I hope Skye will jump with me.

22

SKYE

I WAKE BENEATH A HEAVY, MUSCULAR ARM, LIGHT exhalations tickling my ear. Milky light spills through the blinds and I can't remember the last time I slept this well. I'm usually up before dawn and perpetually tired.

This morning is different, though. I'm well-rested, my body supple and languid. Might have something to do with the amazing sex last night.

Or it might have something to do with the man holding you safe in his arms right now.

Yesterday comes tumbling back to me in a messy rush —going out to the ranch to tell Roman I'm off the case, confessing everything about my dad, spending Christmas day with his family.

Then spending the entire glorious night with him, naked and tangled up in his sheets.

I really hope there's more where that came from.

"Morning, beautiful." Roman's chest rumbles against my cheek, his voice gravelly with sleep.

How is it possible that he's even sexier this morning?

"Hi." I peer up at him, suddenly shy. Being here, like this, somehow feels more intimate than fucking him in the alley.

"How'd you sleep?" He smooths hair back from my face, the rough pad of his thumb lighting up every inch of my skin he touches.

"Good. No, great, actually."

He brushes his lips against mine and I surrender to the kiss. Long and slow, unrushed, heat flushing my chest as our tongues collide. Circling, teasing, whispering unspoken promises of things to come.

His hand splays across my belly and my thighs clench, muscles contracting in anticipation.

"You hungry? I can make us breakfast."

"I kind of have other things on my mind right now." I reach down, encircling his thick cock in my hand. He's already hard, the skin velvety-smooth against my palm as I slide up and down the shaft.

A sharp hiss falls from his lips. "Fuck...Skye..."

"Are you good with that?" I stare up into his deep blue eyes, the pupils wide and dark.

"I'm never gonna say no to that. You honestly don't even need to bother asking." The corner of his mouth tips up in a smile as I slip down his body, licking at the crown of his cock. Swirling my tongue around, I press into the slit and lap at the salty drop of pre-cum beading at the tip. His fingers twine in my hair and I open wider, taking more of him into my mouth. I know it's going to be a struggle, fitting him all the way in due to his size, and I'm not sure I can do it.

I relax my jaw and breathe through my nose as I move up and down his steel rod, licking and sucking.

"Fuck, baby, that feels so good." His hand's on the back of my head, but I'm still in complete control. I suck harder, his length pulsing against my tongue. Reaching up, I massage his balls and he lets out a long, low groan, bucking his hips.

I smile, satisfied at the sound of his pleasure. With my other hand, I grip his thigh for better leverage as he pulls me in, closer to him. The musky scent of sex fills my nostrils as I breathe in and out, my mouth filled.

"I'm close, if you want to stop."

I shake my head *no*, instead picking up my pace and sucking harder. I want to give Roman this gratification.

Hot, salty fluid hits the back of my throat and I swallow down as fast as I can, taking everything he has to give. His fingers knit in my hair, holding me still on his cock as he spurts again and again into my mouth. The strong muscles of his abdomen twitch beneath me, tiny vibrations against my skin, and my nipples harden against the sheets. Wetness pools between my thighs as he finishes, finally releasing me and pulling me to him.

"That was amazing." He wraps me in his arms, his fingers trailing up and down my arm, over my breasts, toying with my nipples. Shockwaves of excitement ripple through me and my entire body's buzzy with desire.

"Thank you." My mind's hazy, and 'thank you' is the only response that comes to me.

Smashing his lips to mine, he claims my mouth in a searing kiss, tasting himself on my tongue. He circles my swollen clit with his finger, lightly flicking at it. On edge, I shudder against his thigh, blood roaring through my veins.

Roman traces his fingers through my slick folds, then slides three fingers deep inside me.

Firm, decisive.

My breath hitches at the intrusion, then my muscles relax and quickly adjust as he scissors inside me. Hitting every spot, every nerve in my most sensitive area. Heat builds from my toes to my calves to my thighs and I'm already dancing close to the edge—and we've barely begun.

"I want to hear you cry out my name." He thrusts, locking his eyes on mine. I whimper, cohesive thoughts escaping me as he assaults me in the best way possible.

"Can you do that, Skye? Can you call out my name?" He purrs my name, pinching and rolling my nipple as my skin puckers with arousal.

"Yes." I bite my lip as my release builds, a tsunami barreling toward the shore.

Thrust. Thrust. Thrust.

He crooks his fingers, hitting my G-spot and a gargled moan falls from my lips.

"I like that." He kisses my neck, licking at the flesh, then nipping with his teeth until I'm in a frenzy, bucking against his hand.

"That's very nice, but I want to hear my name. Got it?" Not really a question, more of a command.

All I can do is nod as he fingers me, stroking and working my muscles. He slides a fourth finger inside me and I'm so full, almost as full as last night when I rode his cock.

"Very good, baby girl. Does that feel nice?" He stares down at me with a lusty gaze, fully aware that it absolutely does and he owns me in this moment.

My eyes flutter closed, bright white spots dancing behind my eyelids, shimmery pleasure rushing through me.

He thrusts harder, pushing up, his thumb circling my hot, swollen clit, and I explode.

"Fuck, Roman!" My voice is high-pitched, shrill and needy, as I shatter on his hand.

"Such a good girl, crying out my name like I asked. So damn beautiful." The calm, soothing tone of his husky voice washes over me as I shudder in his arms, waves of the orgasm rolling through me. My body's limp now, every muscle weak and spent.

"I love watching you come." He presses a kiss on my forehead and I breathe him in, his clean pine scent mixing with the smell of sex.

Intertwining my legs with his, I snuggle against his chest, wishing we could stay here in this warm, safe nest forever.

After a few long, blissful minutes, I finally open my eyes. "Thank you. That was fantastic."

"Anytime, baby. Ready for breakfast now?"

I grin up at him. "Yes, please."

Roman throws on a pair of gym shorts, then proceeds to the kitchen to whip up scrambled eggs, toast, and coffee, insisting I sit at the table and do nothing to help.

It's difficult, but I manage, instead passing the time studying his taut back muscles as he works, a vein popping in his forearm while he whisks the eggs.

The man is beyond gorgeous. It's a real shame he put shorts on because he has a fantastic ass, high and round.

And the dip of his hips leading to his cock.

Oh my word.

Something that sexy should be illegal, honestly.

"Why do I feel like you're staring at me?" He glances in my direction, a cocky smirk on his face.

"Because I am. Can't help it, when a man as sexy as you is working in the kitchen shirtless."

He shoots me a playful grin. "What can I say? The less clothing, the better. I like you walking around shirtless too."

I blush as he winks at me before scooping up the food and carrying it to the table.

"For you." He sets the plate down with a flourish, hands me a fork before claiming my lips in a kiss.

"About my shirts..." I say when we finally break away from each other. "After we eat, we should head to my house. I need to grab some stuff—my charger, toiletries, maybe some clothes..."

"Shame..." His gaze drops to my bare legs and I blush.

"As much as I'd love to stay here naked, I do have a few pressing issues to attend to. Like employment. And the fact the Capellis need my dad's debt repaid."

The ugly situation hangs in the air between us, sullying our perfect morning.

Roman reaches across the table, squeezes my hand. "We'll figure something out. Don't worry."

Despite the amazing orgasm, tension's creeping back into my shoulders.

I am most definitely worried.

"I don't know how to fix this, Rome." I toy with a bite of egg, prodding it with the tine of the fork.

"Maybe it's not your problem to fix, Skye." His words both shock and reassure me and the contradiction's unsettling. Confusing.

I've always been a fixer.

I get things done.

I do shit.

But this? This?

I'm out of my depth and I'm scared. The coffee burns in my gut, churning, and all the blissful vibes from earlier vanish.

"Hey." Roman tips my chin up, forcing eye contact. "I get it. You're worried about your father. Let's finish breakfast, then we'll grab your things and kick around ideas. Okay?"

Pressing my lips together, I take a deep breath.

It's a good plan. And for once, I'm going to let someone else take charge.

"Okay."

He laces his fingers in mine, drawing my hand to his mouth and grazing my knuckles with his lips. So lightly the touch barely registers, yet somehow manages to send butterflies zooming around my stomach.

I'm confused about a lot of things right now, but one thing I'm sure of—I'm falling fast and hard for Roman Montgomery. And I don't ever want to hit the ground.

23

ROMAN

After breakfast, I drive Skye over to her house to get her things. The streets are still empty, most people enjoying a long holiday break. She's silent on the way over, her brows knitting with worry. Her right thumb rubs her ring over and over and I feel bad for her. Over the last few days, she's made some tough choices, and those choices had consequences I doubt she anticipated. I'm certain she'll come out of this thing better – and stronger – than before, but right now the stress is obviously intense.

I reach over, covering her hand with mine. "Hey. It's going to be okay."

She bites her lower lip and nods. "I know."

Tiny frown lines tip her mouth down, her toe tapping on the truck floorboard. She's not a great actress.

"Turn here." Skye points at the corner and I make a right turn into an older neighborhood consisting mostly of Florida ranchers, with the occasional historical Craftsman.

"That's my street."

I follow her directions, making a left turn on Neptune

Circle and driving to the end of the cul-de-sac. We park in the driveway of a small sage-colored bungalow and she takes a deep inhale.

"I'll be quick."

"Take your time. Get everything you need for a few weeks."

"A few weeks?" Her voice rises in surprise.

"Yeah. Just to be on the safe side."

Her pretty pink lips press into a tight line. "Good point."

Straightening her shoulders, she tugs the sleeves of her sweater down and hops out. We walk up to the house, me trailing slightly behind her and scanning the area. Everything appears normal, nothing amiss. No neighbors in sight, the only noise the low hum of the oversized inflatable snow globe blowing in the yard next door.

"Freeze." My voice is quiet, but firm, and I grip Skye's elbow before she can move any closer to the house.

"Rome, what—"

That's when she spots the bloody mess sitting on the welcome mat in front of her door. The decapitated head of a chicken, its black eyes bulging, beak wide open in a silent squawk.

Skye's arm is shaking, her face deathly pale. "What the hell?"

A note's taped to her front door, CHICKEN written in all caps in bright red ink.

"Oh my god, Rome..." Her fists clench and she stumbles backward into my chest. "What sick fucks they are."

"The Capellis being the *they* in this scenario, I'm assuming." I press her body behind me, shielding her from the ugly sight of the chicken carcass. A few mosquitos swarm around the stinking head, specks of blood crusting on the front porch.

"I can't believe this." She pulls her phone from her purse, leaning around me to snap photos.

"Here." I pry the cell from her hand, zooming in for close-ups, then out for a wider view. "We should probably go to the police."

"And do what? What are they going to do, realistically?" She's visibly shaking, the skin on her neck a mottled pink.

"Put a restraining order in place, for one."

"I've seen how effective those are, Rome. You know a piece of paper's not going to stop the Capellis."

"It's better than nothing, Skye." I cup her chin, force her to face me, mainly to tear her eyes away from the nasty pile of bloody feathers on her step.

"Here's what's going to happen. You're going to wait in the foyer while I scan the house and make sure it's clear. Assuming it is, you're going to pack as much as you want or need as quickly as possible while I clean up the chicken mess. Then we're going to the police station to get a restraining order against the Capellis."

"But we have no evidence it was them." She fiddles with a stray thread on her sweater, fear in her brown sugar eyes.

"I have connections in the force, I'll handle it." I clutch her hand, try to reassure her.

"What about my dad?"

"I'm still putting it together, but I think I have a plan there. Let's focus on your safety right now, though. We need to get you out of here."

She nods, a grave look on her beautiful face. "Okay."

Skye doesn't move, though. Just stands there, staring at the chicken head.

"Let's go, baby." I take her keys and rub circles on her back, trying to ground her while pushing her inside the house.

Pressing my finger to her lips, I urge her to hold still and be quiet. Then I leave her in the dim foyer while I do a quick search of the house, gun drawn.

I'd love nothing more than to pop a Capelli right now, but I doubt even they're dumb enough to be inside Skye's house. They knew she'd come home eventually, but they're trying to intimidate her, if I had to guess.

"All clear."

Skye's chest deflates, a huge sigh of relief rushing out of her. "Thank goodness."

"Even Jagger's not stupid enough to stick around. Go on—" I urge her toward the bedroom. "Pack and I'll clean up the chicken."

She nods and hustles off, hips swaying as she moves double-time down the hallway. I head to the kitchen and find a trash bag under the sink, along with a container of bleach. Grabbing some paper towels, I get to work on the crime scene. First, I snap a few more photos and send them to my buddy Nate at the police station. Then I shove the poor chicken into the trash bag, grateful it's cold outside. This task would be a hundred times gnarlier in the summer. I chuck the bloody welcome mat into the bag too, white feathers flying through the air. I do the best I can with the feathers, trying to scoop as many of them into the bag as possible before dousing the concrete with bleach. The astringent scent burns my nostrils, but the smell's one-thousand times better than the decaying chicken head.

Jagger's a fucking sick piece of work.

Hot rage bubbles inside me as I scrub the blood from Skye's front stoop. What kind of twisted fuck beheads an innocent chicken to make some kind of point?

The dude needs to be behind bars. He's crossed a line this time, gone way too damn far.

If he so much as lays a hand on Skye, he's a dead man.

Tying the trash bag closed as tightly as possible, I circle around the back in search of Skye's trash can. Flipping the lid open, a nauseating stench assails me.

"Fuck—"

Laying at the bottom of the trash can is the rest of the chicken, along with an entire family of flies crawling over the corpse. I suppress a dry heave, taking a deep breath of fresh air before untying the bag and upending the contents of the can into the plastic bag. The flies scatter as I flip the can over and pour enough bleach in to cover the bottom.

"Fucking disgusting." I tie the bag for the second time, praying I don't discover anything else repulsive. After a few seconds, I dump the bleach on the grass and toss the garbage bag into the empty can, slamming the lid down.

Hopefully, Skye's trash pickup is soon.

I head back into the house, scrubbing my hands with hot, soapy water over the kitchen sink. I'd love a hot shower, but figure now's not the time.

My cell vibrates in my pocket and I dry my hands, read the text.

Nate: Nasty shit. I'll start the paperwork
for the restraining order

I send over the photos of the decapitated chicken, then head down the hallway to Skye's bedroom.

"How's it going?" I survey Skye's room, absorbing more detail this go-round. Her room's feminine, but not overly so. There's a queen-sized bed with a dark wood headboard. Lots of whites and lavender, with some touches of dark purple. No family photos, only a few black-and-white photos of her with a group of women, presumably friends from college.

Skye peers over her shoulder at me from the closet, pulling a silk blouse from a hanger before folding it neatly and placing it in a rolling suitcase.

"Good. I'm almost done. Give me like two more minutes."

"Need help?"

"I'm good. Oh—can you check the fridge? Make sure I don't have anything that's going to spoil."

"On it."

I clean out her fridge, making my second trip out to the trash. No way am I letting Skye out here. The scent of bleach takes my breath away when I lift the lid, but it's better than rotting chicken flesh.

Back in the house, I scrub my hands again and then Skye's next to me, suitcase in hand.

"Ready."

"Good." I bend down, brushing my lips against hers. Trying to reassure her, let her know she's safe with me. She relaxes against me and I figure she gets the message.

We lock up and she surveys the front step, now clean and feather-free.

"Thanks, Rome. That was super gross."

"Sure." I shrug, not wanting to think about the chicken any further. "I talked to my friend at the station. He's expecting us."

"Oh. Okay. Although I don't really believe it's necessary."

I grip her forearm, hold her still for a second. "It is. If Jagger or his brothers try anything, you'll have instant back-up. In case I'm not around."

Her eyes widen, fear flashing in her eyes.

"Come on."

One hand on her back, I lead her to the truck, loading her suitcase into the back before helping her into the cab and shutting her safely inside.

I start driving before I say anything further, the low hum of the engine a soothing backdrop to what I'm about to say.

"We need to get your dad out of town. For good."

She sucks in a breath, biting down on her lip. Shakes her head no, her eyes welling with tears.

"It's the safest thing, Skye. For him and for you." I run my hand over her thigh, a lone tear trailing down her cheek.

"What about the money, though?" Her voice is soft, reedy with worry.

"I can lend your dad the money. He can pay me back."

"He won't, Rome."

I shrug. "Maybe he'll surprise you."

"Like I said—he won't. But I'll pay you back. Promise."

I squeeze her leg. "It's fine. I have a buddy from the

Marines who lives in south Georgia, fixes up old cars. Your dad know anything about cars?"

Skye tips her head. "Probably. I seem to remember him doing odd jobs for a mechanic a while back."

"Great. I'll have my buddy put him to work and he can send me part of his earnings. Cut your dad out of the entire transaction."

She's quiet, but her brow relaxes, her chest rising a little slower with this plan in place.

"It's a good plan. But we have to get my dad to agree to it."

"He doesn't have much of a choice. From what you've said, if he stays here, he's in danger. And after the chicken incident—I don't think Jagger's bluffing."

I slide the truck into a parking space in front of the police station. "C'mon—let's get this taken care of, then we can worry about your dad. My first priority is keeping you safe."

Skye glances over at me, tears shining in her eyes, glistening on her dark lashes. "Thank you, Roman. Seriously. No one's ever taken care of me before. You don't know how much I appreciate this."

I lean over, pressing my mouth to hers, her lips soft and pliant against mine.

"You're welcome. I've got you, okay?" I run my thumb over her smooth cheek, swiping at the wet skin.

"Okay."

"Now let's go, before Jagger figures out our next move."

24

SKYE

I can't believe Jagger chopped off a chicken's head and threw it on my doorstep, all to scare me. To send the message that he's the biggest baddie in town.

Well, joke's on him because I'm not scared.

Okay, maybe a tiny bit scared. But not when I'm with Roman. There's no way he'll let Jagger come near me.

And now neither will the police. I have an official restraining order against all three Capellis and I'm ten pounds lighter without the burden of anxiety bearing down on me.

So fuck you, Jagger.

"Now what?" I peer over at Roman, his jaw tense as he throws the truck in reverse and we leave the police station behind.

"Much as I'd love to head straight to your dad's, it's not the best idea. Jagger's probably watching, waiting for you to react to his stupid little chicken prank."

I grimace, my mind flashing back to the grotesque sight of the chicken head on my porch, his yellow beak wide, probably squawking until the bitter end. I shudder, a chill racing down my spine.

Jagger truly is a sick individual. I'm glad I'm no longer the Capelli's attorney—the less face time I have with them, the better.

"I need to give him a warning, though. Some kind of a heads-up." I toy with a loose thread on my sweater, winding it around my finger.

"Why? You think he's going to need a lot of time to pack? The less notice he has, the better. We don't want him talking, giving away his safe location."

Roman's right. My dad does have a big mouth, especially if he's been drinking. Which is pretty much all the time, let's be real.

"Fine, I agree. So when are we going to pick him up? Tonight, after it's dark?"

He pauses for a long time and my stomach rolls, a crushing dread heavy on my chest.

"*We're* not. I don't want you to come."

The words echo in my head, banging over the rush of blood roaring through my ears. I'm hot all of a sudden, my hands shaking.

With anger and with fear.

"What? Of course I'm coming."

Roman turns off the main road, pulling down a side street and idling along a deserted curb. The cheery holiday decorations—bright red bows on mailboxes and life-sized twig reindeer statues poised on lawns—seem strange, at odds with the maelstrom of negative emotions swirling inside me.

Throwing the truck into park, a vein throbs in his neck. "No, you're not coming. It's too dangerous. I can protect your dad better if it's only the two of us. You're staying here."

Hot tears prick at my eyes, and I can't decide if I'm more mad, sad, or scared. I decide to go with mad because it's easier, safer.

"I appreciate your concern, but I'm a grown-ass woman and I can do what I want."

Roman locks a steely gaze on me. "Not this time. Typically, I'd respect that. Women's lib and all that. But like it or not, your dad's in danger—and by extension, so are you. You're staying here."

"But won't I be safer with you?" My voice tips up into hysteria; I don't like this out-of-control feeling.

"Not on the open road. I'm taking you out to the ranch. You can stay at the house with King. The Capellis don't dare go near the ranch. Plus, they won't be looking for you out there anyway, they'll assume you're with me. We're going to get your car now, then we'll drive it back to your house. I'll tail you, make sure no one follows. Then we'll leave your car at your house, and Parker will come get you, drive you out to the ranch. Meanwhile, I'll grab your dad and head out of town."

The tears spill over, too much emotion bubbling around inside for me to control. I'm breathing fast and hard, the world spinning impossibly fast.

"I don't get to say goodbye to my dad?" I whisper, hot panic flooding over me.

"It's not a great idea."

I clutch at his arm, desperate. "Please, Roman. He's my dad."

His face softens, and he lets out an exasperated sigh.

Peering up at the ceiling of the truck, he mutters something under his breath I can't quite make out before turning to me.

"Fine. But let the record show this is against my better judgment. Call your dad and have him meet us behind The Tipsy Taco at five p.m. Parker will swing you over there before he drives you out to the ranch."

I throw my arms around Roman's neck, giving him a huge bear hug. "Thank you, Roman."

He pats my back, shaking his head. "I hope I don't regret this."

ROMAN AND I DRIVE OUT TO THE RANCH TO PICK UP MY car, the only sound in the truck coming from the radio. The local station's still spinning holiday tunes and Roman's so distracted he doesn't even bother to fight with me to change it. He checks the rearview roughly every thirty seconds, deep worry lines etched on his brow.

"I'm sorry I dragged you into this mess." I finally break the silence once we're out of town and it seems like we're in the clear.

"It's fine."

His tone's flat, the words inconsistent with the tension in the truck right now. My stomach turns, a hot flush climbing my neck.

"It's not fine. Ever since you met me, your life's been screwed up."

He licks his lower lip, the tip of his tongue darting out and moving slowly across in a straight, pink line.

"You're wrong about that."

My breath hitches, my throat dry. I want to believe him. Desperately, in fact.

But I don't.

"Really? First, it was the trial and your family inn at risk, and now you're protecting me and my father."

"Listen—the Capellis have been the bane of our existence for decades. You can't take full credit for that." He shoots me a wry smile, the edges of his eyes crinkling. "And I don't mind helping out your dad. And definitely don't mind watching out for you."

He reaches over and squeezes my hand, and my gut unclenches a teensy bit. I still can't shake the feeling that this is all my fault, though.

I slump back against the seat, allowing Michael Buble's crooning about a white Christmas to wash over me, lulling me into a semi-calm state.

What choice do I have?

My dad got himself into this predicament and dragged me down with him. I need help and Roman's offering it to me.

"Everything's going to be fine. Trust me." Roman strokes my hand with his thumb and I cling to his words with every fiber of my being.

Maybe if I focus on them, everything really will work out.

25

ROMAN

I hate seeing Skye cry. And I didn't mean to be a dick about her coming with me. But she'll be safer tucked away out here on the ranch with King watching over her.

I know it's for the best, but it doesn't take away the pain in my chest, the rolling in my gut as tears cascade down her face.

Fuck.

This whole thing got real complicated, real quick.

I'm glad my buddy Dustin can take her dad in, for a while anyway. Hopefully he won't be too big of a pain in the ass. Dustin owes me a favor—I had his six on a mission we did together in Afghanistan back in the day—but still. You can only ask so much. And I have a feeling that Skye's dad might be too much. But I guess I'll have to wait and see.

We bump down the gravel drive and I pull around back. I need to talk to King, get him on board with the plan. Not that he'll say *no*, but I do have a nagging feeling that he's not going to be thrilled with this turn of events.

Dude's got major trust issues, and he and Skye didn't exactly get off on the right foot, what with the trial and all.

"C'mon, King's probably in the stables, feeding the horses." I take Skye's delicate hand in mind, slamming the truck door shut behind her before we cross the yard and head back toward the barn.

"Wow, I didn't realize your family had so much land." She gestures at the open fields beyond the paddock and stables.

"Yeah, our great-great-grandparents had the ranch first. Then as Seaglass Beach developed, our great-grandparents saw the potential in town and built the inn."

"Best of both worlds. How did all of you end up in town, but King's out here?"

I shrug. "My brother doesn't much care for people. He's more at home out here, with the open space and the horses. Poppy and Parker thrive on the energy of others, so they always knew they'd live in town. I could go either way."

"Interesting." She chews on the corner of her lip, sizing me up, and I wonder if that's the correct answer.

"What about you? Do you like the country?"

"I've never lived anywhere rural. Seaglass Beach is about the smallest place I've ever been. I like it fine. Better than a city, I suppose. Minus the Capellis."

"A lot of people would agree with you on the Capelli part." Opening the gate for her, we cross through the dusty paddock.

"King?" I peer into the stable, my eyes adjusting to the lower light.

As suspected, my brother's feeding the horses. He

glances over his shoulder, tying a bale of hay up in the hay net.

"Hey, Rome. What's up? Didn't expect you out here today. Skye." He tips his hat at Skye and she blushes.

"Yeah, wasn't planning on coming out. We kind of have a situation."

"The trial?" King continues working, moving on to the next net. Lifting a bale of hay and tipping the straw on end, he pulls the net closed and cuts the string.

"Not exactly."

King stops, standing up straight to face me, brows furrowed.

"Jagger left a chicken head on Skye's front porch sometime last night."

King's lips thin, pressing together hard. He folds his arms over his chest, widening his stance.

"Really? That's harassment."

"Yes, I know. We filed a police report and I had my friend Nate at the station help me get a restraining order against all of the Capellis for her."

"Good."

"There's more..."

"Go ahead—"

"Her dad's in trouble."

King's frown deepens, his eyes narrowing. "How so?"

Skye shuffles next to me, her boot kicking at the loose straw lying on the ground. I glance her direction, sizing up her reaction to me sharing details with my brother. She nods her head ever so slightly, so I keep going.

"He owes Jagger some money. I'm going to get him out of town tonight, and we'll pay that little weasel whatever her dad owes."

"It's a long story—" Skye cuts in. "I took the case to repay the debt. But when it became clear that I couldn't with a good conscience continue to represent them, Jagger went off the deep end. I guess he heard I dropped the case and is trying to send me a message. The next logical step will be going after my dad."

"If you figure he's logical. Verdict's definitely out on that," King says, shaking his head. "But I see why you'd be concerned."

"The point to all this is we need your help. Right now, we're getting Skye's car and driving it back to town. Parker will pick her up and drive her out here to stay with you until I get back."

King rubs his jaw. "Where you going? How long you planning on being gone?"

"I'm going to take him up to south Georgia and he can stay with one of my Marine buddies until he gets his new life together. He can work off the debt and get back on his feet. I'll head out of town as soon as it's dark and I'll try to be back by tomorrow morning. The less time I'm gone, the better. Even someone as dumb as Jagger will be able to put two and two together eventually."

"Seems like a reasonable plan." King's jaw flexes and I sense a big ole' *but* coming. "Can I get a word?" He motions to the corner of the stable and I follow behind him.

"I'll step outside, give you two some privacy." Skye waves her hand at the blue sky beyond the stables, already moving in that direction.

As soon as she's out of earshot, King pivots and glares at me. "You sure you know what you're doing, Rome? You barely even know this girl and now you're swooping in to rescue her dad, repay his debt to the Capellis. You're acting like this is some kind of special mission or something."

I scrub a hand over the back of my neck, trying to get a hold of the simmering aggravation running through me right now.

"Yeah, I'm sure. And I'm not playing special ops, either. He's really in trouble, King. You're telling me that if Juliet was in danger right now, you wouldn't drop everything to help her out?"

King's hands ball into fists on his forearms and I know I touched a nerve.

"Leave Juliet out of this." His voice is gruff, but I can't help but poke the bear.

"It's the same thing, though. Don't you see that?"

"No, it's not. Juliet and I have history. You've known Skye for three damn minutes. For all you know, she's using you to pay back the Capellis."

I inhale a sharp breath, pressure building behind my ribs. Now I'm seriously pissed.

"Fuck off, King. Just because I can open myself up to the possibility of a relationship with someone doesn't mean that I'm getting played."

"Just sayin'. The thought never crossed your mind?" He rubs at his jaw, goading me.

"No, dickhead, it did not. And you know why? Because she had no idea any of this would happen. Jagger left a *dead chicken* on her porch, King. Feathers and blood, the whole nine yards. That's next level. And he did it because she dropped him as a client to protect us. So to answer your question—no, I don't think she's using me. But thanks for the vote of confidence in my people skills."

King and I face off for a long minute, locked in a cold stare. The blood roars in my ears and I'm seriously amped. I want to punch him in his smug face, maybe have another round of wrestling in the hay. But I kind of need him to watch over Skye while I'm gone, so I force myself to resist, instead shoving my hands in my pockets.

"Go slow. That's all I'm saying."

I swallow hard over the lump in my throat, still angry but willing to move on because we're brothers and he's my closest ally.

"I will. Take good care of her."

"Will do."

I start walking out, but stop halfway, turning around to face my brother. "Have you heard anything from Juliet?"

King scowls, shakes his head *no*. "Not yet. Soon as I do, I'll let you know."

I gauge my brother's reaction to the question and decide he's telling the truth. King wouldn't screw the family over just to avoid one brief, unpleasant encounter with Juliet, I'm sure of it.

"Okay, thanks."

I'm almost out of the stable when I hear my brother's deep voice calling after me.

"Rome—be careful."

Without so much as a backwards glance, I shoot him a wave over my shoulder, keeping my eyes trained on the ground.

I sure as hell don't need to go getting all emotional with my big brother right now.

"Everything okay?" Skye runs up as soon as she spots me leaving the stables, her eyes wide with worry.

"All good. Let's drop your suitcase off at the house and then we'll get going."

Lacing my hand in hers, we head back to the house, the threat of the Capellis hanging heavy between us.

26

SKYE

Back at my house, I follow Roman's instructions and call my dad promptly at four p.m. He picks up after about five rings.

"Hey, Chicky. You calling to wish me a Merry Christmas?" He slurs the words *merry* and *Christmas* together, a jumbled mish-mash of sounds tumbling from his mouth.

"That was yesterday, Dad. And I did call, but you didn't pick up. Everything okay?"

"Perfect. Watching some boxing on the old boob tube. I made five hundo today." The sharp clang of a bell pierces my ears—the boxing match playing at deafening volumes on the television. "Damn. Down a hundo now."

"Quit while you're ahead and you can use that money to repay the Capellis. Listen—I need you to meet me behind The Tipsy Taco at five today."

"Huh? Wha-for? Way too many townies hang there for my liking. I only go there for those five-dollar margaritas."

There's a loud slurp on the other end of the line, followed by a lip smack.

Wonderful. He's still drinking.

"I'm calling you an Uber now. You shouldn't drive."

"Ha! I can drive, Chicky. 'cept my truck's up on blocks, 'member? But why you need me to come all the way into town? Why can't you come out here? I have another sixer."

"I can't come out there, Dad. I need to see you in town. And don't tell anyone."

"Who would I tell, Chicky? I don't even have a damn cat." He cackles maniacally at his stupid joke and disconnects, leaving me with a sick feeling low in my gut. I push it away, instead clicking on the Uber app and ordering my dad a car.

"You good?" Roman asks, glancing over at me from the couch.

I huff out a breath. "Yeah, fine."

"Alright, get anything else you might need. Parker's on his way."

I do a quick spin of the space, shoving my laptop and a notebook into my bag, and then I'm ready to go.

Roman cracks the blinds, peers out the window to make sure no Capellis lay in wait for us.

"All clear."

A cool breath of relief hisses through my lips, my muscles loosening a bit. I've been on edge since this morning when we found the chicken. The whole situation's so untenable, so twisted. I can't believe that just yesterday I was with Roman's family sharing a holiday dinner and now today, I'm hiding out like a fugitive.

"Hey—" Roman comes up behind me, wrapping his strong arms around my waist and holding me to him. His warm breath feathers my hair, chill bumps rising on my neck.

I love this man.

But it's way too soon to make those sorts of declarations; he'll think I lost my mind.

Instead, I tip my head back and gaze into his deep blue eyes. "I'm going to miss you."

"Me too. But I won't be gone long. Promise."

He nuzzles my neck before dropping his lips to mine, claiming my mouth in a searing kiss and sending my heart rate skyrocketing.

A bright light beams into the dim room, creeping through the slats of the blinds. Roman unwinds his body from mine, cracking the blinds.

"Parker's here. Let's go."

Roman steps out and I trail behind, clutching my bag and locking the front door. No evidence of the dead chicken remains, save for the concrete reeking of bleach. Parker waves at us from his SUV, a huge grin on his boyish face, and I instantly relax. Unlike King, he's easy to talk to —and doesn't distrust me, so there's that.

"Thanks for helping out, Parks." Rome opens the door for me, leaning in to chat with his brother. "Circle around the back of The Tipsy Taco and I'll meet you there. Don't get out of the car until you get the go-ahead from me."

"Cool, cool. So will that be like a super-secret signal? A thumbs-up? What should I be looking for?"

Roman shakes his head, a vein pulsing in his neck. "I'll text you, how about that?"

"Oh, okay, cool. Using technology. Smart."

Rome taps the roof of Parker's SUV, sending us on our way before he climbs into his truck and follows behind. He's careful to keep at least a few car lengths between us and I have no doubt he's surveilling the scene. Parker chats at me the entire drive, although to be honest, I have no idea about what. He asks me zero questions requiring responses, and for that I'm grateful.

"Alrighty. Here we are, in the back of the Tipsy Taco. Reporting for duty." He throws the car into park, but leaves the engine running. We sit and wait for a text from Roman. I'm searching everywhere for my dad, but see no sign of an Uber. He'll probably get dropped in the front.

Roman's name pops up on the infotainment screen signaling receipt of a text message. Parker taps his phone, reading the text.

"Looks like it's go time."

My stomach's fluttery with nerves, my heart racing. Hot panic pricks the back of my neck and I hate that I'm so weak. I can't believe I'm letting stupid Jagger intimidate me like this. But a decapitated chicken will do that to someone, I suppose.

I move to open the door, but Parker reaches out, grabbing my arm. "Wait. Rome said he'll come around back in a sec, hang tight."

"Seriously?" I scan the small, empty lot, but stay put, drumming my fingers on my jeans. A minute later, Roman's truck pulls around and he cuts the lights so we're in full darkness.

Then Roman's opening the door and ushering me out by the elbow.

"Sorry to do this to you, but make it quick. I don't have a great feeling about this." Roman's voice is stern but sympathetic, and my stomach pitches and rolls.

"Chicky, what the hell's going on?" My dad stumbles out of Roman's truck, almost falling from the running board.

Shit, the man's plastered. I feel terrible for Roman, having to spend a couple hours with my father in his current condition. Maybe he'll pass out.

"Dad—" My voice breaks, a swell of sadness rushing through me. Although he isn't the most upstanding citizen—and an even worse father—he's still mine.

And he's all I've got.

He wobbles over, unsteady on his feet and swaying slightly as if being blown around by a strong wind. I embrace him, the hoppy smell of beer strong on his breath, rolling off his skin. He's frail now, no longer the man I remember from childhood, a lifetime of drinking, smoking, and gambling having taken its toll.

My dad bucks in my arms, pushing me away. "What's wrong, Chicky? Why'd you need me to come to town?" He scrunches up his gray brows in confusion.

I swipe away at the tears stinging my eyes, embarrassed. Roman and Parker are standing off to the side, giving us space, but they're still within earshot and can definitely see the entire encounter.

"Dad, listen to me. You're in danger. Roman's taking you somewhere you'll be safe."

"What? Hell no. I'm not going anywhere."

I grab onto his thin arms, shaking him. "Yes, you are. This is happening. You're going with him now. Tonight. And you're not coming back."

"The fuck I am—" His face flushes, white spittle flying out of his mouth.

"You don't have a choice about this, Dad. Jagger and the Capellis are dangerous. They already tried to set your trailer on fire and today they left a dead chicken head on my porch. They mean business, this isn't a joke. You're going with Roman and you're going to work off your debt."

"Shut the hell up, Skye. I'm not going nowhere." He wrestles away from me and the familiar rise of panic hits me in the gut, bile rising in my throat and burning my esophagus.

"We've got to go. Now." Roman cuts in, taking my father's scrawny arm in his firm grip and guiding him over to the truck. My dad writhes and squirms, but it's futile. Roman's taller, stronger, and sober.

He shoves my dad into the back of the truck, tossing him a blanket. "Lay down and cover up. I'm going to pretend you're not there. Maybe you can sleep it off, be fresh when we get to where we're going."

My father shakes his head *no*, but does as instructed, lying down on the leather seat. Rome covers him with the blanket, tucking him in like a naughty child.

"Oh, one more thing." Roman pops the blanket up. "Give me your phone. We have to get rid of it."

"What? I need it. How am I going to get in touch with my pals?"

"We'll get you a burner phone. This is too easy to track." Rome takes the cell from my dad's outstretched hand, clawing it away from him. "Night-night."

Rome slams the door of the truck, then jogs over to the dumpster near the back door of the restaurant. He tosses the phone over the side of the green waste container, the metal landing with a dull thud.

Then he joins me outside of Parker's SUV, wrapping me in his arms. "I'm sorry, Skye."

He holds me while I let the tears fall, my entire body shaking in anguish. Deep-down, I understand I'm being irrational. My dad's the reason I'm in this mess in the first place. But still, I'm filled with regret.

Regret that I can't do more, be more.

Regret that I never had the childhood I wanted.

Regret that now I'm alone.

"Sshh." Roman strokes my hair as I cry, letting the pent-up emotions flow out of me. "It's okay, everything's going to be okay."

I sniff, the tears slowing.

"It's not your fault, you know," Roman whispers against my neck and his words soothe me, the truth a balm to my bruised soul. "I'm sorry, but I need to go. I'll be back as soon as I can."

I tip my head, gazing up at him, white moonlight shining around him. I take him all in—the dark scruff on his defined jaw, his high cheekbones, those beautiful cobalt eyes.

In that moment, I know I'm wrong.

I'm not alone.

I have Roman—and he's a million times better than I ever could have dreamed.

I rise on tiptoe, pressing my lips to his in a soft kiss, trying to convey all my emotion in this one small, simple gesture. "Be safe and hurry home."

Running his thumb over my jaw, he smiles before dropping his mouth to mine in one last, possessive kiss. "I will. See you soon."

Then he hops into his truck and drives away, leaving me standing in the empty lot bathed in the red of his taillights.

27

———

SKYE

THE DRIVE OUT TO THE RANCH IS A LITTLE AWKWARD, although Parker does his best to lighten the mood, telling me funny stories about working at the tiki bar. It's an uphill battle, though, because I'm a sad ball of anxiety and I already miss Roman. I'm not looking forward to spending the next day or two stashed away out here with King—even if that means I'm safe from Jagger and his motley crew.

Of all the siblings, King's the toughest to talk to. Why does it have to be him and not Parker or Poppy? The twins are fun, easygoing. King seems so serious all the time. I have a sneaking suspicion I'm going to be spending a lot of time hiding in my room.

"Here we are—home, sweet home. I hope I earned a five-star review." He grins at me and I can't help but laugh. It's funny how he's so different from Roman, yet I see the similarities in the line of his nose, the shape of his eyes, the way one side of his mouth tips up a half-second before the other when he smiles.

Montgomery genes must be strong.

"Absolutely. I'll leave you a rave review."

He chuckles, coming around to open my door for me. A true Southern gentleman, another trait all the Montgomery boys share. I trail slightly behind him up to the house, the porch light glowing in the darkness. We're far from the city out here, and it's much darker, no ambient light at all save for the twinkling stars in the sky.

"Hey, King," Parker shouts in the direction of the kitchen. The canned laughter from a TV sitcom bounces off the high wooden rafters, echoing in the quiet space. King's in a leather armchair, one foot resting on his knee, sipping a glass of whiskey on the rocks. He nods when we enter the room, but doesn't get up.

"Everything go okay?" King directs the question at Parker instead of me, and that really grinds my gears.

"Yes." I jut my chin out, folding my arms over my stomach. Defiant and nervous at once, and King's definitely smart enough to read my vibe.

"Good." He takes a sip of his drink, remains seated.

"Listen, I'd love to stay and hang out, but I have to get back. I promised Liv I'd help her with the wedding thank you notes. Call if you need me." He squeezes my arm on the way out the door, panic clawing at my chest.

I'm going to be alone out here with King for at least tonight and tomorrow.

I shuffle from foot-to-foot, feeling like a captive in the spacious family room. Yesterday, this room felt warm, cozy, inviting. Tonight, it's a whole different ambiance. The air temperature's fine, yet I'm chilled, and despite the noise coming from the TV, I swear I hear an owl hooting from all the way out in the barn.

"You can sit down, you know. You don't have to stand until Roman comes back to fetch you."

His deep voice startles me and I try to stifle my instinct to jump.

I take a seat on the leather couch, sinking down into the oversized cushions. "Thanks."

Figure I might as well play nice. Maybe I can win him over in the next day or two.

"You want something to drink?" King glances over at me, his gaze neutral, the corners of his mouth downturned. Like he's sizing me up.

"That would be great, thank you. I can get it." I go to stand, but King presses his palm down against the air.

"Sit. I'll get it. Beer, wine, whiskey, or water. That's all I've got." He crosses over to a mini bar in the corner I didn't notice yesterday.

"I'll take wine, thanks."

"Red good with you?" He plucks a wine glass from the hanging display and starts pouring the red liquid.

Good thing I'm not that picky.

"Sure."

"You have anything to eat yet?"

"No."

"I'll fix you a plate."

"I'm not that hungry."

He hands me the glass of wine before moving to the kitchen, ignoring my hunger strike.

"Rome'll be pissed if I don't at least feed you. It's nothing fancy, just leftovers from yesterday."

Opening the fridge, he pulls out ham, scalloped potatoes, green beans, rolls. He heats the food up in the microwave before grabbing silverware and carrying the dinner over to the couch.

"Here."

I take the food, my stomach rumbling. "Thank you."

King resumes his spot in the chair and turns his attention back to the television, giving me space to eat in peace.

Kramer and Jerry argue about what exactly a tax write-off is on the screen, and King's chest rises with a silent chuckle.

Funny. I wouldn't have taken him for a Seinfeld fan. He strikes me as a news-and-weather guy, to be honest.

Maybe I should relax and give him a chance. Roman likes him—trusts him—so he can't be all that bad.

"You want more to eat?" He points at my empty plate, every last bite of food consumed.

"No, thank you. I'm stuffed."

"I have some leftover cake." His voice tips up, trying to tempt me.

I'm full, but don't want to be rude.

"Fine. I'll have some cake."

I stand up to carry my plate to the sink, but King once again motions for me to sit. Not one to argue with a man in his own home, I plop back on the couch while he slices up a thick piece of chocolate cake I doubt I'll be able to finish. Then he brings the dessert over, refilling my wine glass.

King's quite the host.

"So. What's the deal with you and my brother?" He peers down at me, wine splashing into the glass.

A hot flush rises from my chest to my neck, King's navy stare boring into me. My breath catches in my dry throat as laughter echoes from the TV, cutting through the silence between us.

I swallow hard, take a sip of wine. "What do you mean?"

"Don't be coy, Skye. You obviously have some kind of hold on Roman. I've never seen him act like this before." He sets the wine down on the coffee table, takes his seat across from me while I process what he just said.

I skim over the *hold* part, instead focusing on the latter information.

Roman's never acted like this before.

My heart flip-flops in my chest and I'm all fluttery inside. I lick my lips, trying to remain calm.

"What are you really asking me here, King?"

He swirls the amber liquid in his glass, one leg propped up on his knee. "I guess what I'm asking is what are your intentions? Because Roman doesn't deserve to be hurt. He's lost a lot in his thirty-some years. I'd hate to see him lose anything more."

A pang squeezes my chest, thinking about hurting Roman. "That's definitely not my intention, King. The last thing I want to do is hurt your brother."

We lock eyes across the room and I hold my breath. I want King to believe me, but he doesn't seem the trusting type.

"Good. Don't hurt him. Once he's committed, he'll go to the ends of the earth for you. Literally."

King leans forward, resting his elbows on his knees, his glass catching the reflection from the television.

"That's not something to be taken lightly."

I nod, the gravity of his words sinking in. "I understand."

"What I'm trying to say here is don't mess with his heart. If you can't love him for who he is, how he is—walk away now."

My chest squeezes tight, King's threat veiled so thinly I can practically see it on his rugged face.

"Got it."

"Good."

King sits back, drink in hand, and watches the rest of the sitcom episode like nothing happened between us. Just a regular fireside chat between two people.

Meanwhile, all I can focus on is how I can possibly prove my love to both Roman and King.

A tiny part of me wonders if this relationship's going to be too crowded, what with the family and all the ghosts of the past.

28

ROMAN

Skye's father snores all the way through Florida. Thank god for small favors because the last thing I want to do is make small talk with a drunk guy.

And by all accounts, we're not gonna have a lot in common anyway. I doubt there'll be much love lost between us, that's for sure. The man's a sorry excuse for a human, let alone a father. The only reason I'm bailing his ass out is Skye.

Because you're in love with her.

I huff out a deep breath, running a hand over my prickly jaw.

Fuck.

The realization hits me hard, socking me right in the gut.

I'm in love with Skye Adams.

I barely know the woman and I'm already over here fantasizing about waking up in bed with her every morning, the two of us making babies.

Get it together, Montgomery. You should probably at least

tell her how you feel before you print up the damn wedding invitations.

But does she feel the same? We haven't even gone on a real date yet.

Nothing about our relationship's been quote-unquote normal. Starting with the hook-up in the alley, right down to this very moment. Our entire time together's been covert, on the run. I'm looking forward to being with Skye out in the open, doing normal couple things.

Buzz, buzz.

I glance down at my phone, quickly reading the text.

> King: Skye's here. All good

My gut unclenches, knowing she's safe out at the ranch. No matter what, King won't let anything happen to her, I'm sure of that. He might not love the situation, but he has my back. Always.

There's a rustle behind me as Skye's dad rolls around in the back seat, muttering. I can't make out any intelligible words. Then the snoring starts up again, louder than before.

Whew. He went back to sleep. I kind of have to pee, but don't want to risk waking the old man up by stopping. To take my mind off my bladder, I flip through the radio stations, settling on classic rock. Some AC/DC thumping should keep me alert.

Trees whiz by as I put more miles between us and the Capellis and soon we're deep in south Georgia. Traffic's non-existent, so I'm making good time.

"Lemme outta here."

The growly voice startles me out of my rock concert reverie.

Shit. Skye's dad's awake, rattling the handle in the back, trying to get out. Good thing I have child lock on. No chance he's escaping before we get to my buddy's house.

"Don't think so." I glance back at him in the rearview. He's scowling, his mouth twisted in a confused sneer.

"You can't kidnap me like this."

I let out a strangled chuckle. "More like rescue you, you mean. You're in deep shit with the Capellis."

"Bullshit." He spits the word out, gripping the back of the seat.

"Did Skye tell you the Capellis left a dead chicken head on her front porch? Or that they wrote BITCH on her car in blood-red ink?"

He slumps back against the leather, staring out the window as the road flies by beneath us.

"No. Why they doing all that?"

"My guess is because you owe them money."

"I told them I'll pay them back. Soon as Bobby G. pays me from the boxing match, I'll have four hundred."

"You owe them way more than that."

"Jagger just needs to be patient."

"I'm not a gambling man, but I'm pretty sure that's not how this works. You pay up what's owed when it's owed. And the Capellis aren't in the loan business."

He says nothing, his face impassive.

"Here's what's gonna happen. I'm taking you to my buddy Dustin's house. He's got a place for you to stay. You're going to work for him and the money you earn will be used to pay off your debt. Once you pay off the money, you're welcome to head out, go wherever you want to, I don't give a shit."

"You can't do this."

"I believe the appropriate thing to say here is *thank you*. I'm saving your ass, and so is Dustin. And to be clear, the only reason I'm helping you out is for Skye. You're her father and she cares about you."

"I care about Chicky too."

Now it's my turn to call bullshit.

"Uh-huh. And that's the last thing—you're not going to contact her. At all. You're going to leave her the fuck alone."

"What? You can't do this! She's my daughter."

"And the only time you ever talk to her is when you need something. Well, that ends now. You get sober, quit gambling, straighten out your life, maybe. Until then—do not bother her. From here on out, your problems are exactly that. Yours. She's not going to be bailing you out again. So I strongly suggest you get your shit together."

I catch his eye in the mirror and glare at him, and he glowers right back, eyes cloudy with booze.

"Fuck you. You're not the boss of me. Or her."

"So you'd rather I turn around? Deliver you straight to the Capelli's doorstep? I'm pretty sure you don't want whatever deal they'll offer you."

He balls up his fists, crushing his gray brows together.

"This is some bullshit—"

"Or a great deal I'm offering you. Take your pick."

Skye's dad leans against the window, staring out into the night like a resigned dog. He doesn't say anything else and I'm glad for the silence. I'm tired of trying to reason with this sorry excuse for a human being.

Finally, we roll into the closest town to Dustin's. It's almost ten p.m. by the time we make it all the way out to his home. He lives way out in the country, not another house in sight for miles.

Good luck getting out of town, especially without a vehicle.

"We're here." I cut the engine, but don't unlock the door yet. "This is my buddy's house and you're going to be on your best behavior. Is that understood?"

Skye's dad scowls at me, but nods his head.

"Don't pull any shit. It's going to take you a few months to pay off your debt. Until then, you better stay clean. No more gambling. No more benders. Got it?"

He grunts something, muttering a string of expletives under his breath.

"I'm going to unlock the doors. There's nowhere to run, so I wouldn't bother. Town's a good thirty minutes away and you don't strike me as a fitness buff."

"Fuck you."

I shake my head, happy I'm almost free of him. "Let's go."

Opening the door, I grip his arm and drag him up to the house. Dustin left the porch light on, and it's a good thing because it's pitch black out here. Quiet too, no passing traffic, only the occasional chirping of a bird confused about the time of day.

I knock and Dustin cracks it open, a wide grin on his face. "Brother!"

He throws the door open wide, embracing me. I keep a hand on Skye's dad the entire time, shoving him into the brightly lit room.

"Hey, Dustin. This is Mr. Adams." I shove Skye's dad forward and he folds his arms over his chest, defensive.

"Larry. The name's Larry."

"I'm Dustin." Dustin thrusts his hand out for a shake and Skye's dad takes it reluctantly.

"Tomorrow we'll get you set up in the guest house—sounds fancier than it is. It's more like a shed, but it's clean. Tonight you can stay in the guest bedroom."

Larry's shoulders slump forward, relaxing, as he scans the small kitchen and living room area. Guess he's satisfied there's no bad guys here out to get him.

"Rome said you worked with cars before?" Dustin's brow raises and Larry nods.

"Yessir. I worked at a garage for a bit. Why?"

"I could use a helping hand out in the shop. Been looking for a mechanic for a while."

"Hmmm." Larry presses his lips together, rubs the gray whiskers on his jaw. "I could probably help you out."

"Great. We can get to work tomorrow. No boozing, though. In exchange for room and board, you can work in the garage with me. Any extra, I'll send to Rome to pay off your debt. Sound good?" Dustin cuts his eyes at Larry, trying to get buy-in.

Not that it matters, this is the deal whether he likes it or not.

"Do I have a choice?"

Dustin guffaws, smacking Larry on the back. "We're gonna get on just fine. C'mon, you should get some sleep. Hit the hay and be ready to go bright and early tomorrow morning. Follow me."

Dustin leads Larry back to the bedroom and I hit the

bathroom, desperate to pee. A few minutes later, Dustin's back and Larry's tucked into bed, safe and sound.

"You want a beer?" Dustin reaches into his fridge, pulls out a bottle and pops the top. Hands it to me without waiting for an answer.

"I was kicking around leaving tonight."

"Leave first thing tomorrow. It's been forever since I've seen you. What was it, two tours ago?"

I nod, take a slug of the cold brew since it appears I'm spending the night. "Sounds about right. Has to have been at least four years."

Dustin runs a hand through his sandy blond hair, a few silvery strands reflecting in the bright light hanging over the dining table. "Damn. Hard to believe it's been that long."

"I know. Sometimes it feels like yesterday."

A long beat of silence stretches between us, both of us wrapped up in our own thoughts. My mind flashes over all the things that've happened since the last time Dustin and I were together—my parents' death, the accident, leaving the Marines.

Life was a helluva lot simpler back then.

"You know I'm happy to help out, but what exactly did I get myself into with this Larry guy?" Dustin tips his bottle back, taking a long slug.

I scrub the back of my neck. "Tough to say. I don't know him that well. At all, really. I only know his daughter, and she's good people. But that's probably in spite of her father, not because of him. If things don't work out, feel free to kick his sorry ass back out on the street."

"Doesn't sound like you're too attached to him." Dustin chuckles, peeling back the corner of the label on his bottle.

"Nope. She's the only reason I'm involved with him at all."

Dustin lets out a low whistle. "She must be something special to get you to drive all the way up here in the middle of the night, go to all this trouble."

My face heats as he studies me, waiting for my reaction. Gazing hard at the beer bottle, I kick around what to say. I decide to go with the truth.

"She is, man. There's something about her that's different, ya know?"

"I do believe that's called love, brother. You're fucking in love with this girl."

Hearing the words spoken out loud somehow makes everything between me and Skye tangible. Real.

I don't know what I was expecting to feel, but it definitely wasn't this. Like my insides are blossoming, warm emotion springing up everywhere, buzzing through every square inch of me.

After a few seconds sitting with this feeling, I grin at him. "Yeah, I guess I am."

Dustin polishes off his beer, then smacks me on the back. "Congrats, bro. Hopefully everything turns out great for you. I'll do my best to keep the derelict dad occupied and out of trouble. If all goes well, maybe he can manage to turn things around. If not, I'll stick his ass on the next bus heading north with a one-way ticket."

I snort, not even letting Larry spoil my mood right now. "Sounds like a plan. Keep me posted. And I'd lock up all the booze and pills you have. Pretty sure that's what got him into this mess in the first place. Well, that and the gambling. How long you think it's going to take him to work off the debt?"

"Six months, probably, if I deduct room and board. Does he have that long to pay it back?"

I snicker, the notion of Jagger waiting six months for his money comical. "Hell no. Me and Skye will pay it off, her dad can pay us back over time. He had to get out of town before Jagger did something bad. It's for his own good, even if he doesn't see it that way."

"I'll try to keep him here and out of trouble as long as I can."

"Thanks. That's all I can ask. And one last favor." I pull out my wallet, handing him two twenty-dollar bills. "Here's cash for a burner phone. We tossed Larry's cell before we left town. Too easy to track. I'm hoping he doesn't have his bookie's number memorized."

Dustin takes the money, shoving it in his pocket. "Alrighty. I can get the man a cheap phone, with strict instructions not to call anyone from his old life. I'm also going to get him hooked up with a men's group in town, try to talk him into AA."

"That'll be a tough sell. The man loves himself some alcohol."

"I'll do what I can."

"Thanks, Dustin. I appreciate it."

"One last thing, Montgomery."

"Shoot."

"Can I plan the bachelor party?"

He grins at me, wide and goofy, and I sock him in the arm. "Sure. Not that I'm walking down the aisle anytime soon."

"Uh-huh. Keep telling yourself that."

I roll my eyes as he stands, grabbing the empty bottles and chucking them in the trash.

"I'll crash on the couch. I'm leaving at dawn, so I may not see you."

"Good seeing you, brother. Take care and be safe, and I'll be in touch. Give you updates on your future father-in-law."

Hearing that phrase, my gut roils. The idea of Larry being my father-in-law isn't exactly palatable.

"Try to keep him here, will ya? He's already caused me a lot of grief."

Dustin chuckles. "Wait until you're related to him."

29

SKYE

King puts me up in Roman's old bedroom. The room's cozy, decorated in navy and white, with dark wood furniture and wide plank floors like the rest of the house. It's evident his parents never redecorated after he left home, his high school baseball trophies still lined up in a neat row on his dresser. The air carries a faint scent of him and that makes me feel a little better.

I settle in for the night, curling up in his childhood bed, snuggling under the striped comforter. Taking a deep inhale of his sheets, I try to relax. Easier said than done because it's eerily quiet all the way out here, except for the occasional tap of a tree branch on the window. And it's so dark, I don't even need to close my eyes.

I manage to fall asleep after counting backwards from one hundred, finally succumbing around thirty-two.

Then the nightmares start.

Jagger, Cash, and Damon chasing me in a field. The grass so tall I can't run very fast, and I keep stumbling and falling, scraping my knees. I'm breathless, panic clawing at my chest.

Then I'm outside my dad's trailer. I pound on the door, shaking the knob, but it's locked. I'm screaming for my dad to let me in, but there's no answer.

Jagger's behind me then, twisting my arms behind my back, pinning me up against the trailer. I try to kick away from him, screaming for my dad to help me, but he never comes.

Now I'm at the office and Jagger locks the door, sits down in the boss's chair. I'm only wearing a bra, panties, and stilettos, and I'm cold, so cold.

"On your hands and knees, Skye." Jagger leers at me from across the room, his voice commanding.

But I'm frozen, terrified. I can't move.

"Now."

Cash and Damon pelt me with dead chicken heads, the pointy beaks stinging my bare flesh. Tears stream down my face and they all laugh, deep, maniacal laughs.

Somehow, I manage to make my body cooperate, dropping to my hands and knees.

"Now crawl. Nice and slow."

I try to move, but my arms and legs are like lead. Cash kicks at my legs, but I stay there, unmoving. Then he's slapping my ass with his hand and I'm screaming, hot tears rolling down my face.

After several long minutes, I somehow manage to move, crawling to Jagger, my knees scraping on the cheap, scratchy office carpet.

"What an obedient little bitch you are." Jagger's gravelly voice sends a cold shudder of fear racing down my spine. I keep my eyes averted, staring at the hunter green floor, trying to figure out how to escape.

But the Capellis have me locked in here, captive.

I crawl across the room to Jagger, stopping at his feet. The smell of motor oil hits my nostrils and I gag, choking on the rising bile in my throat. His hand darts out, grabbing me by the hair and yanking me forward so hard my neck cracks, a loud pop echoing in my ears.

"Eyes on me, bitch. You're going to pay off Daddy's debt now."

I realize his pants are unzipped. He reaches down between his legs and pulls out a thick red fire hose. He points straight at me and a cold jet of water pours out, straight at my face. Now I'm soaking wet and trying to scream, but no words come. Cash and Damon take turns pawing at me, alternating between slapping my flesh or tickling me with chicken feathers.

Jagger's hand darts out and holds me still, gripping the back of my head, and I'm gagging on my tears and then he's shooting the hose straight at my mouth and I'm positive I'm going to die. Thick streams of water hit me and I'm choking. I can't breathe.

He finally lets go of my head, and I try to crawl away, but I still can't move. I'm frozen in place and time stands still.

Jagger leans down, his eyes glued to my throat, his breath hot against my ear. "You're mine now, Skye. I own you. You're having my baby."

"No, no, no!"

I wake with a start, sleepy half-screams caught in my throat. The comforter's on the floor in a heap and my body's sticky with sweat.

Cold fear grips me, and I clutch the sheets tight to my chest.

I'm not naked.

No one's here.

I'm safe out at the ranch, in Roman's bedroom.

The first weak rays of sun slant through the curtains and I try to catch my breath. A rooster crows in the distance and I shudder, the memory of the chickens haunting me.

But I'm definitely not having Jagger's baby. He can leave a whole freaking platoon of chickens on my doorstep, there is no way I'm going anywhere near his dick.

I grab my phone, check the time. Six thirty.

I wonder if Roman's awake yet.

Skye: You up?

Brushing hair sticky with sweat from my eyes, I stare at the screen, willing it to light up with a text.

Roman: Morning, sunshine. How'd you sleep?

I debate telling him the truth, knowing he'll worry if I detail the nightmare. Probably best to keep that to myself.

Skye: Fine, except for a nightmare. I miss you.

Roman: I miss you too. You okay? I wish I were there to hold you, kiss the nightmare away

Skye: Me too. I'm okay, though. Don't worry. What time will you be back?

Roman: Leaving now. Should be home around ten and I'll come get you.

Skye: Everything go okay with my dad?

Roman: Your dad's fine

Skye: Good. Thank you for helping him.
And me

Roman: You're welcome

Three dots appear, then disappear, then appear again. Disappear. He's taking a long time to respond and I wonder how long this next text will be.

Roman: Ask King to show you the horses. He loves giving tours

I laugh, smiling at the message. King loving the tour guide gig?

Skye: This I doubt

Roman: Seriously. Gives him a chance to show off his skills. He's better with horses

Roman probably has a point here.

Skye: Ok, I will. Be careful

Roman: I will. See you soon

I send him a heart emoji and climb out of bed, eager to brush my teeth and take my birth control.

I need to scrub the ickiness of Jagger off me. Even a nightmare with him in it sufficiently grosses me out.

30

ROMAN

I start typing out **I love you**, then stop myself.

Type it again.

Delete it again.

It's too much, too soon. I need to go slower, take my time.

What if she doesn't feel the same way?

I'll ruin things before they really get going.

Better to play it safe and guard my heart. Even if it's plainly evident to everyone around us, maybe King's right —I should be careful.

You've never done this before.

But safe's not your style. You take risks. It's who you are.

Not in love, though. I don't do relationships. Or romance.

Historically, I stay detached. No one gets hurt, and my singular focus can be on serving my country, doing my duty.

You don't have that obligation anymore. You can take a chance.

Man up and go for it.

But instead of manning up, I text Skye back, telling her to hang out with King and the horses and reassure her I'll be home soon. Then I go to the bathroom, taking a piss and brushing my teeth before creeping out the front door as quietly as possible. I don't feel like making small talk this morning, and I definitely don't want an ugly confrontation with Larry.

I'm halfway back to Seaglass Beach when I get a phone call from a number I vaguely recognize as a municipal line.

"Hello?"

"Where are you?" It's my buddy Nate, his voice tense.

"Just across the state line, heading back home. Why?"

"A call came in. There's a trailer fire on the outskirts. We're on our way, but the neighbor said it looks real bad."

Anger grips me, clawing at my insides as I white-knuckle the steering wheel and press down harder on the accelerator.

I have to get back to Skye. Protect her and keep her safe.

"You have any more details?" I grit the words out, trying to keep my emotions in check.

"Nothing concrete. By his report, he didn't see anything, only heard an explosion then saw the flames."

I know it's Jagger, but without proof the police can do nothing.

"Thanks for the heads-up. I appreciate it. I suppose y'all will canvass the area, search for evidence of arson?"

"Of course. But you know how it is out there. Nobody sees or hears anything, ever. Unless there's concrete evidence, nothing's going to stick."

And the Capellis are motherfucking Teflon.

"Maybe they got sloppy."

"We can hope. That would solve all your problems."

"Yeah. Doubt I'll get that lucky, though."

"You should stay away. Keep your distance from this mess."

I'd love nothing more, but there's not a chance of that happening. Not with Skye involved.

"Noted." I keep my tone flat, non-committal. "Keep me in the loop if you can."

"I'll do my best." Nate disconnects and I accelerate, inching up to twenty over the speed limit.

I need to get to Skye before she hears about this and does something that puts her in danger.

LESS THAN AN HOUR LATER, I'M BACK AT THE RANCH. The main house is empty, so I head out to the stables. Although I know she's fine out here with King, I'm still eager to see Skye, verify she's safe.

I hear her before I see her, the sweet, melodic notes of her giggle floating across the field. Air fills my lungs, my chest lightening. She's sitting atop one of the smaller horses, a halo of sunshine shining around her dark hair. My lower body tightens as she smiles sweetly at King, throwing her head back and laughing at whatever he's saying. I'm too far away to hear, and wouldn't be able to, anyway, over the hammering of my heart.

She's so damn beautiful, so perfect.

I've never felt this way about anyone before.

A ripple of panic swells in my gut, but I squash it down.

Get your shit together, Montgomery. You're a Marine.

"Rome!" Skye spots me, waving. The horse shakes her head, neighing a little, and she strokes the golden mane, calming the horse down.

She's a natural. Who'd have guessed?

"Pretty good for a city girl," King jokes, keeping his gaze pinned on her. Making sure she's steady and safe.

"Aww, thanks. Such flattery." Skye's tone is teasing and I swear King blushes.

She pats the horse a thank-you, then dismounts, allowing King to help her.

"Thank you for the lesson. I'm sure that will come in handy in the courtroom one day."

King tips his hat at her. "You never know."

He leads the horse back to the stable as she unlatches the gate, running out to greet me. Throwing her arms around my neck, she brushes her full lips against mine. Her vanilla lip balm tastes sweet as she opens her mouth, slips her tongue in.

"Hey," I murmur, gripping her by the hips and pulling her in tight. "I missed you."

She shimmies against me, and I'm instantly rock hard in my jeans.

"Me too. I'm glad you're back." She twines her fingers in my hair and we kiss for a long time under the canopy of the oaks, the bright sun warm on my back.

I'd love to stay out here all day, kissing her. Or maybe duck into the stable, lay a blanket over a bale of hay and make sweet love to her all afternoon. Lick, suck, and fuck until we've had our fill of each other's bodies and we're fully satisfied.

I break away, stroke the soft skin of her cheek. "Listen—"

Her eyes darken. "What? What happened? I don't like that look—"

She searches my face for clues and I take a deep breath. "Your dad's fine. But there's a fire on the outskirts. Trailer explosion."

Her hand flies up, covering her mouth and she trembles in my arms. I grip her tighter, grounding her.

"The good news is we're all safe. You and your dad."

Dropping her hand, she shakes her head, her cheeks flushed. "It was Jagger. I know it."

"Most likely. But the police will need evidence, and I doubt he's that stupid."

"I need to go." She starts pulling away, heading back to the house, visibly shaking now.

I squeeze her arm, hold her still. "No. You should stay here, with King. You're safe out here."

Skye spins on her heels to face me. "No. No more. I can't hide out here forever, Rome. I appreciate you rescuing my dad and I went along with the plan because it made sense. I didn't want to put any more on you. But this? I need to see the damage for myself, see if anything's salvageable—" Her voice cracks, eyes shimmering with tears.

I scrub a hand over the back of my neck, sighing. "Fine. I'll take you out there. But I wouldn't get my hopes up. Nate said it looked bad."

She presses the corners of her eyes, inhaling, trying to stop the tears from falling. "I'll take my chances."

Then she stalks toward the main house, her hips swaying side to side with pent-up anger and frustration. I hustle after her, wondering what exactly could come from an excursion to the outskirts.

A few minutes later, Skye bangs through the front door of the ranch and heads straight upstairs to get her stuff. Wanting to give her space, I make my way to the kitchen for a drink of water.

"Hey, how was the trip?" King's at the kitchen counter, making a sandwich. "Want one?" He gestures at the loaf of bread and the turkey.

I'd low-key love a sandwich right now—all I've had today is gas station coffee and a banana—but figure it's probably not the best time to grab lunch.

"Nah, I'm good. Thanks. Trip was fine. Skye's dad is squared away in rural Georgia, for the time being at least. It's gonna be tough getting out of there, too. Hopefully he can get his act together, for Skye's sake."

King pushes an aqua envelope across the counter. "You recognize that handwriting or return address?"

The letter's addressed to our mother, who's been dead for three years.

"No. Do you?"

King shrugs. "Nope."

"When did you get this?"

"Came in the mail today. First I've seen of it."

We both stare at the blue envelope, silent.

Finally, King breaks. "Should we open it?"

Curiosity tugs at my gut, my fingers tingling as I reach out and touch the paper.

There's literally no way in hell I'm *not* opening this letter.

"Yeah. What if it's important?" I raise a brow at him, snatching up the letter.

"Who sends a letter to someone who passed away?"

"Someone who doesn't know the person's gone." I slice

through the thin stationery with the bread knife carefully, holding my breath, and pull out a letter the same color as the envelope.

Dear Mrs. Montgomery,

I hope this letter finds you well. I'm sorry to be reaching out to you like this, after all this time. But after my adopted mother died, I felt the time was right to try to contact you. I've longed to reconnect with my birth mother ever since I found out the truth.

My stomach lurches, banana-flavored acid hitting the back of my throat, the room spinning. I glance over at King. He's standing stock-still, his sandwich hanging mid-air.

Our mother had another child. A secret child none of us knew about, judging by the look of shock on my older brother's face.

Holy shit.

31

ROMAN

THE GROUND BENEATH ME SHAKES, THE ENTIRE AXIS OF my world shifting.

My mother—the single most important woman in my life, the center of my entire universe—had another child.

I guess has, technically.

Which means King, Parker, Poppy, and I have a half-sibling.

I wish I never opened that letter.

The thought sucker punches me in the gut, but it's too late now. Pandora's box—er, letter—is open now.

I keep reading:

I'm sorry to spring this on you. And if you don't want to reach out to me, I totally understand. I know you didn't have a fully open adoption and that's all part of the deal.

A little about me: I'm doing just fine for myself. I live in Peachtree Grove, Georgia, and have one daughter. I was married—briefly—but that didn't work out. But Opal and I are fine by ourselves, we still have good kin here. I'm a third-grade teacher and have a fine life.

I'd love to meet you, if you'd be up for it. If not, I understand. If it wouldn't be too much to ask, could you please write me back and let me know you received this letter? Or give me a call, that would be lovely as well. I've spent a lot of time thinking about you and pray that you might want to connect with me, too.

Sincerely,

Lacey McCauliffe

A leaf of lettuce falls from King's sandwich, plopping onto the counter. The roughage goes unnoticed by him as he stares slack-jawed at the letter in my hand.

I don't even know how to react. My throat's tight, my mouth bone-dry, a dry heave threatening.

"Well, fuck me." King's growl shocks me back to reality. I drop the letter, the aqua paper fluttering down to the granite surface. "Our mother had another kid. You think Dad knew?"

A swirl of confusion whirs inside me, churning. "I don't know. Do you?"

The sandwich twitches in the air, forgotten. "Doubt it. If he knew, the two of them would have reached out before, included her in the family."

"So our mother—the most loving, decent human being we know—had another child and didn't tell her spouse of several decades about it? That feels off to me, King."

"How do you reconcile that with how Dad was, though? He was a family man, always wanting everyone together. If he knew Mom had another kid, don't you think they would have gone to look for her?"

"You read what the note said. It wasn't an open adoption. Maybe there are rules or something, I don't know—" My voice trails off as a million possibilities run through my head.

If Dad knew, how did he feel about it? If he didn't know and found out, how would he have felt?

A sharp pain stabs at my gut, the same pain that's been fading bit by bit over the past three years. Remorse, anger, sadness—grief, rearing its ugly head.

I'd been making good progress, but here it is again, stabbing, stabbing, stabbing. Tearing off the scab and slicing straight through my flesh, cutting down to the heart. My chest open, blood pulsing around the open wound.

Thud, thud. Rage surging in and out with each beat of my heart.

Why our parents? They were in good health, not ready to die.

They had so much life left to live.

It's fucking unfair and now I have questions, so many questions.

Questions that will go unanswered forever.

"What should we do?" I glance over at King, looking for answers. He's the big brother, the leader. He'll know what to do.

"Fuck if I know." He huffs out a breath, his face pale. Sets the sandwich down on the counter, untouched.

"We have to tell Poppy and Parker."

King presses his lips together, tipping his head back to the ceiling. "Shit. Do we have to?"

"Yes, we have to. It's the right thing to do."

"Poppy's going to freak." King states the obvious.

Poppy freaks about everything.

King rubs a hand over his jaw. "How do we know this Lacey person's telling the truth? We just taking her at her word?"

"I'm sure with a little bit of digging, we can find the birth record. We have all of Mom's personal info, I'm sure we can piece it together." I thrum my fingers on the counter, nervous energy running through me.

"Do that. Let's verify before we go telling Poppy and Parker anything."

I nod. "Okay. I should be able to gain access to our mom's info through the county. I have to make a trip to the outskirts first, though."

"Why?" King's brows knit together.

"Trailer explosion. And I bet you can guess whose trailer it was—and who did the exploding."

"Shit. Jagger's kicking this up a notch, huh? Arson's pretty extreme, even for him."

"I know." I lower my voice, figuring Skye'll be coming down any second. "I think he's sending a message. And it's not necessarily aimed at Skye anymore. You hear anything more from Juliet? We really need to get this trial over with."

"I was gonna talk to you about that. She messaged me last night. Wants to meet up after dark."

I run a hand through my hair, blow out a breath. "Great. Let's do it. I hope she has something concrete we can use to shut this whole thing down."

"Me too. I'm tired of the whole mess. Jagger's such a little shithead."

"Yep. Set up the meeting with Juliet and text me the time and location. I'll hide in the shadows, she won't even know I'm there. I don't want her to get spooked."

"Alright." King gazes out the window, clearly twisted up in his own thoughts. I say nothing, giving him space. The two of us are good about that sort of thing—unlike Poppy. She's all Labrador retriever energy, bounding into everybody's business, and that does not sit well with our older brother.

"Rome, you ready to go?" Skye interrupts the quiet, suitcase in hand. Shoulders square, she's on a mission.

"Yeah." I slide the letter back into the envelope, folding it in half and discretely shoving it into my back pocket.

A secret mission for later.

"Watch your back, Rome." King shoots me a concerned look, navy eyes serious.

I give him a two-finger salute. "Will do."

He nods and picks up his sandwich, waves to Skye. Guess they have a nice little détente going and I'm here for it.

I can't handle any more feuds at the moment. The Capellis are plenty to deal with.

Taking Skye's suitcase, I wheel her belongings to the door. "Let's see what the Capellis did this time."

32

SKYE

Roman's not exactly chatty, but he's unusually quiet, even for him. Worry lines crinkle the corners of his eyes and his lips press together in a tight line.

"You okay?" I gaze over at him as we speed out of the country toward town. His square jaw's peppered with dark scruff, and he looks tired.

Still hot as fuck, mind you. But tired.

"I'm fine." Gripping the wheel with both hands, he stares straight ahead at the seemingly endless stretch of road.

"Okay." I lick my lower lip, nerves humming just beneath my skin. Anxiety about our trip to the outskirts, but also the tension in the air.

I lower my voice and take a chance, resting my hand on his muscular thigh. "If you decide you want to talk about it, I'm here for you."

He swallows and his Adam's apple bobs up, then down.

"I can't believe I'm telling you this—" His voice is a low rumble, barely above a mutter.

I squeeze his leg, encouraging him. He remains focused on the road as we coast through Seaglass Beach, the trees morphing from oaks to palms. I don't press any further, sitting back and waiting for him to open up. I've been an attorney for a while, and sometimes these things take time, like an oyster popping open over the hot coals during a roast. You can't rush the process, everything has to align—the temperature, the timing—and be ready.

"I think my mother had another child."

I suck in a breath, my skin tingling all the way to the tips of my fingers. "What? Why would you think that?"

"This person sent a letter to the house, addressed to our mom. King and I opened it." His voice cracks and he bites down on his lip, trying to rein in his emotions. "King wants me to find out the truth. See if this woman really is our half-sister."

"Wow. Rome—I don't know what to say."

He sighs, hanging a right and gunning the truck down the dirt road leading to the outskirts. "Can't blame you there. I don't know what to say either."

"That's a lot to process."

"Yeah." He goes silent for a long minute as the grass grows taller and the road gets bumpier. "Don't worry about me. You have enough shit going on right now."

"Hey." I move my hand from his leg to his arm, squeezing, and he cuts his eyes at me.

Dark lashes frame sad cobalt eyes and my stomach clenches, my heart aching for him.

Roman—strong, tough, capable Roman—looks like a lost, scared little boy. I want to wrap him in my arms and hold him tight, tell him everything's going to be alright again, sometime soon. Promise.

But that's not a promise I can make.

What I can do is be there for him, just like he's been there for me.

It's the best I've got.

"Anything you want, anything you need—I've got you. I need you to know that."

A small smile pulls at the corner of his mouth. Kind of a pitiful attempt, but he tries.

"Anything?"

"The attorney in me might need to throw in a few parameters. Hard limits, I believe they're called," I tease and that at least elicits a low, rumbling chuckle.

"Tell me more about your hard limits, Skye Adams." He shoots me a sly grin and the mood shifts a little, lightening.

"Permanent physical harm or disfiguration—"

"Um, not my thing. I wouldn't want to deface a masterpiece."

I blush, my cheeks heating. "Thanks. Exhibitionism, like other people watching."

"Babe. We had sex in the alley."

"True. But it was dark and I doubt anyone saw."

"Fine. Point taken. So no sex on the beach in broad daylight. Fine."

"Oh, here's a good one. Definitely no video recording."

"What? Really?"

"Yeah, really. That could fall into the wrong hands and be a total disaster, career-wise."

"Killjoy." He winks at me and I'm happy to catch a glimpse of a happier Roman. "I didn't hear you rule out a bunch of other things, though."

I gnaw nervously on my lip, noticing we're getting closer to my dad's trailer. This conversation's been a nice distraction, but reality's quickly flooding back. The acrid stench of burning metal permeates the cabin, seeping through the air vents of the cab, and the sky's gray with the low-hanging smoke.

Trying to block out my nerves, I drop my voice. "What exactly are you looking for?"

"The kinkier, the better." He shoots me a wide grin, winking, and butterflies flap wildly in my stomach.

This man could be the death of me. Hot as sin, a fierce protector, with a kinky side?

Sign me the fuck up.

"Sadly, we'll have to finish this conversation later." He pulls up behind a police car, red-and-blue lights flashing. The area teems with first responders: police officers, firefighters, and a man in a suit I recognize from the courthouse, a detective. Hopefully working the arson angle.

I go to hop out of the truck, but Rome stops me, grabbing my arm. "Listen—I know this has to be tough for you."

A lump forms in my throat, the playful atmosphere totally dissipated now, as I lock eyes with him.

"I'm sorry about all this with your dad. But we need to let the police handle it from here. I don't want you getting further mixed up with Jagger and the Capellis." His jaw tenses, deep worry lines etched on his face.

Rationally, he's one-thousand percent right. Clearly, Jagger's fucked up in the head. I should stay as far away from him as possible.

But I need to see if there's anything my dad left behind, anything with meaning.

Anything at all.

And I need to make Jagger pay for his crimes.

"Why do I get the feeling you're not going to listen to this little pep talk even one little bit?"

"Because you already know me better than most people." The truth falls from my lips and we both sit with it for a second. Then Roman leans across the seat, pressing his mouth to mine in a kiss so tender, so sweet, I almost melt away.

"Don't do anything stupid," he whispers against my lips. "And stay with me the whole time."

I nod, adrenaline pumping through me. "Got it, boss. Can we go now?"

"Go." He shoos me out of the truck and I race immediately to the smoldering remains of the trailer, black smoke still lingering in the air, yellow caution tape taut across the metal door.

"You can't go in there." A male voice sails through the air, domineering and authoritative.

Rome trots up, flashing his ID badge. "Checking out the scene."

The detective eyes us suspiciously. "You're on holiday break, Montgomery."

"The mayor needs a report on this. Wants to know if the explosion was a one-off thing or something his office should be concerned about."

"You can tell the mayor Detective Truett said we're all good here. No concerns. Doesn't appear to be foul play involved. Left a cigarette burning and the gas was on. Kaboom!" The detective flares his hands out and I flash back to Jagger doing the exact same thing a few days ago.

"Really? You have evidence suggesting that?" My tone drips with sharp disbelief, but at the moment I don't give a shit.

"Not exactly." Detective Truett shuffles his feet in the grass, averting his eyes.

"The mayor's expecting a little more than that, I'm betting." I spit out the words, hot anger bubbling inside me. The "incident" is going to be swept under the rug because it happened in the outskirts. Or worse—the Capellis paid someone to cover this up.

"We're conducting a full investigation. Happy to send a copy over to the mayor myself once we're done."

"He'd appreciate that, Detective. Thank you." Rome squeezes the inside of my arm and I begrudgingly take the hint. "Have a good day."

Roman waves at him, acting all friendly, but I don't have it in me to fake that level of nice. Detective Truett saunters away, leaving us standing right outside the door.

"So much for letting the police handle it." Rome rolls his eyes, keeping a firm grip on my arm.

I crane my neck to peer inside the trailer, but there's nothing left, only charred outlines of the furniture. The couch is blown to pieces, scraps of the frame scattered around what used to be the living room. Every window's blown out, glass littering the ground. The metal stove stands, along with the fridge, but the TV is gone.

"There's nothing left, Rome." My voice wobbles, eyes welling with tears. Which is stupid because it's not like I lived here with my dad or anything. I have no attachment to this space, except for the fact that my dad used to live here.

"I know. I didn't think there would be." He drops his lips close to my ear, his breath warm on my skin. "I'm glad your dad wasn't here. Can I please take you home now? Get you out of here?"

I nod, ignoring the pain in my chest at the mention of my dad.

Even though he's been a shitty excuse for a father, I still didn't want this for him.

He truly has nothing left now.

33

—————

ROMAN

"I have no food at home. So we're either going to starve or we need to stop and pick something up. I vote for the latter."

I glance over at Skye, her face pale as she rubs at her ring. The surface must be glass-smooth by now, as much as she rubs that piece of silver.

I'm sure she doesn't feel like eating right now, but I can't let her waste away to nothing.

"I'm making the executive decision to stop. You want tacos? Pizza? Sandwiches from the deli?"

She shrugs, staring out the window as we move further away from the outskirts. Trailers turn into houses with driveways and mailboxes, then we're back in town.

"How about sandwiches? That will be the fastest." I pull into the lot of the best sandwich place in town, creatively named The Deli.

"Come on, food always helps." I come around the truck, taking her by the hand and helping her out of the cab. Gone is the fiery Skye from the courthouse. This version of Skye is withdrawn, lost.

Wrapping an arm around her narrow waist, I bring her in close to me. "It'll be okay, baby. We'll nail Jagger, don't worry."

She tips her head up at me. "How? He's managed to evade everyone—the police, all of you. That asshole never gets caught."

"He'll slip up, he's not that smart. Let's not waste any more energy on that weasel today, okay? I want tonight to be about me and you." I squeeze her hip and the corners of her mouth turn up. It's a tiny smile, but it's something.

"There you go. We'll pick up food, watch a movie back at the house. Forget all about everything for a little while. Deal?"

"Deal."

We head into the deli and Skye spends a few minutes studying the menu. "What's good here?"

"Everything."

She chuckles. "Helpful, Rome."

"My favorite's the pastrami on rye, but honestly, you can't go wrong with anything here."

Wrinkling her nose, she squints at the choices, finally deciding on turkey and Swiss on wheat. We place our order, grabbing chips and drinks while we wait.

"You okay if I hit the restroom?" I survey the empty deli, gauging the risk to be low.

Skye nods. "Yes. I'm fine, go." She waves me off and I hurry to the back, ducking into the closet of a restroom.

I'm gone less than five minutes, but walking out, my blood runs cold. Jagger's holding Skye by the arm, Cash and Damon circling around the two of them like sharks sniffing blood in the water.

"You've gotta be kidding me..." I mutter, hustling over.

"Well, well, well. I didn't know you brought your little attack dog, Romeo, with you. Y'all on a date? How cozy." Jagger gives me a once-over and blood roars in my ears.

"Fuck off, Jagger. And take your hands off her. She has a restraining order against all three of you, so you need to bounce." I squeeze his wrist until he winces, dropping Skye's arm.

"Really, Skye? You went to the police? After all we've been through together? I'm hurt." Jagger blinks, trying to cull up tears but failing.

"And Romeo, that's not a very nice way to speak to me. Especially when you're running around town with our ex-lawyer. Who still owes me a whole lotta cash, by the way. Skye, when you paying up?" He stands taller, pressing closer to us, and I tuck Skye behind me.

She doesn't stay tucked away, though. Folding her arms over her chest, she glares at Jagger.

"I'm pretty sure we're square. You blew up my dad's trailer. We're even."

"How dare you accuse *me* of such a heinous crime." Jagger splays a palm on his pumped-up chest, feigning indignance. "I'd never do such a thing."

He drops his voice lower. "And there's no evidence, right?"

Then that little fucker purses his lips and winks at Skye and she loses it, storming straight at him, punching at his chest. He laughs as her fists pound on him, again and again, bouncing off with little effect. The dude has to be on 'roids.

After a few seconds of her boxing efforts, he seizes her forearms and she winces. "Guess I need a restraining order now. Romeo, get your bitch off me, will ya?"

Cash and Damon laugh like hyenas as Skye kicks at Jagger's ankles. I step in, grasping Skye's waist and pulling her away from him. She's breathing hard from her efforts, her face flushed.

"Hope that was as good for you as it was for me." Jagger leers at Skye and she scowls in his direction.

"Fuck you, Jagger." She emphasizes each syllable and he clutches at his heart.

"Ouch. Such nasty words, Skye. And after I gave you extra time to pay off Daddy's debt too. Really though— how are you going to repay me?" He runs his finger down her arm and she shudders beneath his touch.

That's the last fucking straw. Black spots dance in my peripheral vision and my heart pounds as I smack his hand away from Skye.

"Don't you fucking touch her, Jagger. You got me?" I block his view of Skye, keeping her behind me as I square up with him. He's considerably shorter than me, and I stare down at his close-cropped hair that could almost be classified as a buzz cut.

"Pretty sure you don't own her, Romeo. I can touch her, lick her, kiss her. I bet I could even fuck her if I wanted to." He licks his thin lips, peering around me at Skye's breasts, and I snap.

Lunging at him, I seize his throat and throw him against the wall. Squeezing his neck hard, his heartbeat speeding beneath the pads of my fingers, his face grows redder by the second. His lips move like a guppy dying on the land, and I'd love nothing more than to keep pressing, crushing the fucker's windpipe and ridding the earth of this miserable human being.

"Don't do it, Rome. He's not worth it." Skye's voice permeates my consciousness and I loosen my grip, allowing Jagger to sip at the air. He inhales sharply, but I keep him pressed against the wall.

Bending in close enough to count the stray whiskers dotting his face, I deliver my message.

"If you so much as touch a strand of hair on her head, I will end you. Are we clear?"

Jagger stares at me, his beady eyes cold. He doesn't respond, and I step even closer to him, kicking at his feet.

"Now's your chance to save your own miserable life. Don't try me, Jagger. I've killed much greater men than you for a whole lot less, I promise you that."

A bead of sweat trickles from his brow, falling onto my knuckle. I give him another little squeeze and he tips his head up, then down, nodding.

I let go and his body slumps for a second before he rebounds, rolling his shoulders and shaking his arms and legs.

"You're a fucking animal, Montgomery. Can't believe they let beasts like you walk around with the civilized members of society. C'mon, boys. Let's leave these two lovers alone. Good luck with that one, Skye. He's a loose cannon."

Jagger motions to his brothers and they all slink out the door, the roar of Jagger's cherry-red truck shaking the building as he guns it out of the parking lot.

"What an asshole," Skye says, sinking into a metal chair. She's shaking slightly, a light sheen of sweat on her chest.

"He won't bother you again." I flex my fingers, cracking my knuckles before taking the seat nearest to her.

"Thanks for the protection, Rome. But are you going to guard me twenty-four-seven? What happens when you have to go back to work?"

"If I weren't here, you'd call the police. He's not supposed to be within fifty yards of you."

Skye sighs, dropping her head in her hands.

"Order up for Roman." The deli worker comes out from the kitchen holding a paper bag with our sandwiches, unaware of the showdown that happened here a few moments ago.

We stand and Skye plucks her satchel from the table, a scrap of paper fluttering to the floor. She bends down to pick it up and her mouth forms a pink 'O,' her face flushing. Her hand's shaking, the paper vibrating in the air.

"What's that?"

Wordlessly, she hands me the paper. A photo of a young Skye—she's probably eight or nine—blowing bubbles, a man in the background wearing a white T-shirt, a wide grin on his face, a beer in his hand.

Skye's dad. A long time ago, but they look happy, if even for this one moment.

A tear trickles down Skye's cheek and pure hatred wells up inside me, rolling around my gut.

Jagger dropped this photo purposefully. The only place that picture could have come from is Larry's trailer. But he's right. There's no way we can prove when he was there or that he had anything to do with the explosion.

Fucker.

"We'll get him, Skye." I wrap my arms around her,

pulling her tight against my body. "One way or the other, we'll get him."

34

ROMAN

I DRIVE STRAIGHT HOME, SPEEDING THROUGH YELLOW lights and passing anyone going under the speed limit.

I want—need—to get Skye back to my place, where she'll be safe.

Hitting the garage door, I slide the truck into the parking spot and quickly close the door behind us. Skye visibly relaxes as soon as the door thuds down against the concrete.

"We're all good now." I lead her into the house, guiding her straight to the bathroom. "Why don't you take a quick shower? I'll get the food ready."

"Okay." She spins around, locking her caramel gaze on mine. "Thanks, Rome. For protecting me from Jagger. And for going with me to the outskirts. I'm sure you have more important things to be doing right now."

With one hand on her waist, I press a finger to her lips. "Sshh. I don't. You're more important than all of it."

Her eyes glisten with tears as I run my finger across her lips, dipping down to claim her mouth. I kiss her, soft and slow, trying to tell her how much she means to me, how I feel about her. She opens to me, winding her arms around my neck and pulling me in close. Our tongues slide together, every beat of my heart belonging to this woman.

After a long minute, I break away. "Take your time. I'll fix the plates."

Leaving Skye in the bathroom, I make my way out to the kitchen. I turn on some music, keeping the volume low enough I can still hear outside noises. Then I pour us two fresh glasses of iced tea and plate the sandwiches.

Ten minutes later, Skye emerges from the shower, her hair damp and cheeks flushed pink from the heat. She seems way more relaxed in a tight little T-shirt accentuating her curves and a tiny pair of cotton shorts.

"Feel better?" I carry the plates over to the coffee table and she sinks down onto the couch, tucking one of her long legs under her.

"Much. Thanks."

I join her on the couch and we eat in companionable silence for a few minutes, the low thrum of country music the only sound in the room. Despite everything that went down today, I'm surprisingly hungry and devour the sandwich in record time. Skye's still only halfway through, taking tiny bites and chewing oh-so-thoroughly as I wipe my hands and set the plate down.

"Wow. Guess you were hungry." She smiles at me and my chest opens, lightening up for the first time today.

"Guess I was. I also don't take bird bites." I nudge her bare foot with my thigh, teasing.

"What? I don't take bird bites." She scrunches her nose up and she's so damn adorable I can hardly handle it.

"You do."

"You've been studying me." She narrows her eyes, her mouth twisting to the side, and my cheeks heat.

Busted.

"I'm a keen observer. All part of running special ops, babe."

"Oh." She nods, sets her sandwich down. "I get it. It's strictly a job requirement, that's all."

"Now I didn't say that." I lock eyes with her, my body tensing as her tongue darts out, licking her bottom lip.

Skye puts her plate on the coffee table, reaching her hand out for mine. "Dance with me."

I stare at her outstretched palm. "I don't really dance."

"C'mon, I love this song." She drags me off the couch, Chris Stapleton crooning about Tennessee whiskey and strawberry wine.

We're in the center of the living room and I encircle her waist, bringing her body in close to mine. She wraps her arms around my neck, the light scent of vanilla drifting off her skin still warm from the shower. We sway to the slow beat of the music and she rests her head on my chest, a golden glow on her face from the kitchen light. My heart's hammering away and I'm sure she can feel the vibrations thumping against her cheek.

I haven't been this happy in a long, long time.

Maybe ever.

My hand drops from her waist down to her ass, palm splaying across the perfect peach of her cheek. She fits just right in my arms. In my life.

The song ends and I lean down, kissing her soft and slow. Urging her mouth open with my tongue, she lets me in.

I want her. All of her. Right now.

I pick her up, carrying her back to the couch and laying her down on the leather cushions.

Wordlessly, I slide her tiny shorts down her legs, peeling them all the way off. Then I drop my head down between her thighs, sucking her clit through the thin satin of her panties.

She twines her fingers in my hair, lightly scratching my scalp and a low moan falls from her lips. I ease her panties off, kissing the inside of her thighs until I come to the apex. Flattening my tongue, I lick through her wetness, swirling her clit, tasting her sweet juices.

"Rome—" She shivers with pleasure and I continue, plunging my tongue inside her as her hips buck up into the air.

With one hand, I hold her down on the couch, making her lie still beneath me until her entire body vibrates. I dip beneath her shirt, tickling the smooth skin of her belly, and she shudders at the touch. I keep moving upwards, cupping her bare breast, rolling her nipple until it peaks in my fingers.

I pull away from her then, tearing off my shirt, my jeans, my briefs. She sits up and takes off her shirt and now we're both naked.

"I want you. Now." She gazes up at me through dark lashes and I've never wanted a woman so badly in my entire life.

"I'll grab a condom." I start to walk away, but Skye grabs my hand, stopping me.

"No. I want to feel you inside me." She licks her lips and my balls tingle, tightening. "All of you."

Although my cock's protesting, I raise a brow at her. "You sure? I mean, that would be okay?"

She nods. "Yes. We're covered on that front."

Lacing my fingers with hers, I pull her up from the couch, then scoop her into my arms and carry her back to the bedroom. She squirms in my arms, giggling as my fingers tickle her bare skin. Her chest, neck, and cheeks flush the prettiest shade of pink and she's so damn beautiful my heart aches at the sight of her.

"I want you so fucking much it hurts, baby." I toss her gently onto the bed, her dark hair spilling over the comforter. She's a sight, all soft curves to my hard edges.

"I want you too, Rome. Please." She bites down on her lip, staring up at me with those wide brown sugar eyes, and my cock dances between my legs.

I fist myself, running up and down the shaft as she watches, her chest rising and falling with shallow breaths.

"How bad do you want it, baby girl?" I tease, pumping.

"Very badly. I've been thinking about you all day."

"Spread your legs and show me. Show me how wet you are for me."

She does as I say, opening her thighs and exposing her pink, glistening pussy to me.

"So nice, such a good girl." I keep stroking myself, inching closer to her. "Will you touch yourself, let me see your arousal?"

Gnawing at her lip, she reaches down, running a finger through her slick folds then holding it up in the air for me to see.

"Perfect, so wet for me."

I move closer to her still, until I'm standing between her open legs. Leaning forward, I suck her finger into my mouth, tasting her.

"So sweet, baby." I wink at her, licking my lips, and she

blushes. Her nipples harden and I palm both of her breasts, cupping her curves. She has amazing tits, full and round, and I massage the delicate flesh until tiny chill bumps rise on her skin.

"I love your tits."

Her head lolls back, her eyes glazing with lust as I fondle her. She wraps her legs around my knees, applying light pressure until I fold down on top of her, catching myself on my elbows. I cage her in between my arms, our faces inches away from each other, our breath syncing as we stare into each other's eyes.

"Fuck me, Roman."

Crushing my lips to hers, I claim her mouth. I want every inch of her body, every part of her she's willing to give me. My cock twitches on her stomach, hard as steel and ready to go. Hot desire hums through me as I push into her wet heat.

"Fuck, baby. You feel so good, so tight around my cock." I ease into her, inch by inch, stretching her. She lets out a whimper as I drive into her, slowly at first, then a little faster. Picking up the pace, our bodies find a rhythm, and she matches me thrust for thrust. Her skin pinkens and she's panting, her face flushing with pleasure. My balls tighten, a hot tingle starting at the base and I know I'm close as they slap against her ass.

I tweak her nipple and she arches up against me. I pinch harder and she lets out a startled cry, shivering with pleasure as I release the sharp point, the blood rushing back into her skin.

"You're such a good girl, fucking me so hard like this," I murmur against the delicate skin of her neck, licking and sucking. She's writhing beneath me and I know she's close to the edge. "That's it, baby. Take it all like a good girl."

I push her over the edge and she cries out, her pussy pulsing around my cock. That's all it takes to send me crashing right behind her. I explode, spilling hot cum into her. Thrusting several more times, she bucks beneath me, taking everything I have to give.

"You're so damn beautiful, Skye." I stroke her as she quivers, her entire body quaking with her orgasm.

She opens her eyes, brings a hand to my face. Cupping my cheek, she runs her thumb back and forth over the scruff.

"I love you." Her voice is a soft whisper floating through the air, her gaze locked on mine. My heart pounds —from the sex, from the rush of release.

From the words that tumbled from her swollen, kissable lips.

"I love you too, baby."

I claim her mouth with mine, sliding down beside her and pulling her onto my chest.

Wrapping her in my arms, I breathe Skye in. Deepdown, I know she's the one for me. Her fiery spirit, the quick wit, even the broken pieces, the bits no one else sees. The jagged edges that hurt.

I want all of her, always.

We drift off to sleep in each other's arms, both of us sated and content in this perfect moment.

35

SKYE

*I'm in a rowboat in the middle of the ocean and it's
night. The waves are big and choppy, tossing me all around, water
slopping over the sides. I drop one of the paddles into the water and
it's sucked down, sinking quickly into the dark blue depths. The boat's
small and tight, and I'm surrounded by stacks of cash. I'm paddling
and paddling, frantically trying to get somewhere, but I'm not sure
where or how to get there. All I can see for miles and miles is water.*

*I scream and cry, shouting for help, but I'm all alone. Lost at
sea with one paddle and a boatload of cash.*

*Then Jagger's behind me in the boat, pulling me by the pony-
tail, yanking my face back to stare up at his ugly sneer. He's laughing, his dark stare cold.*

*"You brought me the money. But that's not all I want from
you." His meaty fingers stroke my neck, curling around my throat,
squeezing until I can't breathe.*

*Hot panic claws at me, my eyes tearing up. He squeezes and
squeezes.*

Suddenly, Roman's in the boat and it's storming, sheets of cold rain pouring down over us. Roman grabs Jagger's arms, picking him up and tossing him overboard. Lightning flashes in the sky as Jagger's body bounces across the water like a skipping rock.

A huge wave rises beneath us, and we're high up in the air. The moon's within arm's reach and huge claps of thunder boom, shaking the boat.

"Roman! What are we going to do?" I scream over the loud rumble, but Roman disappears and I'm alone again. The wave breaks and I crash down, down, down to the water, sinking all the way to the bottom of the ocean floor.

My mom's there, her lifeless body lying on the sand. My dad too. But he's still alive, his face twisted in a silent scream. Jagger's sitting on top of him, choking him and laughing as phosphorescent fish swim by, oblivious.

I scoop piles of money into my arms, but I'm stuck in the boat, my feet shackled to the seat. Water's filling my lungs and I can't breathe.

Roman swims up, ripping me from the boat, stacks of bills falling from my arms. I'm trying to gather as much as I can and swim back to my dad to save him, but Roman's gripping me by the waist and pulling me up to the surface.

I'm torn, wanting to go with Roman, but also needing to save my dad.

"I can't leave him, Rome." I'm crying and trying to swim down, down to the deep. I can barely see my dad and Jagger now, the glow of the fish fading as we get closer to the surface.

"You have to leave him. Make a choice, Skye."

"I can't." I'm pummeling his hard chest with my fist and I still can't get enough air. I'm drowning as I try to swim against the current.

"You can. Be with me. I need you. I'll save you."

"I can't, I can't." I keep crying and shaking my head, my arms flailing as I try to swim away.

The moon fades and we're back on land, standing on bright green grass. The sun's shining and a bird chirps in the distance.

My arms feel heavy and I gaze down, expecting to see money.

Instead, I stare into the cobalt blue eyes of my baby.

I wake up in a cold sweat, my heart racing, Roman's heavy arm slung over me. His fingers graze the bare skin on my arm and I try to catch my breath.

It was only a dream, Skye.

The pit in my stomach's real, though. The loss, the fear. So real I taste it, bitterness coating my tongue.

Am I making the right choice? Can I abandon my dad, leave him stuck in rural Georgia forever, along with what little past I have left?

Am I making Roman's life harder, more complicated with my family drama? Adding more fuel to the fire between the Capellis and the Montgomerys?

I love Roman, but is that enough?

"Babe, you okay?" His voice is deep, husky with sleep. His hand moves from my arm to my waist, pulling me in closer to him, his breath warm on my cheek.

"Yeah, I just had a bad dream."

"You're safe here with me. Go back to sleep." His fingers splay across my belly protectively and I snuggle into him, breathing him in. The crisp, masculine scent so familiar to me now I'd recognize it floating on the wind. Like standing in the middle of the forest after a light rain. I time my inhale to his, match the exhale until we're breathing as one.

Sharing the same air, the same space, I nestle into his arms and drift back to sleep.

THE NEXT TIME I WAKE UP, GOLDEN SUNLIGHT'S streaming into the bedroom. Despite everything that went down yesterday, I feel lighter than I have in months. I roll over, fully expecting Roman's handsome face, but I'm alone, his side of the bed cold.

What time is it?

I check my cell. Damn, it's already ten a.m. I haven't slept this late in ages. I stretch, my body deliciously sore, then throw on my T-shirt and pad out to the kitchen in search of Rome.

"Hey." My voice echoes through the space, breaking the silence.

Rome's sitting at the table with a laptop, his back to me. He doesn't turn around, just sits and stares at the screen, his shoulders slumped forward.

Not good.

I tiptoe up behind him, unsure if he wants to be disturbed. He's staring at the computer, the white glow of the screen highlighting his high cheekbones, his square jaw. He sits perfectly still as a clock ticks in the corner, *tick, tick, tick.*

"Rome? You okay?"

My voice seems to register this time. He swivels around slowly, glancing up at me, his deep blue eyes dazed.

"It's true." His voice is hollow, his face slack.

I squint at him, trying to figure out what he's talking about. "What's true?"

"I have a half-sister."

36

———

ROMAN

Our mother had—has—another child.

I have another sister out there.

I stare at Skye's light blue T-shirt as the bottom drops out of my world and I free-fall through space. Everything's cold—my arms, my hands, all the way down to the tips of my fingers. I'm frozen, I can barely blink. My heart thuds hard in my chest as the clock bangs in the distance.

tick. Tick. TICK.

Each second louder than the last.

A scream builds deep inside me, but it's stuck, tangled in my throat.

Skye reaches out and touches me, her hand resting on my shoulder, but I feel nothing.

I'm totally numb.

I never expected it to be true.

It's true.

I thought for sure that letter was a hoax, a prank, a trick.

It's true.

The baby was born here in Seaglass Beach, five years before my mom had King.

It's true.

No father is listed on the birth certificate I tracked down. Only my mother's name.

It's true.

The baby's sex was recorded as female. Born in March, weighing six pounds, five ounces.

It's true.

But I'll never know the real truth.

Who was the father? Did my father know? What happened? Why did our mom give up her firstborn baby?

She's gone and there's no way to find the answers to these questions. I'll never know how she felt, the motivations behind her actions.

Another family secret.

One my mother kept buried her entire life.

Until now.

"Rome?" Skye's voice cuts through my thoughts and I gaze up at her. Everything's moving so slowly, like I'm suspended in slow-motion. My mouth's dry as cotton, and I swallow hard over the lump in my throat.

"I can't believe this."

With shaking hands, I pass the thin aqua paper to Skye and she scans the words.

"Wow, okay—" She scrunches her lips together, re-reads the letter.

"I thought it might be bullshit. My family's an easy target, what with the inn and all."

Skye nods, her dark hair rustling over her shoulders.

"But it's true. My mother had another kid. Before King was born, before she married my dad." I push down the sour taste of grief, but it bubbles around my gut. A sharp pang of disappointment stabs me in the chest and I try to ignore it.

Keep pretending my mother was perfect.

I thought I knew her. She was wonderful, sweet and kind and loving.

Not someone who would give away her baby.

Skye rubs my shoulder, massaging my tense muscles. I shake my head side to side, cold shock still gripping me.

How?

Placing one finger under my chin, she tips my face up and stares at me, straight into my soul.

"It's going to be okay, Roman. Whatever you and your family decide to do with this information, it's going to be okay. Your mom is still everything you always knew her to be."

Her words buoy me, bringing me back to the surface. I inhale, the tightness in my chest easing just enough to allow me to breathe again.

She slides into my lap, wriggling in between my thighs, her face close to mine. Pressing her lips to mine, she kisses me, her mouth warm. Thawing me from the inside out, Skye brings me back to life.

I allow myself to melt into her until I'm not sure where she ends and I begin, my arms wrapping around her body. I hold her tight, and she anchors me, rooting me to the ground.

I've never needed anyone as much as I need Skye right now.

I deepen the kiss, our connection, slipping my tongue into her mouth. We tangle together, tasting and teasing, our bodies tensing. My dick swells, hardening in my shorts and I press against her. Letting her know how I feel.

She reaches down, stroking me through the mesh fabric. I pulse beneath her touch, ready. Wanting and willing.

Skye pulls back, lifting her shirt over her head and dropping it to the ground. Taking my hand in hers, she guides me to her breasts, urging me on.

I need no encouragement, squeezing and fondling her luscious tits. Rolling her pink nipples into diamond-sharp points until she squirms in my lap. Sucking first one, then the other into my mouth, alternating between the two until chill bumps rise on her skin. Peppering her chest with kisses, nipping at the long column of her neck.

"Straddle me, baby." I cup her ass, and she stands up, peeling her panties off. Then she positions herself, wrapping her legs around me until we're face to face. Her skin's soft and warm against my bare chest, grounding me in this moment.

I dip a finger in between her legs, trailing through her wetness before slipping into her. She tightens around me, hips rocking, and I work another finger, then another into her until she moans into my neck. Her breath skates over my skin as she grinds on my hand, her arousal slippery on my fingers.

"Always so wet and ready," I murmur, kissing the nape of her neck, her hair tickling my cheek.

"I want you, Rome." Her voice is high and reedy with need, my cock standing at attention.

"I want you too, baby."

Skye reaches down, freeing my cock from the shorts, circling the crown with her thumb. Rubbing the drops of pre-cum into the hot flesh, she glides her hand up and down the steel shaft. Fiery desire coils tight within me, my balls tightening.

"Fuck, baby, that feels so good." I practically grunt the words, trying not to piston into her hand. Holding on to my release until I can feel her tight pussy around my cock.

"Come inside me, Rome."

She doesn't need to ask me twice. I slide my hand away and she lifts up slightly, positioning her hips at a good angle. Then I sink into her, driving into her wetness. Her muscles stretch to accommodate me, then contract around my dick.

"Skye—" I hiss as she rides me, her tits bouncing against my pecs. Her chest flushes pink, her breathing shallow, eyes squeezed shut. Tiny lines of concentration furrow her brow and I thrust harder, staring as she bobs up and down on my lap. I smack lightly at her ass and her eyes fly open, then she smiles at me. I swat the other side and her pussy quivers around me.

I'm close, the base of my spine tingling as pressure builds.

"Come for me, baby. Let go." I squeeze her ass, pushing my cock even deeper inside, swiveling my hips to hit her most sensitive spots. She tremors, then explodes, crashing over the edge. I keep fucking her, watching as her body convulses with pleasure.

Finally, I erupt. Spilling my hot cum deep inside her pussy, over and over again, until there's nothing left. She collapses against my chest, wrapping her arms around me. I kiss her forehead, breathing her in.

We sit still together for a long time, her heartbeat

thudding against me at first, then slowing back to a normal rate.

"Thank you." I smooth dark waves over her shoulder, running my palm over the silky strands.

Lifting her face, she gazes up at me through dark lashes, pupils still wide. "For what?"

I respond by crashing my lips to hers. Such full, perfect lips—I never want to stop kissing this woman.

"For saving me," I murmur into her mouth, trailing my finger over her cheek, my heart full.

She presses her hand to my chest, resting her palm over my heart. "You saved me, Rome. More than once. I didn't do anything special."

Lacing my fingers with hers, I raise her knuckles to my face, graze them with my lips.

"You did, baby. You gave me hope. I haven't felt that since before I left home and joined the Marines. After everything that's happened—" My voice wavers and I take a deep, shuddery breath, centering myself before I continue.

"I didn't know it, but I was dead inside. Numb. But with you here—" I squeeze her perfect peach of an ass. "I'm alive again. Even when things are confusing, you center me. Ground me, bring me back to life. I love you."

She cups my face, kissing me gently, an unspoken understanding passing between us.

This is forever, and we both know it.

"I love you, too, Rome."

My cell chirps on the table, vibrating against the wood. I ignore it, but it chirps again.

"You should get that." Skye eases off my lap, standing. "I'm going to shower."

I grab at my phone, tapping the screen. "I'll join you in a second."

King: Juliet wants to meet tonight at the lake. 9 p.m.

Huffing out a breath, I type back:

Roman: I'll meet you there

King: Find anything out about the letter?

Feels like maybe this should be a phone call and not a text. I hit the call button and King picks up on the first ring.

"You alone?"

"Yeah. Just me and the horses."

"I'd sit down on a bale of hay if I were you—"

"Shit. So it's true?"

I scrub a hand over the back of my neck. "Yes. I found the birth record. No mention of the dad. The baby was born five years before you."

King's silent for a long time, the horses neighing in the background. "Thanks for looking into that."

He doesn't say anything else, doesn't ask any questions. Typical King behavior.

"See you tonight." He disconnects, leaving me with silence.

37

ROMAN

After much debate—mostly on her end—Skye ends up coming with me to the lake. Truth be told, I didn't feel great leaving her home alone and she wanted to come. King's just going to have to deal with it. Besides, she's in the mix already and knows more than most about the situation.

More than Poppy, and I hope that doesn't end up being a problem. I figure as long as I can deliver good news, she'll get over it. The last thing I'm gonna do right now is bring Poppy out here and scare Juliet off. We need information and I'm banking on Juliet delivering tonight.

It's the only plan I've got.

We ditch the truck and hike the half-mile out to the lake, the full moon lighting our path. An owl hoots off in the distance and a light wind rustles the leaves that rebelled, still clinging stubbornly to their branches. Neither of us speak, fully focused on the mission. Skye's jumpy, her head swiveling at every snap of a twig. I press my hand to her lower back, reassuring her and letting her know I'm right here behind her.

Finally, the trees open up and we're in a clearing, the lake in sight. The moon's bright in the inky sky, a white glow shimmering over the glassy surface. King's standing near the edge of the water, hands shoved in the pockets of his jeans. I shoot him a text.

> Roman: Here

He reads the text, his cowboy hat jerking up. Glancing around, he searches for me in the dark.

> King: I don't see you

> Roman: That's kind of the point

King shakes his head, his teeth gleaming white in the dark. We're about fifty yards away and I hope we'll be able to hear their conversation. I don't dare risk getting closer, though, because there's nowhere to hide. Here we're at least covered by the trees.

Two bright beams of light cut through the darkness.

Headlights.

It's go time.

The lights disappear, and Juliet steps out of the car. She's alone. Even from this distance, I can sense King's apprehension. His shoulders square, posture ramrod straight.

Juliet moves quickly toward him, clutching something in her hand, a folder or papers or something. It's tough to tell from this distance. She's nervous, glancing over her shoulder every few seconds.

"Thanks for meeting me." Juliet's voice drifts over the clearing, carrying on the wind.

"Sure." King's gruff voice is easier to hear, his words clipped and tight.

"King—" Juliet reaches out, touching his arm. King stiffens, stands stock still.

Undeterred, she steps closer to him and he doesn't recoil, allowing her to move into his space.

A long moment passes, the two of them staring at each other. Skye cuts her eyes at me, brows raised, but I stay quiet. Now's not the time to delve into my brother's past. Besides, it's not my story to tell.

Finally, King breaks the silence. "We need to make this quick. You shouldn't be here with me."

Juliet lifts her hand to King's chest and Skye gasps beside me, her hand flying up to her mouth to muffle the sound. I elbow her, remind her to be quiet. We can't scare Juliet off now.

Juliet rests her hand on my brother's chest for a minute, and surprisingly, King allows the contact. The two of them lock eyes and I'm as shocked as Skye.

No one touches King like that. Dude's never even had a real girlfriend.

King clutches her hand on his chest, moving closer to her still, their bodies almost touching. Then he lowers her arm down, placing it back by her side before easing the folder away from her.

"Thank you." King's deep voice breaks the silence and Juliet's head bobs.

"You're welcome. That should be enough to kill the lawsuit."

"I'll leave your name out of it. And if Jagger or your other idiot brothers so much as lay a finger on you—" King trails off, his empty fist clenched.

"They won't. They're jerks, but they're still my brothers. Besides, you could have gotten that information anywhere. They'll never know it was me."

King reaches out, tucks a stray lock of Juliet's hair behind her ear, his hand lingering on her skin. Juliet wraps her fingers around his wrist, holding his arm to her body, leaning into his touch.

Well, I'll be doggone.

I did not expect this moment of tenderness between my brother and Juliet. King avoids running into her at all costs, like she has the plague or something. When he does bump into her around town, he seems angry.

Besides, at the end of the day, she's a Capelli and he's a Montgomery. We don't get along and haven't for many generations.

And we sure as hell can't be together.

Skye's brows scrunch in confusion and I shrug, watching as the two of them gaze at each other in the moonlight.

After another long moment, King lowers his hand and steps back.

"Go. I'll follow behind in a few minutes, give you a head start."

She says something, but her voice is such a low whisper I can't make out the words. Then she spins around and jogs back to her car. She reverses and drives away, leaving King standing alone next to the lake.

Once she's gone, he stares out over the lake for another long minute before walking back to his truck, turning the engine over. He speeds away, leaving me and Skye to hike back on our own.

"Did you know, Rome?" Skye breaks the silence.

I kick around what to say here, not sure how much of my brother's story I can share without betraying his confidence.

"Know what?" Averting my gaze, I play dumb and begin the hike back, dead leaves crunching beneath my feet.

"Know they have a thing." Skye catches up, trotting next to me for a second. The trail narrows and I press the small of her back, pushing her ahead.

"They don't have a thing."

"Come on. Of course they do. I could see it all the way from the woods, in the dark. Something's going on between them."

I grip Skye's hand as she climbs over a fallen log, her fingers chilly from being out in the cold so long.

"Let's pick up the pace. You're freezing."

"Nice tactic, changing the subject." She raises a brow at me and my gut churns. I don't want to lie to her, but I'm not sure how much I should say.

"Anything that happened between them is in the past. That's all I can tell you."

"You'd make a good lawyer, Montgomery. That's just enough info to piss me off and answer none of my questions."

I shrug. "Sorry. My reputation as the vault's on the line."

"Judging from that exchange, I'd say your brother and Juliet definitely still have something between them."

Smashing my lips together, I swallow hard before answering. "I can neither confirm nor deny. I don't really know."

"Vagueville."

"Best I can do, babe. Sorry."

We're back at the truck and I unlock the door, helping her into the cab.

"You're a good brother, Rome." She leans in, brushing her lips lightly against mine. "And at least I know you can keep a secret."

"It's my best thing." I kiss her again, winking, before slamming her door shut and heading back to town.

38

ROMAN

THE NEXT MORNING WE HEAD OUT TO THE RANCH. THE trial's set to start in a few days, as soon as the holiday break's over.

"Did King text you anything last night?" Skye glances over at me as we bump down the gravel driveway of the ranch.

"Only that he got home okay and Juliet did everything she said she'd do."

"That sounds promising."

I nod, throwing the truck in park behind my sister's old blue Bronco. "It does. How'd Poppy beat me here? I wanted to get the download first."

Hot aggravation churns in my gut as I scowl at Smurfy, my sister's vehicle.

"I'm sure it's fine, Rome. Worst case, I'll distract her and you can talk to King in private." Skye strokes my arm, calming me down.

I shoot her a grateful look. "Thanks."

We head inside, Poppy's loud voice echoing all the way down the hall.

"You met Juliet without me?" She's pacing in front of the stacked stone fireplace when we walk into the kitchen.

As soon as she spots me, she glares. "Did you know about this, Rome? Because we had a deal." Crossing her arms over her chest, she taps her foot hard on the wood plank floor.

"I did, and I'm real sorry about not looping you in, Pops. But we couldn't risk Juliet getting spooked."

"You two are unbelievable!" Poppy throws her hands up in the air, screeching. "Always going behind my back, even though I'm the one with the most at stake." Her lower lip juts out in a pout and King shakes his head.

"You want to know what we found out or are you gonna rant all day?"

"Rude." But Poppy takes a seat at the long dining room table next to King. An olive green folder sits in front of him.

"I'll take a walk. I can't be privy to anything about the trial." Skye squeezes my hand, then starts walking out.

"Don't go too far." My heart pounds, my chest tight. Probably irrational anxiety, but I don't like the idea of Skye being out there alone.

But she's correct. We don't want there to be any hint of impropriety—we're already toeing the line.

"I won't. I'll be fine." She smiles at me, then heads outside.

King waits until the screen door slams shut before he opens the folder, pulls out the contents.

"Is that the land survey?" I squint down at the paper as he unfolds it on the table.

"One of them."

"Wait—what?" Poppy holds up her hand. "What do you mean, one of them? There should only be one land survey."

"Bingo." King's voice booms around the room and my pulse picks up speed. I flash back to the night I ran into Skye at the inn, standing on the eastern corner.

"Holy shit. She knew..." I mutter under my breath, grabbing at the folder. I unfold the second survey, honing in on the far-right corner and comparing.

"There." I point at the spot, lining the edges of the two surveys up together and holding them against the window. Sunlight streams through, the paper transparent on the glass. A distinct rectangle of disparity is plainly visible in the upper right corner.

"Those pieces of shit forged a fake land survey." King's voice is a low growl in my ear.

"Skye must have figured it out and that's when she dropped the case and got fired." I lower the papers to the table, face my siblings.

"She got fired?" Poppy tips her head, her honey hair falling over her shoulder.

"Yes. She went to the judge and got dismissed from the case, then told her boss and he fired her."

"Over our case?" Poppy bites at her lower lip.

"Yes, Poppy."

"She must really love you, Rome." My sister locks eyes with me, and my heart flip-flops in my chest.

I shrug. "More that she wanted to do the right thing."

"Maybe." Poppy twirls her hair between her fingers, considering. "I like her. You should marry her."

All the breath evaporates from my lungs. "What?"

"Yeah. She's great. Anyone that would quit their job to

help our family is a winner in my book. Don't let her get away, Rome."

"Thanks for the dating advice, Pops." I run a hand through my hair. Probably the only person worse than King to be doling out relationship advice is my kid sister.

King stands, pushing away from the table. "I'm gonna call Cleet and tell him what we found. See what he wants to do."

"Is this enough to get the case dismissed?" Poppy's voice tips up in a hopeful lilt.

King shrugs. "No idea, but I've gotta think so."

"I just want this all to be behind us." Poppy sighs, but she's more relaxed than I've seen her in months, ever since this whole mess started.

I rise, ready to find Skye, but Poppy grabs me by the arm. "Rome—"

"Yeah."

"Thanks for everything. You're the one who did all the legwork."

I shake my head. "King put in some effort, too. Don't discount that."

"Yeah, but you pushed him. There's no way he would have done all this without you standing behind him. So thank you."

"You're welcome, Pops. We good?" I raise a brow at her and she nods.

"Yeah, we're good." Then she throws her arms around my neck, squeezing me tight, and we share a rare moment of peace and quiet.

She finally drops her arms, and I pat her on the shoulder. "I'm gonna go find Skye."

Poppy grins, making kissy noises at me.

"You're so immature," I grumble at her, my cheeks burning.

"Go get 'em, tiger." She smacks me on the back and I roll my eyes, move down the hallway toward the front door.

"Shut up, Pops." I shake my head, but I've never felt lighter.

39

———

SKYE

That night, Roman takes me home and makes love to me.

It's not just sex or fucking, far from our first time together in the alley.

He peels back each layer of clothing, stripping me down until I'm naked before him. My skin warms beneath his heated gaze, flushing as he presses his mouth to the dip at the base of my neck, my pulse fluttering beneath his lips. He rains kisses up and down my body, every inch of my skin touched and worshiped. His breath skates over my sensitive skin, a shiver of pleasure rushing through me, straight to my core. My thighs clench, muscles coiling in anticipation.

I love this man.

Everything about him. His beautiful face, the raw strength running beneath his skin, his cobalt gaze as he drinks me in. Like I'm the first and last sip of water he'll ever take and he's going to savor every drop.

He strips out of his clothes unceremoniously before

laying me down on his cool sheets, arranging me on his pillows. Lowering himself down between my legs, he licks and sucks, lapping at my arousal like a sweet nectar. I run my hands up and down his muscular back, caressing the sinewy muscles outlined by the moonlight slanting through the blinds. Scratching my nails lightly across his back, every inch of him flexed and hard. He lavishes me with kisses, swirling his tongue on my most sensitive spot until I'm writhing beneath him, begging for more.

He dips into my wetness, and I arch up to meet him.

I want more.

I want all of him.

We lock eyes and I wrap my legs around his waist, pulling him in closer. Inhaling his heady masculine scent, tickling my nose as I breathe him in. Our chests rising and falling together.

I lean up and he crushes my lips in a searing kiss. Saying so much without ever speaking, our tongues sliding across and tangling together.

I love you.

Withdrawing his hand from me, he raises my arms above my head before tiptoeing down my body, brushing the pads of fingers against the puckered points of my nipples. Circling the sensitive flesh, he teases me with his thumb. One large hand splays across my belly, cupping my sex.

He eases into me, inch by inch, fusing my body with his. He's all the way inside me now, no space between us at all, and we are one.

Lacing his fingers with mine, he rocks in and out gently, driving me close to the edge. I'm so close, shimmery pleasure dancing at the corner of my eyes. My eyes lock on this gorgeous man hovering inches away from me. He thrusts in and out, our bodies slapping together as we climb up, up, up.

Roman never breaks his gaze, pupils dark as he watches me buck beneath him. Taking him in, accepting everything he has to give, everything he is.

I squeeze his hands, the peak close, so very close. He drives in harder, grinding into me, and I cry out, shattering around him. My body contracts and convulses, shuddering with pleasure. He follows right behind, filling me with his hot release, tensing and uncoiling inside me.

"I love you." The words slip from my lips so easily now, as natural as breathing.

"I love you too, baby." He kisses me, soft and slow, his tongue darting out as he takes his time. Enjoying the taste of me, the taste of us.

Sliding out, he rolls onto his back, pulling me onto his chest. His breath feathers my hair, my sensitive skin lighting up under the light strokes of his fingertips.

This thing between us—this man—the two of us together.

This is forever.

40

ROMAN

MY CELL RINGS AT NINE A.M. THE NEXT MORNING. I can't believe I'm still in bed, but I didn't want to disturb Skye, her sleeping body curled up tight against me.

"Hello?" I'm groggy, rubbing away sleep as my eyes focus on the stunning naked woman next to me.

"Rome? Hold on, I'm adding in Poppy, then Parker," King says.

I stroke the side of Skye's bare breast, her dusty pink nipple puckering under my touch as I wait. Her chest rising and falling in a slow rhythm, the corners of her full lips tipping up even as she sleeps.

"Hello?" Poppy's chipper voice rings down the line.

"One sec," King growls into the phone, placing Poppy and me on hold again.

My fingertips caress the long plane of Skye's torso, running over each individual rib before I drop down, splaying my palm over her flat belly. She nuzzles into my touch, moving her body up against mine, her hair tickling my shoulder.

"Hello?" Parker's on the line. The gang's all here.

"Hey. So I just got off the phone with Cleet." King forges ahead with no preamble and I hold my breath. "He already contacted the judge. It's done."

I exhale, long and loud, close my eyes as a cool rush of relief washes over me.

It's done.

The Capelli nightmare's over. A pressure lifts off my chest, a heaviness I'd learned to live with but certainly won't miss.

Jagger can go fuck himself.

"What did the judge say exactly? Is Jagger going to get into trouble?" Poppy chimes in, wanting all the details.

"Not sure how the court's going to handle that. All I know is we're good and can go back to business as usual."

"Awesome news, King," Parker's voice booms down the line. I can picture him pumping his fist in the air triumphantly. "Great work, guys. Appreciate the effort."

"I want Jagger to pay," Poppy says, her tone brusque, not her usual sunshine-and-rainbows lilt.

Skye shifts next to me, her brown sugar eyes fluttering open. She smiles up at me through dark lashes and I want to sink into her, get lost in her body. Jagger Capelli's the furthest thing from my mind right now.

"There's not much we can do about that, Pops," I say, cupping Skye's full tit, kneading her warm flesh, a soft moan falling from her lips as she cuddles up to me. She rolls on top of me, straddling my waist, and I move my hips, adjusting to accommodate her.

She's so fucking beautiful, all soft curves, dark waves of hair cascading around her shoulders. Her fingers smooth over my bare chest, tracing the outline of my pecs, fanning over my skin. She rocks her hips against my pelvis, her pussy already wet for me. My cock lengthens and hardens, jumping to attention.

Reaching down, she strokes my shaft, and I grow larger for her. Pulsing in her hand, my balls rise as she pumps up and down. She circles the swollen crown, her fingers velvety on my tender skin. Blood roars in my ears, and I'm not sure if my siblings are still talking, all attention focused on Skye and what she's doing to my cock.

I want to plunge inside her, feel her tight pussy quivering around me, spasming as she screams my name.

"There's nothing we can do?" Poppy's whining down the line and I'm over this conversation for now.

"I'll talk to Cleet about it, Poppy," King says, trying to appease her.

I guess that's good enough because Poppy drops it.

Hitting the speaker button, I drop the phone onto the bed and sink into Skye's hot pussy. She gasps and I press my finger to her lips, a silent warning to be quiet so my family doesn't hear. Her mouth tips up in a smile as she squeezes, her muscles contracting around my cock. I piston into her, hard and fast, pushing her to the edge.

Perversely, I want to make her scream, call out my name.

I want everyone to know Skye is mine.

Reaching up, I tweak at her nipples, pinching until the blood drains from the skin. Her pussy tightens, spasming on my cock as her mouth forms a silent 'O.' I release the sharp points and her muscles clench again, milking me.

I move my hips in a circle, hitting all her sensitive spots as she grinds against me, slick and wet. Parker's saying something, but all my attention's on Skye right now. Her luscious tits bouncing up and down, her skin satiny smooth, flushing pink in my palms.

Our bodies slap together, again and again, as I drive into her. The base of my spine tingles and I'm close, my release building. I smack her ass lightly, careful not to make too much noise as Poppy and Parker talk about New Year's Eve at the inn.

She spasms on my cock, unraveling, and a low moan vibrates deep in her throat. I continue surging into her until I explode with such force that it surprises me.

"Roman?" My sister's voice chirps beside me and Skye claps a hand over her mouth, stifling a giggle.

"Yeah?" My voice is husky as I continue convulsing inside Skye, spraying hot cum deep inside her. She strokes my chest, chill bumps rising on my skin.

"You okay? I thought I heard a scream or something."

Skye's body shakes with her giggles and I swallow down my laugh. "All good. Y'all need anything else from me right now?"

"No, we're good," King says, his voice definitive. "Good work."

"Thanks, Rome," Parker and Poppy both say, agreeing for once.

"See y'all later then." I disconnect and Skye bursts into laughter, the sweet, melodic trill filling the room.

"You're a bad, bad boy, Roman Montgomery." She gazes down at me, her thumb stroking my jaw. "And I love it."

Bending down, she claims my mouth in a scorching kiss and I'm not sure I ever want to leave this room again. Everything I'll ever need is within these four walls and I've never been happier.

41

SKYE

Roman and I ring in the new year with his family at the Seaglass Inn, dancing and laughing under the stars. Near midnight, everyone makes their way out to the beach with champagne glasses in hand.

The night's beautiful, clear and crisp, the waves crashing against the shore. Practically the entire town's out here on the sand, waiting for the clock to hit midnight so we can all usher in the new year.

Poppy leans against Griffin, his arms wrapped around her shoulders, dwarfing her small frame. Liv and Parker stand next to them, Parker's arm slung around her waist. Even King left the safety of the ranch to be here tonight and celebrate with his family.

They have a lot to celebrate, the nightmare of the trial behind them. Jagger may have dodged the law once again, but at least he won't be owning any part of the inn.

Roman tightens his grip around me, bringing me in closer to him, his chest hard and muscular against my back.

I nestle against him, his warm breath skating across my cheek.

"Ten, nine, eight—" the crowd chants, the countdown on.

"Seven, six, five—" I gaze out at the calm water, lightness filling my chest.

A year ago, I wouldn't have believed this is my life. Surrounded by people who care about me, wrapped in the arms of a man I adore with my whole heart.

The mayor even offered me a job in his office, overseeing town housing laws and the protection of lower-income rental properties, including the outskirts. I'm certain I'll be seeing more of Jagger, but I'm confident I can handle him. I have the full protection of the office of the mayor—and Roman—behind me now.

"Four, three, two—" I take a deep breath, a twinge pulling deep in my stomach. Butterflies zoom around as I spin to face Rome, his lips brushing against mine.

"One! Happy New Year!" Fireworks boom in the sky, white bursts exploding over the ocean. Smoke mixes with the salty air as everyone kisses and claps, singing Auld Lang Syne and clinking champagne glasses.

"Happy New Year, baby." Rome's deep voice vibrates against my open mouth and I breathe him in, all his strength, goodness, his raw masculinity.

"Happy New Year, Rome." I smash my lips to his, drowning in his touch, the perfection of this moment.

"Come on, walk with me." He breaks away from the crowd, lacing his fingers in mine, and my heart stutters in my chest.

I follow him, moving away from the crowd, down the

beach to a much more secluded area. The tide's rising, the water crashing higher on the shore as we walk.

"I'm glad you're here with me tonight." Roman's thumb strokes soft circles on my hand, electric shocks pulsing up my arm.

"Me too. I had the best Christmas, now I'm having the best New Year's Eve. It's going to be hard to top this." I smile over at him, his cheekbones bathed in the glow from the fireworks still exploding overhead.

"That's actually what I wanted to talk to you about."

My heart lurches, a lump forming in my throat.

And here I thought everything between us was perfect...

"Um, okay—" My voice falters, the happiness ebbing from me quickly.

We're all alone on the beach now, far away from the crowd. Roman wraps his arms around my waist, pulling me in close. I gaze into his blue eyes, marveling at how I got so lucky.

"I know you're thinking about moving back home—"

I take a deep breath, unsure where he's going with this. He lifts his hand to my face, tucking a stray hair behind my ear.

"But I don't want you to. I want you to stay with me."

"Ahh—" I exhale and smile up at him, relief whooshing through me all the way to the tips of my toes. "Are you sure, though? You're not just worried about Jagger coming after me?"

Rome dips his head, kissing me square on the lips. "I'm sure. This time we've spent together has been amazing, some of the best days I've had in a very long while. Maybe ever. Even with all the crap going on, you somehow made me smile, laugh."

He trails his thumb over my cheek, caressing my skin, and my heart is so full it may burst from the happiness.

"What I'm trying to say is I love you and I want to be with you." Rome's deep voice sends a shiver of pleasure racing through me.

"I want to be with you too, Rome. I've never felt this way about anyone before." My voice wobbles, tears springing to my eyes, and I will myself not to cry. "I love you."

He swipes away the tears, brushing his lips with mine. "It's decided then."

Digging in his pocket, he pulls out a key. "For you."

I take the shiny metal, cool in my palm. "You were pretty confident I'd say yes, huh?" I tease.

"I like to be prepared. Come on, let's go home." He gives me one last kiss on the beach before taking my hand in his. Lacing our fingers together, we walk hand in hand into the new year.

42

SKYE

TWO MONTHS LATER…

"Rome, where are we going?" I peer out the window as we pass through town, the moon shining bright overhead.

"Since it's not as cold tonight, I thought we could take a stroll over by the inn."

"Oh. Sounds great. I need to walk off the tacos anyway."

Rome cuts his eyes at me, shakes his head. "Babe, you could eat twenty tacos and you'd still be perfect."

My cheeks heat, blushing under his praise. I've never known anyone as sweet as Roman. Under all that Marine bravado, he's the kindest, gentlest man I've ever met.

We pull into a vacant spot near the inn and park the truck, Roman circling around to get my door like always. Taking my hand, he helps me down, wraps his arm around my waist. I sink into him, inhaling his clean, familiar scent. He leads me down the sidewalk and I flash back to the early days of the trial, how he snuck up on me and jump scared me.

"What are you smiling about over there?" Rome glances over at me, his lips quirking up.

"I was just remembering how you caught me sleuthing that night."

He chuckles. "Oh, I remember. I wanted to throw you over my shoulder and take you home with me."

My face flames, heat unfurling low in my belly. "I wanted you to."

Roman rubs his thumb over mine, and I'm so glad we're not fighting each other anymore. I much prefer being on the same team.

We stroll past the inn, taking a right turn, the ocean pounding the shore in the distance. During the winter, it seems like the ocean's louder—less people and trees to block the noise, I suppose. The air's cool and crisp, the salty humidity pulling out the waves in my hair. I snuggle into Roman, happy to have his warm arm slung around my shoulders, protecting me from the wind.

There's an open grassy space, a white gazebo standing in the center, all lit up with twinkly string lights. We cut across the lawn, heading toward the gazebo.

Climbing the wooden steps, I notice a silver chiller with champagne and two flutes set out on a bench.

"Rome, did you plan this?" I narrow my eyes at him.

"Guilty, Counselor." Then he sinks to one knee before me and my heart pounds hard in my chest, blood roaring in my ears.

Roman pulls a small black box from the pocket of his jeans. "I've been wanting to do this for a while now, but never found a good time." He pops the lid of the box, a round diamond set in a simple silver band winking at me in the glow of the twinkly lights.

"Oh my god, Rome—" I stare down at the ring, one hand clutching my chest.

"Skye Adams—" He reaches for my left hand, running his thumb over my bare ring finger. "I know we haven't known each other that long, but I've never felt this way about anyone before. I'm in love with you, and I know I will be for as long as I'm alive, until I take my last breath on this earth. I want to wake up every morning and fall asleep every night holding you in my arms. I will provide for you, protect you, love you with every fiber of my being. Please will you marry me and be my wife?"

With a shuddery breath, I caress Roman's face—his cheeks, his jaw, his amazing lips—every inch of him gorgeous, perfect.

Mine.

Tears shimmering in my eyes, I lean down and brush my mouth against his. "I love you, Roman Montgomery. With every cell in my body. Every beat of my heart belongs to you. I wake up in the morning thinking of you and fall asleep every night doing the same. I want to love you, take care of you, be there for you for the rest of my days. So yes, Rome. Yes, I will marry you."

His face breaks into a huge grin, his teeth shining white against the darkness as he slips the ring onto my finger and stands, spinning me around in a circle.

"I love you, Skye." He tilts my face up to his, crushing his lips to mine.

"And I love you."

I melt into him—his strength, his love, his warmth—and know I'm finally home.

#bestdayever

EPILOGUE: ROMAN

ONE MONTH LATER...

Living with Skye is easy. We fall into a nice rhythm, drinking our coffee at the kitchen table before driving to work together. She still wears her sexy pencil skirts, gauzy blouses, and stilettos, giving me plenty to look at on the days when I'm in the office with the mayor. She loves the new gig, helping the citizens of Seaglass Beach access affordable housing. She especially loves getting to go after Jagger, the greasy slumlord that he is. More than once, she's been able to slap him with a hefty fine for breaking some city ordinance or other.

Poppy's thrilled to be getting another sister. She loves Skye, she and Liv looping her into chats about shopping and interior design. Glad they have each other to talk to because I have zero interest in either thing. The three of them have girls' nights, and I can only pray they don't discuss our sex life. Not because I'm embarrassed, I just don't want the other guys to feel inadequate.

Parker's jazzed that he's not going to be the only married guy in the Montgomery family, and he's been hinting at Griffin to pop the question to Poppy. Mainly because he's really into baseball now, but also because Poppy is considerably calmer and less annoying when Griffin's around.

King's been quiet about the whole thing, but I'm not offended. I wouldn't expect him to have a lot to say on the matter unless he opposed. So it's a good thing that he hasn't said too much about it one way or the other. He did offer up more horseback riding lessons to Skye, so I take that as a good sign.

"Rome! Can you please come here?" Skye shouts from the bathroom.

"Yeah, just a sec." I hit the timer on the oven before hustling down the hallway. Her voice is shaky—I hope she's not getting sick.

Skye's leaning against the counter, her arms folded across her stomach, bright splotches of pink coloring her cheeks.

"You okay?" I rush in, wrap my arms around her. She's trembling and now I'm worried, a gnawing deep in my gut.

She nods, nuzzling against me, her skin warm and soft against my neck.

"I have news." Her voice is a quiet whisper, a prick of fear tingling down my spine.

Skye reaches behind her back, holds up a pink-and-white stick. "I'm pregnant."

The bottom falls out of my stomach, the air punched from my lungs as I stare at the bright pink plus sign.

"What? How?"

"Um—didn't you learn how this happens back in school?" She squints at me, teasing. "Could be the unprotected sex we've been having almost every day since we met. Call me crazy..."

"You know what I mean. I thought we were careful, you're on birth control." My mind's whirling, all the times we had sex playing on loop in my brain.

"There was that time last month where I got food poisoning after the potluck. Then I might have missed another day or two. And it's not 100 percent effective you know—" Her voice trails off, wobbly with emotion. Tears shimmer in her eyes and I brush her cheek, swiping them away.

"Babe, don't get me wrong. I'm thrilled. Shocked, but thrilled."

Her face breaks into a huge smile, brighter than a thousand sunbeams. "I was hoping you'd say that!" She throws her arms around my neck, laughing and crying into my skin.

I run my hands up and down her back, the world righting itself again, the spinning stopped.

"We're gonna have a baby." My voice is low, filled with awe, as I reach down and spread my hand over her still-flat stomach.

She beams up at me. "We're having a baby, Rome."

I brush my lips with hers. "I love you, Skye. And I already love this precious baby we made."

"The next generation." Skye laces her hand in mine, splayed across her belly, and we both stare down in awe.

She's carrying my baby and we're going to be a family.

I didn't think I could love this woman any more than I already do, but I was wrong. She brought me back to life, and then we made new life, created out of our love for each other.

I know, deep-down in my soul, nothing will ever beat this moment, top the incredible, powerful feeling sweeping over me right here in this bathroom.

"I love you, baby." I gaze straight into Skye's brown sugar eyes, knowing my love for her and our baby is, and always will be, unrivaled.

Want an invite to Roman and Skye's wedding? Subscribe to my mailing list and you'll get instant access to an exclusive bonus scene!

Want more in the Seaglass Beach series? Keep reading for a sneak peek at King and Juliet's book, UNDONE!

UNDONE SNEAK PEEK

KING

Present Day

Errand day.

Twice a month I head into town to get supplies, rain or shine. Today's that day.

I don't much care for errand day. Leaving the wide-open space of the ranch and venturing into Seaglass Beach—where there are bound to be tourists and, let's be honest, other people too—isn't my idea of a good time.

But it must be done. Much as I'd love to be 100 percent self-sufficient, I still need gas, supplies, and the occasional taco.

Although it's not seven a.m. yet, I'm already bumping down the long gravel drive toward the main road. The ranch fades in my rearview as I pick up speed, the ground changing to smooth pavement beneath my tires. At least the sun's peeking out, turning the sky a dusty blue. We've had a ton of rain this past week. Good for the grass, not so great for the mood.

I crank up the radio to Chris Stapleton belting out "White Horse," roll my window down to catch the first scent of the ocean. One of the only redeeming factors of town, really. That and my siblings, I suppose. All three of them live up here. I usually make at least a half day out of the trip, catching up with Roman or Parker for lunch or the occasional beer before heading back home. Sometimes I even swing by the inn to say hi to Poppy, but she's usually bustling about, helping guests. I need to make a freaking appointment to get face time with my sister.

Traffic's light at this time of day, the streets almost empty. People will be stirring soon, heading off to work, school, or the beach, but I'll be knee-deep in horse feed by then.

After glancing down at my gas gauge, I make a quick turn into the only station in town. I still have a quarter of a tank, but might as well fill up while I'm here. Maybe grab a quick coffee to go.

I pull up next to an empty pump and hop out of my truck, going through the familiar motions. I slide my credit card into the reader and am busy selecting the fuel grade when a white blur slams into the open spot directly across from me. I glance up, wondering what the damn hurry is as the driver flies out of the beat-up Toyota SUV and rushes to the pump.

Shit.

My gaze locks on an all-too-familiar pair of hazel eyes, fringed by dark lashes, and my entire body tenses. The pump beeps at me to remove my card—*beep, beep, beep*—

loud and insistent, but I'm frozen in place. Heart pounding double time, palms sweating, my mouth dry as dust.

Juliet squares up, flips her wavy hair over her shoulder, and blinks. Once, twice. A soft pink flush creeps up her neck all the way to her cheeks, and her full lips press into a tight line.

"King."

Her voice is neutral, giving nothing away.

"Juliet." I tip my hat at her, all cool, calm, and cordial, even as my gut churns.

She turns her attention to the task of pumping gas, and I try mightily not to hyperventilate.

I know running into her is a risk I take every time I leave the ranch, but it doesn't make it any easier when it happens.

It's like my worst fears colliding—peopling and *her*—all before eight a.m.

"You gonna take your card out, or are you gonna let it beep in there all morning?" The corner of her lip tips up, and I'm rocketed out of my trance.

"Oh. Yeah. Right." I snatch the card out of the machine, and the word *ERROR* flickers on the screen in front of me. "Shit," I mutter, jamming my card back in.

CARD READ ERROR.

"What the—" I fumble with the card, pulling it back out.

Backward. I put the damn thing in backward.

Trying again, I shove the card back in and wait for the go-ahead to enter my zip code. I try to focus on the pump and not the woman on the other side, a mere foot away from me.

Not on the way that black T-shirt clings to her curves,

not on the smattering of freckles dancing across the bridge of her nose, not on the delicate slope of her neck, the dip of her collarbone, where her skin's so soft and tender. Like a ripe, juicy peach at peak harvest you're dying to sink your teeth into.

The card reader beeps, and this time I manage to pull the plastic out successfully and punch in the right numbers. I lift the gas nozzle, tap the "Regular" fuel button, and start pumping, averting my eyes from Juliet. Instead, I focus on the convenience store, drumming my fingers on the yellow rubber handle to pass the time.

Which crawls, by the way. This must be the slowest gas pump on the whole fucking planet, swear to goodness. Juliet finishes up—the scrape of metal on metal alerts me to the fact—and I breathe a tiny sigh of relief as she opens the door of her vehicle.

But she doesn't climb in and drive off into the sunrise.

Nope. Instead, she grabs her purse and sashays past me into the building, hips swaying side to side.

Damn. I really wanted a coffee too.

At this rate she'll probably be done in there before I finish pumping.

Thump. The lever pops up, signaling the tank is full. I replace the nozzle and shut the gas tank door.

Should I go in there? Stall here until she comes out? Or forget the whole coffee plan altogether?

Taking a deep breath, I weigh my options before deciding to just go for it. I'm a grown-ass man, and I want a coffee, dammit. It'll only take a few seconds—what's the worst that could happen? So I see her again, no biggie.

After locking my truck, I head across the parking lot, shoving a hand in my pocket. All nonchalant.

I push through the door into the small space and shoot a quick wave at Barty, the twentysomething-year-old kid standing at the register.

"Morning, King."

"Morning," I half grunt, rounding the corner and heading back toward the coffee station.

"Aah!" A high-pitched squeal startles me as I collide with an outstretched Styrofoam cup, hot coffee splashing down the front of my flannel shirt. A dark-brown stain blooms over the blue-and-white-checked fabric, now sticking to my skin.

"Well, shit." I pull my shirt away from my body and shake off as much of the hot liquid as I can, then stalk over to the Formica counter, where I pluck white square napkins from the tall pile.

"Oh my gosh, I'm so sorry, King." Juliet trails behind me; then her small hands are dabbing at my shirt, trying to sop up the spill with flimsy gas station napkins. Tiny pulses hit my chest, and my heart's banging so hard I'm certain she can hear it, feel it beneath the wet material.

She's inches from me now, her fresh cotton scent mixing with the strong smell of dark roast and hitting me straight in the nostrils. Every inch of me prickles like I'm on fire as I fight against the sudden hard-on springing to life in my jeans.

Hopefully she stays focused on my chest, because that situation's gonna be pretty damn obvious in a few seconds.

It's her voice that gets to me. Every single time. Soft, seductive, almost a purr deep down in her throat. The vibrations so low only the two of us can hear.

Sexy as hell.

I shouldn't have come in here. This was a big mistake.

"It's fine." I step back, putting space between us. Her hands flutter through the air, suddenly taskless, clutching the soggy napkins.

Against my better judgment, I let my eyes slide to hers, sending a sharp jolt straight through me.

I'll never get over those eyes, the bright ring of green blending into a cocoa center, with gold flecks that sparkle in the sunlight. The way she stares straight at you, all wide-eyed and innocent.

My mom used to say her eyes were *beguiling*. I didn't even know what that meant until I looked it up in the dictionary.

Beguiling /be·guil·ing/ (*adjective*) : charming, enchanting. Highly attractive and tempting.

Tempting is right.

Heat creeps up my chest to my face, and I'm having a hard time getting air into my lungs. A warm cup of joe is no longer important—I need to get out of here right fucking now.

"I can't believe I did that. I'm really sorry." Juliet gnaws at her bottom lip, and damn if I can't stop staring.

Tearing my gaze from her mouth, I somehow force words out, my voice harsher than I mean it to be.

"Whatever, it's fine. I have more shirts."

She swallows hard, and I'm in a weird time vortex where everything's moving fast and slow at the same time. I shove my sweaty palms into my back pockets, try to act casual and downplay the panic attack I'm about to have right here in the gas station.

Taking a step to the right, I attempt to move around

her. Juliet moves to her left, and we're still face-to-face with each other.

"Sorry." She blushes, her cheeks bright-pink splotches, and moves in the other direction at the same moment I slide over to the left. Now we're boot to sneaker, locked in an awkward dance.

"Sorry," I grumble, tipping my hat to her. "Ladies first."

I take a big step to the side, giving her ample space to pass.

"Thanks. I'm just gonna get a refill." She waves her mostly empty cup in the air, her glossy lips screwed up in embarrassment.

"I'll get out of your way then."

Without another moment of hesitation, I hustle out of the gas station, not even bothering to wave goodbye to Barty.

Head pounding, I bolt to my truck, then unlock the door and launch myself into the driver's seat. I slam the door shut, fire up the engine, and peel out of the lot before Juliet exits with her refreshed coffee.

It's been a helluva morning, and it's not even eight a.m. yet.

UNDONE IS AVAILABLE NOW!

ALSO BY KARA KENDRICK

SEAGLASS BEACH SERIES

Unmistakable

Unstoppable

Unrivaled

Undone

PEACHTREE GROVE SERIES

Rushing Into Love

Turning Up the Heat

Chasing After Forever

MAN OF THE MONTH CLUB: STARLIGHT BAY

New Year's Renovations

Love in Bloom

Stars & Sparks Forever

MAN OF THE MONTH CLUB: SYCAMORE MT.

Snowbody But You

MAN OF THE MONTH CLUB: CANDY CANE KEY

Reeling Him In

Lights, Camera, Christmas

HOLIDAY NOVELLAS

Christmas in Cayman

Mr. Right Under the Mistletoe

My Charming Holidate

Snowed In With the Scrooge

BILLIONAIRE SERIES

Charming the CEO

Flirt Like a (Fake) Groom

HEART OF A WOUNDED HERO SERIES

Soldier On: Heart of a Wounded Hero

WILD BROTHERS SERIES

Forever Wild

Find them all at www.karakendrick.com

ABOUT THE AUTHOR

Kara Kendrick writes fun and flirty small-town romance destined to give you all the feels. A reformed English major, she also has a master's in counseling and was an elementary school counselor in her pre-mom life.

She loves the beach, wine, and rock-hard abs, not necessarily in that order. When she's not dreaming up Happily Ever After's, you can find her chasing after her boy-girl twins, working out semi-hardish, or walking her adorable Shiba pups with her husband, who's not too bad himself.

Let's be friends! You can be the first to hear about upcoming releases, promos, and giveaways.
Find her at www.karakendrick.com

ACKNOWLEDGMENTS

Deepest gratitude to all the people involved in helping me put this book out into the world:

My alpha readers, my sisters and mom; Valentine Grinstead and the entire Valentine PR team; Virginia Carey, editor; Sarah Sentz at Enchanting Romance Designs; and my ARC team and all the bookstagrammers and bloggers who took a chance on me.

Last, but never least, thank you to my home team—Lance, Luke, and Kinsey. I love you all and am so grateful for the opportunity to pursue my passion. Xoxo.